Christel Detsch

ON THE EDGE OF TOWN

This book is licensed for your personal enjoyment only. Thank you for respecting the hard work of this author. To obtain permission to excerpt portions of the text, please contact the author at christeldetsch@gmail.com.

All characters in this book are fiction and figments of the author's imagination.

Published by Christel Detsch
Copyright © 2016 Christel Detsch
All rights reserved

Cover design by Joe Ottoson

ISBN: 978-0-692-66055-3

For H. Sch.

Chapter 1

The man stared straight ahead at the gray road with the continuous white line on the right side and the broken yellow line in the middle. He knew it was crucial to stay between the two lines. Every so often sleep invaded his brain like a soft scarf. More than once he had swerved too far to one side or the other. One time he nearly hit a marker. It left him shaking with fear and exhaustion. But he had continued, and now they were nearly there.

The man looked at the little girl next to him. For a brief moment he felt an ache in his chest, right down to his stomach. He had felt it several times during the last few days when he looked at her and she was not aware of it. He didn't know that love could hurt so much. Then the fear came back: what if they were found, if they took her away from him? His lips compressed into a hard line, his eyes squinting against the sun.

The land was flat. Pastures and fields of corn lined both sides of the road. Cows, like black dots, stood behind barbed-wire fences, and a pale sky arched over the huge, empty expanse. It was twilight, and he was driving west toward the sun that hung low on the horizon. As the car purred over the asphalt, the sky in front of him changed from blue to purple with streaks of gold and orange. The road pierced the colors like a straight arrow, and he wondered when they'd reach the town. He glanced at the little girl again. She was still sleeping. An hour ago, she had told him that she was hungry, but he didn't want to stop. He wanted to get to their house. They'd be able to eat something in town and then go home. Home—his thin mouth curved into a bitter smile. He was afraid, not for himself, but for Emma, the little one, who trusted him and could sleep so innocently and peacefully next to him. There was no return now. For a short moment the sun blinded him, and he adjusted the sunshield. And then there was only the road again, straight, rigid, inevitable.

A car was passing him, another was approaching from the opposite direction. It would not be far to Junction City now. The man strained to see signs of the town, but he could barely penetrate the golden haze which cast an eerie spell over this monotonous land. In the distance, a tower rose beside the road, round and white. A grain elevator. Within minutes the sun disappeared, leaving behind a thin line of light at the horizon. And then that also vanished, and dusk closed in on him. The man felt nervous as the grain elevator grew larger. He could now read the words that were written in big, black letters on the dirty white metal: Junction City Co Op. He drove on, past a lot with used cars, another lot with green and yellow farm machinery, and a Texaco gas station. Then he was downtown. Several blocks of false-front buildings lined both sides of the street.

He switched on his headlights and drove by houses that appeared deserted. For a moment, he was afraid they had arrived in a ghost town, but then he saw the bar with a bright blue neon sign over the door— Dub's Tavern. Slowly he steered the car toward it and parked between two pickups. The door to the bar was open, and he heard the hum of voices intermingle with the sounds of country music. The man turned around and looked at Emma. To his relief, she was awake now. She didn't move, but her eyes were open. Curiously she gazed at the garish lights. He wondered how much she knew, how much she guessed. He didn't know how much a six-year old could understand. She smiled at him, and he smiled back. He was not a religious man, and he had little liking for religious imagery, but if there were angels, they would look like Emma. Her round face was flushed from a deep, untroubled sleep.

2

Her blond, soft curls had become moist and stuck to her temples and forehead. Suddenly the ache was back in his stomach, and he was afraid that it would make him weak.

"Do you want to eat something here, honey?"

She shook her head. "Are we home now?"

"Yes, we are. This is our town. You were hungry a little while ago, Emma. You should eat something."

She looked through the windshield at the bar and shook her head again. He realized she was right. This might not be the place to take a six-year old for dinner.

"I want to go home." There was a quiver in her voice, and a tear rolled over her round cheek, and then another and another. The man felt panic rise in him as it always did when she acted in an unpredictable manner. Most of the time she was full of joy, but there were these moments when she cried over nothing or was moody.

The short bout of panic had drained the last of his energy, and he suddenly felt weary. He knew he wouldn't be able to look for the house now. It was nearly dark. He needed to sleep so he could think, make plans, take care of Emma, and feel like a normal person again.

"Honey, there's a motel over there. Let's stay here tonight. I'll get something to eat, and tomorrow we'll go to our house." He didn't know if he sounded convincing, but he was clever. He knew that Emma loved to stay in motels because he let her eat chips, drink pop and watch TV until she fell asleep.

A smile stole onto her face, and she nodded her head. "Doritos and those round, little donuts," she said as she wiped her cheeks dry.

He put the car in reverse and eased it back onto the street. A bright sign ahead announced that the Sunshine Motel had vacancies. He sighed as he came closer. By now, he was all too familiar with cheap motel rooms that had mold in the bathroom and unidentifiable spots on the bedding.

It was a long white building. At one end was the office, and next to it were the rooms, not more than ten. A few cars were parked in front

3

of them, but all the windows were dark. A handful of young people were sitting on a bench by the office. He was apprehensive as he steered his car toward them. Quickly he glanced at Emma and was surprised, as he had often been lately, how quickly tears could vanish from a child's face. She was rosy-cheeked now, happy about another night in a motel with junk food scattered around her on a big bed. She would stare at the TV, watch vulgar shows that she did not understand, and fall asleep amid half-eaten donuts and broken chips. He smiled at her. It was time to change her life.

He parked the car in front of the office next to a beat-up blue pickup. When he told Emma to get out and come to the office with him, she shook her head. He asked her again, but she remained stubborn. This had been another surprise. He had been convinced that a child that looked as perfect as Emma would have an angelic personality. On their long trip, he had learned she could be obstinate. He never liked to scold her because he didn't want her to be afraid of him. He preferred to bribe her.

The people in front of the motel, three men and two women, were watching them. They were young, in their late teens or early twenties. They had stopped talking, and their eyes were dull and hostile. He didn't like to be scrutinized, especially now. Their demeanor was not threatening but not reassuring either.

With the promise of more candy and more soda pop, he finally coaxed Emma to come with him. When they entered the office, one of the women got up and followed them. She stepped behind the counter and looked at them indifferently.

"I'd like a room, two beds." It smelled of stale cigarette smoke in the office, and he wondered if there was a point in asking for a non-smoking room. "Non-smoking."

"For one night?" She was searching for something in the desk drawer.

He nodded his head. He didn't care if there were holes in the blanket or if the room smelled like smoke if he could just sleep. The prospect of stretching out his legs between clean sheets, no matter how threadbare, was like a promise of the good life that he intended to live now. He took Emma's small, sweaty hand into his and smiled down at her.

"How long are you going to stay, sir?" Hadn't she seen him nod his head? The young woman pushed a sheet of paper toward him. There was a guarded weariness in her eyes that he found irritating.

"One night," he said gruffly. He let go of Emma's hand and filled out the form. Name: Michael Barron, Residence: Rural Route 2, Junction City. He observed the woman closely when he handed the form back to her. She looked at it but didn't say anything. There was no sign of curiosity on her face. Either she had not read his address or she didn't care. She gave him the key to room number six and told him that there would be coffee and donuts for breakfast in the office. He nodded his head, took Emma's hand again, and left.

Chapter 2

The young woman picked up the form and studied it closely. She recognized the words Junction City quickly. His name took her a little longer. She pursed her lips in the effort to sound out the letters and tried to fight down the all too familiar feeling of terror that always gripped her when she tried to read. It didn't make sense, she thought. The man, Michael Barron, had given a local address. Why did he stay at the motel?

From outside she heard laughter, and then somebody yelled, "Hey, Tif, what's takin' you so long?"

It was dark now. Scraps of music and laughter drifted lazily from the tavern through the quiet street. She put the paper in the drawer and slowly went outside.

The dusty Buick of the new customers was now parked in front of number six. The curtains were closed, and light shone through a thin gap. It was not a busy night. There were only two other customers. One worked for a crop insurance company. He came to Junction City several times a year. The other was a retired teacher who had been staying at the motel for a week now. He was a history buff, he had told her, looking for spearheads, beads, bones and other Indian artifacts.

"Where's the guy from?" one of the young men asked.

"I don't know."

Ed broke into a high, cackling laugh. "Can't read the form, right, Tif? Bring it here."

Blood rushed to her face. She knew Ed didn't want to be mean. It made no difference to him if anybody could read or not. But it hurt her when he talked about it in front of other people. He could read easily, even though he wasn't clever, and he never read anything if he didn't have to. The others could also read, at least she thought so, but they only read the sport's page or the funnies. It wasn't that she couldn't read at all. It just took her a long time because she got the letters mixed up. She didn't know why she had so many problems when nobody else did. Sometimes she told herself that there was nothing wrong with her. Then she'd pick up a newspaper, but it never worked. The words never came. The sentences never made any sense. She saw only letters and spaces, scrambled and unfamiliar, and then panic would rise in her, and hot, desperate tears would burn in her eyes.

"His name is Michael Barron. He put down a local address, Junction City, Rural Route." She sat down between Ed and Marty. She didn't like to sit close to Marty because he was big and fat and always looked unwashed. So did his clothes. Even new clothes looked dirty on him. Sometimes she thought of him as an oversized toddler who couldn't stay clean. She tried not to show her antipathy because Marty was not a bad guy. He was good-natured and simple-minded and did what Ed told him.

"He lives here?" Marty asked while he was shaking a can of beer. His big, flabby body quivered, and his mouth opened into a foolish grin. She jumped up and ran a few steps away from them. He would open the can, and beer would spray all over, and he would find it very funny. She hated him all of a sudden.

"Don't do it, you idiot!" Ed shouted. He raised his bony fist and punched Marty in the arm. Marty leaned away from him to avoid the blow, only to be pushed back by the young man who sat on the other side. Ed laughed and took a deep gulp from his beer can. "Come back here, Tif." He motioned for her to sit down again. "What d'ya mean? He put down a local address? There ain't nobody here with that name. Did he say somethin'?"

7

She sat down again, close to Ed, trying to leave a space between herself and Marty.

"No. I think he was very tired."

"How long's he stayin'?"

"One night."

"His license plate's from Iowa. He's from Iowa," said Marty.

"He don't look to me like somebody from Iowa," said Ed. "Lemme see that form, Tif."

She got up and went back into the office. It had been a dull evening, and she could tell Ed was bored. The stranger would be good entertainment for lack of anything better. She had avoided looking at the man too closely because she was shy and there was something forbidding about him, but he was nice enough with the little girl. Maybe he was her father or her grandfather. He looked old to her.

"She's right," Ed said after reading the registration form. Then he laughed in his high, shrill cackle. Tiffany felt cold and pulled her loose, gray T-shirt closer to her body.

In loud voices her friends debated what this news meant while they emptied one beer can after the other. She didn't drink. It made her sick. The others often teased her about it but took advantage of having a sober companion. Since high school, she had been the designated driver, and it had worked well. She always brought them home safely.

Tiffany hoped that Mr. Wiederspan, her employer, would not come by tonight. He didn't like it when Ed and his crowd were visiting her at the motel. Bad for business, he said, even though there was never much business. But she had to agree with Mr. Wiederspan: it didn't look good to have a group of beer drinkers sitting in front of the office. The man, Michael Barron, had looked at them angrily. She was sure that he didn't like staying in a motel like this. He was probably used to better places. The little girl had looked around curiously and had smiled at her.

"I wanna know how come he's with that li'l girl," Marty said in a loud, slightly drunk voice. "Where's the mom?"

"Yeah, Marty is right. It ain't regular that a man travels all alone with a small kid. Men don't do that. They don't like that." Ed tilted his head back and drained his beer can.

"Maybe he's the father and the mother is dead." She wished they would all go home, so she could sit in the office by herself and think about the man and the little girl and invent a story about them. That would keep her busy till she closed the office at midnight.

The night was black when they finally left. She was too tired to invent stories about strangers; as a matter of fact, she had nearly forgotten about the man and the child. As always, she turned on the TV and watched a late-night talk show. It seemed to her that she had seen it before. Her father had told her that it was the result of spending too much of her time in front of the tube. "But what else is there for you to do, Tiffany? You can't read," he had said and smiled at her sadly. Her father always called her Tiffany, not Tif like everybody else. She liked that.

All of a sudden, there was a noise at the door. A shiver rushed through her, and for two heartbeats she held her breath. A stray cat or dog? She tried to calm herself. Had she locked the office door as Mr. Wiederspan always told her she should? The dark glass pane of the door stared at her. There it was again, a dull thump. Her eyes focused on the doorknob that wiggled loosely in the lock, and then she heard it again. Something invisible bumped against the lower section of the door.

"Are you in there? It's me." The high voice of a child penetrated the thin panels. "Let me in."

Tiffany rushed to unlock the door. In front of her stood the little girl from number six.

"Daddy isn't moving." Her eyes were large and dark, and her lips were compressed as if she was trying to swallow her fear. Tiffany stared down at her unsure what to do or say. When the silence lasted too long, the little girl frowned. She took a deep breath and with quivering lips continued, "You see, I slept a little, and then I woke up, and I tried to wake Daddy, but he didn't move, and my bed is not right." Suddenly her eyes were flowing over with tears. Her head dropped on her chest, and she clasped her hands convulsively.

Tiffany knelt down and put her hand under the soft, round chin. She was surprised how sweet the child's face felt in her palm. "What's with your bed?" Wild thoughts raced through her head, and she was afraid to think them through. He was her father? Why did she complain about the bed? Tiffany got up and reached for a Kleenex. Gently she dried the girl's cheeks.

The child sobbed softly. "Daddy always turns the lights out and tucks me in. But the lights are on, and he isn't moving." She sniffled and Tiffany gave her a Kleenex.

What was she to do? Had the man abused the girl? There were stories about this kind of thing on TV all the time. What if he was dead? He didn't look well. She pulled the child to her. Tiffany had worked at the motel for three years, night after night, with hardly any time off, and had never encountered a real problem. Sometimes a drunk man would call her from his room and pretend that he needed her help with something. Of course, she never responded to such requests. But this was different.

The little girl became restless and strained in her arms. Tiffany looked at the clock on the wall behind the desk. Should she call Mr. Wiederspan? Eleven thirty. Mr. Wiederspan would hardly be glad about a disturbance now.

The girl twisted out of her embrace. She took her hand and pulled her toward the door. "Come."

When Tiffany hesitated, she tugged more strongly, leaning her whole body away from her. Hesitant and uncertain, Tiffany let the child drag her outside, past the row of dark windows to room number six.

The girl walked quickly. It was chilly, and she only wore a thin cotton dress. When they reached the room, she let go of Tiffany's hand to open the door, but swiftly grabbed it again and pulled her inside, as if she was afraid that Tiffany might turn back. The lamp on the nightstand between the two beds was on, throwing its dim light over the cheaply furnished room. The man was lying on his back in the bed closest to the door. His inert body was uncovered to the waist, revealing a tanned and muscular chest. It seemed strange to Tiffany that his shoulders and arms could look so young and strong and his face so pale and old. She felt uneasy, a trespasser catching a forbidden glimpse. The sheets on the other bed were in disarray, food scattered all over them. Colorful pictures flitted across the silent TV. The girl hurried to her father and then turned to Tiffany, waiting for her to follow. Slowly, she did so. As she reached his bed, the man moved and turned over to his side.

The child looked up at Tiffany and whispered, "He's moving." There was so much relief in her voice that Tiffany threw her a surprised glance. She had her own experience with nightly watches and the anxiety that came from observing a lifeless body. But such a young child?

There was nothing wrong with him. He was probably just exhausted. The little girl gazed tenderly at the sleeping man. With her little hands she clumsily tried to pull the sheets over her father's chest. Whether she touched him by accident, Tiffany didn't know, but the man unexpectedly opened his eyes. He grabbed the girl's arm and stared at her wildly.

"Emma, are you all right? Why aren't you in bed?" His speech was slurred.

Hastily Tiffany backed away from them toward the door. He must have seen her move because he turned his head and tried to focus his bloodshot eyes on her.

"It's all right, Daddy," Emma said. "You didn't move, and . . . and . . . ." Her voice faltered and an expression of fear flitted across her face. "I was scared. I asked her to look at you."

"I'm sorry," Tiffany stammered. She wished she was invisible.

"Wait," the man murmured in a muffled voice. Slowly, he sat up and swung his legs off the bed. He rested his elbows on his knees, his face buried in his hands. Then he rubbed his eyes as if trying to massage the sleep out of them. "Wait."

When he took his hands down, she was surprised again that his face looked so different from his body. With red-rimmed eyes he stared at her. There was more than annoyance in his cold gaze. Fear. It seemed silly, but he reminded her of that rabbit that Ed and Marty had chased around in her backyard not too long ago. The rabbit had darted right and left trying to escape its tormentors. Then it stopped, sat still, and stared at them, its eyes big and sad and fearful. That's the way the man looked.

"You are the girl who checked us in. Is there anybody else with you?" His voice was still thick with sleep.

"Your daughter came to the office. I think she was worried about you. She thought there was something wrong because you didn't move." Normally Tiffany was tongue-tied with strangers, but this man was weak and helpless. It was easy to talk to him.

"Come here, honey." He pulled the girl close to him, and Emma leaned her face against his chest. "I was very tired. I'm sorry. I guess I fell asleep."

The child suddenly leaped out of his embrace and ran to her bed. "Look at my bed. It's wet. I can't sleep in it."

The man wore nothing but a pair of boxer shorts. He asked Emma to throw him his T-shirt and pulled it over his head without haste. Then he grabbed his jeans and put them on.

"What's your name?" Emma called to Tiffany. It was obvious that she was not tired at all. Now that she was sure that her father was well, she seemed intent on enjoying the nightly excitement.

"Tiffany." It was time to go. She glanced at her wristwatch, past midnight.

"Tiffany," the man repeated absent-mindedly without looking at her, "like Breakfast at Tiffany's?" He walked to Emma's bed and lifted the sheets.

Tiffany hated it when people referred to the movie. When she was little, she didn't know what it meant. She thought they were making fun of her. When she was fourteen she saw the movie on television. She

12

loved Audrey Hepburn and found her extraordinary, as extraordinary as New York with its skyscrapers and its fancy jewelry store. It had nothing to do with her life in Junction City. After that, when people mentioned the movie in her presence, she felt ashamed. It had been thoughtless of her parents to give her such a ridiculous name.

"Do you need new sheets?" she asked briskly.

The man didn't answer. Emma explained that she had spilled a whole can of soda pop. When she had tried to wake her father to tell him about it, he had not moved. He had lain there like he was dead, and she had become afraid.

"But now everything is all right, isn't it?" She slipped out of her sandals and jumped on the bed. Her father caught her in his arms.

"Emma, it's the middle of the night. I am dead tired."

She put her arms around his neck. "Don't say that, Daddy! You're tired, not dead." She broke into a happy laugh and affectionately leaned her head against her father's cheek. "I'm not tired. And Tiffany isn't tired, right?"

Michael Barron turned to her and tried to smile, but it looked more like the grimace of an exhausted man.

"I'm sorry she bothered you. Emma slept all day in the car yesterday. Normally she falls asleep before I do, but I guess not tonight."

"I can fix the bed, sir."

Emma struggled in her father's arms, and he put her down. With a mischievous smile she said to Tiffany, "He's not sir. He's my daddy, or he's Michael." Then she turned to her father. "Oh, please, please, tell her to stay for a little bit."

"No, Emma, we have to sleep and so does . . . ." He paused and looked puzzled. "Ah, yes . . . Tiffany. We have a big day tomorrow. Maybe we can have breakfast with Tiffany in the morning. Not at Tiffany's but with Tiffany, right?" He raised his eyebrows, and the corners of his thin lips lifted into an amused half-smile.

Did he find her name silly? Was he laughing at her? Tiffany

blushed. Yes, he was making fun of her and her stupid name.

"You said there were donuts for breakfast in the office?" he added.

Tiffany nodded her head.

"We have a big day tomorrow," Emma repeated her father's words. "We're going to our new house."

When Tiffany came back with a clean set of sheets, Emma wore a pink nightgown. They had already stripped the bed. Michael Barron tried to help her remake it, but he was clumsy. He smiled when Emma told him to sit by the TV and let her and Tiffany do the job. There was much concern and affection between father and daughter. It reminded her of another little girl at another time, a memory that belonged to a past lost forever. She lingered over the bed a little longer than she had to. When she was done, Michael Barron got up from his chair and walked her to the door.

"Tiffany," Emma called from her bed, "will you have breakfast with us tomorrow? Please."

"I'm sorry. I won't be here tomorrow morning. Liz will be in the office." She would have liked to have breakfast with them, to hear Emma's chatter and watch an indulgent father listen to his precious daughter.

Michael Barron opened the door for her. "I'm sorry for the disturbance. It's past midnight. You must be tired."

"Tiffany, will you come to our house?" the headstrong, little girl shouted. Tiffany couldn't see Emma because her father's tall frame blocked the doorway. "It's in the country, and Daddy says it's very nice."

Chapter 3

Ed was a bit annoyed with Tif because she didn't want to hang out with him after her shift was over. It was much more fun to drive around with a crowd. When the other two split, he was alone with Marty. Marty was all right. He'd listen to Ed and ask him questions, and Ed always knew the answers. Marty was dumb, maybe even a bit retarded, but it didn't bother Ed because Marty knew that Ed was the mover and shaker, and he showed him respect. Tif should be the same. If he told her to hang out with him, she should do so. But with her, it didn't always work out that way. He didn't exactly know why, except she had her hands full with her father right now. That explained some things. She was also dumb, but in a different way from Marty. In school he used to help her. Nobody else would. She would have failed a lot of English tests, had he not given her the correct answers. Not that he was a great star in school. The way it worked out, they both barely squeezed through. He almost didn't get his credits together to graduate, but at least he could read. He thought it only right to treat Tif the same as Marty, yet she wouldn't let him. She was kind of stubborn.

It had been a lame night, just like the night before and the night before that. He was out of a job right now but still had enough money from the last one to buy himself and Marty and Tif a good time. Well, now it was just him and Marty. Deep inside, he could feel the first signs of anger building up. He never knew if it had anything to do with drinking beer or if it came out of the blue. Sometimes the anger started with little things; sometimes it lingered for a while; sometimes it went away quickly. Sometimes he forgot that he was small and skinny and not very strong. Then he looked for a fight and was ready to take on anybody. He got a chipped tooth that way, and his nose had been broken twice. That's why it was crooked now. But most of the time he was lucky because he was with Marty who always protected him. Marty wasn't especially strong, but he was big. Good as a shield. The others would pummel him, and he would stand there, never fighting back, until they got tired of him.

They were driving through the night silently. Once in a while Ed took a deep gulp from the beer can he held between his legs.

"What ya think 'bout the man with the li'l girl?" Marty asked.

"Michael Barron. That's his name. Nice car he got, brand-new Buick." Ed took another sip and burped loudly.

"I figure there's somethin' fishy 'bout 'im."

"Gimme a cigarette. I need to think."

Marty fumbled in the darkness for the half-empty pack of Marlboros that Ed had earlier thrown on the cluttered dashboard. He was trying to quit, but every time he drank beer, his body yearned for the bitter taste of smoke in his mouth. It calmed him down. And now with the anger coming on and nothing to relieve it, he had to be good to himself. He inhaled deeply and felt a lot better right away. If it weren't for Tif's father, he wouldn't even think of quitting. But the old man wasn't doing too well. It was kind of scary.

"Where we goin'?" Marty asked.

"Casey's." Ed wanted to tell Casey about Michael Barron. Nobody else would know about him yet. Pretty little was happening in Junction City, and anything new was a welcome diversion. Besides, he liked sitting around at Casey's, drinking beer, playing cards, talking. Sometimes he'd stay till two or three in the morning. Hanging out there with other guys who liked shooting the breeze felt better than working. That's why he only worked off and on, just enough to get by. Work never made anybody feel good.

Ed turned sharply off the asphalt street onto a dirt road. Without slowing down, he drove through several potholes, and the truck's frame shook violently. Marty's head hit the side window.

"Hey, watch it!" Marty shouted. He had dozed off.

"Shut up! You're fat enough. A little bump don't hurt ya."

Ed could bully Marty, and his friend never complained. Maybe that was the main reason why Ed let him follow him everywhere. With other people he had to be more careful. But there was something else. Once Marty had the flu. He couldn't get out of bed for a whole week, and Ed had missed him. There was nobody to talk to, nobody to yell at, nobody who listened to his outbursts and agreed with him on everything. He never forgot that.

The pickup came to a halt in front of a long, narrow trailer that was surrounded by a high, chain-link fence. The windows threw a pale glow on the barren front yard. Dogs were barking in the dark, and when they hurled their large bodies against the fence, it rattled ominously. Ed couldn't see the animals, but he knew that Casey's dogs were monsters. From somewhere a loud voice yelled at the animals, and they quieted down.

He hated those dogs and wished Casey would keep them chained. But Casey insisted he needed to let them run free in his yard to protect him and his property. He had once lived among survivalists, anti-government people, ten, twenty years ago. Ed was not much concerned with those people. He found their ideas boring, and the government didn't interest him. As far as he was concerned, he wanted nothing to do with the authorities. He had never been to jail and didn't plan on going there.

Casey had given up that life and was now driving a cement truck. At least that's what he said. Most of the time he stayed at home and had people over and gave them a good time. There was quite a bit of high-stakes card playing going on. The police knew about it and had tried to close him down, but they couldn't do a thing about it because there was no proof that Casey took a percentage of the winnings. All they knew was that Casey and his friends had a friendly game going. Ed played when he had money. When he had no money, he watched and drank. Some took their women along. Casey liked that because it made it look more like a social gathering. Ed had once taken Tif, but that had been a complete failure. She just sat there. She didn't drink, didn't play cards. She watched TV and didn't talk to anybody. They had teased him about her later, and he had never taken her again.

"It's me, Casey. Ed."

"It's okay. Come on in, guys," Casey shouted.

Ed decided to trust him about the dogs that he could hear growling somewhere in the dark. Marty stumbled out of the car and followed him. The smell of cigarette smoke and beer greeted them, as they got closer to the trailer. Casey was standing in the brightly lit doorway, a cheerful-looking man with a round belly, massive shoulders and a smiling, bearded face. The poker players didn't lift their eyes from the cards when Ed and Marty walked past them. Two couples were sitting on a sofa in front of a large, old-fashioned TV set. Except for the two card tables that were lit up by bright ceiling lamps, the room was in semi-darkness.

Behind his kitchen counter, Casey dropped into a wide wooden chair with a generously curved back and an upholstered seat, suitable for a man of his size.

"What's up, Ed? Ready for some poker?"

"Maybe later." Ed tried to be cool. Casey was an intimidating person, even if he looked like a Santa Claus in the shopping mall. "Just met a guy in town. Michael Barron. Drives a nice car, brand-new Buick. Must have money. Funny thing about 'im. He stays at the motel, but gives a local address. Rural Route."

Calmly, Casey surveyed the living room, an expression of goodwill on his face, but Ed knew he was thinking, weighing the information, figuring things out. If only Ed could be so confident and calm and secretive.

"Interesting." Casey motioned with his head toward a small

18

refrigerator. "Have a beer, you two."

Ed reached for the handle and helped himself to a can of beer. Marty stood so close behind him that he could feel his warm breath on his neck. Irritated, he pushed another can into his friend's hand.

"Hey, gorgeous, come on over here." Casey's voice was deep and gravelly.

Ed tried to follow the older man's eyes. One of the women on the sofa lifted her head. She briefly looked at the three men, then turned her attention back to the guy whose hand hung over her shoulder and limply stroked her breast.

"Let her go, Kyle. I need to talk to her."

Slowly the woman peeled herself out of the man's embrace. Without hurry, she lifted herself off the couch and walked over to them, her well-rounded hips swinging and her breasts gently moving under a thin, tight blouse. Now Ed recognized her. Only one girl in town could walk like this and drive everybody crazy. It was Grace, Tif's older sister.

"Hi, Grace." He felt nervous and cursed himself for his voice that sounded squeaky and hoarse at the same time. Would she acknowledge him, maybe ask how he was doing? She should. There was a time when she had been a hot item and had ignored ninety percent of the boys in town who were after her. But that was in the past. Things had changed.

"What you want, Casey?" She smiled at the three men. Her voice was deep and rich, as seductive as her body. She was unsteady on her feet and leaned against Casey's knee.

"Didn't you tell me earlier that the Nielsen house has been sold? You know who bought it?"

Ed was surprised that Casey could be so matter-of-fact with a body like Grace's touching him.

"Yeah, I heard it at work last week." She paused and looked at them, confused, as if she wasn't quite sure what she had really heard last week. Then she shook her head and continued. "Melanie Branson sold it to somebody from a big city, Los Angeles or New York. No, it was someplace in the south, I think. I forgot."

She giggled and swayed. Ed reached out and steadied her. Her arm was soft and warm and full of promise. The touch sent a hot shiver through him.

"Michael Barron? That his name?" he stammered.

"Yeah, that sounds right."

Grace put her hand on Casey's thigh. Ed wished he could trade places with him. When Casey led her back to the couch, Ed's eyes followed her hungrily.

Marty was standing silently next to him drinking his beer in small, nervous gulps.

"What's she mean," he asked, "that man bought the Nielsen house? That's a bad buy."

The place had been empty for years and was a wreck. Everybody, even Marty, knew that.

"Yeah, it's a bad buy," Casey repeated when he took his seat again. He told them to pull over some chairs. "Tell me what you know," he said softly, leaning in close. Ed understood. This was a private conversation, just between him and Casey. Casey didn't drink much, and he didn't play cards, but he liked to know what was going on in Junction City because he worried a great deal that somebody from the government was after him.

The Nielsen house had been empty for eight years, since the day when old Dan Nielsen had died. For the first three years, there had been a for-sale sign on the property, but nobody was interested. Eventually some kids tore down the sign, or maybe the wind did it, and the house began to decay. It was an old Victorian with little turrets, pretty balconies and a spacious porch. The Nielsens had built it. They were frugal dirt farmers who raised their children with a taste for poverty. Ed remembered his father saying that the old folks only came to town to buy coffee, sugar, cans of peaches, large sacks of noodles and fat rolls of bologna. Every day, they ate noodles and bologna for dinner, and as a treat for dessert, they had canned peaches. Old Nielsen hunted rabbits, ducks and pheasants with his two boys, the twins Dan and Jack, and they gave up bologna during hunting season.

When the parents died, the brothers continued to live in the house. Mabel, their younger sister, had left some time before. She couldn't stand the old man. Nobody knew where she was. The twins continued to live the way their parents had taught them. Eventually, Jack turned crazy, and Dan became a recluse, but their lives didn't change. Three or four times a year Dan went into town to buy canned peaches, bologna and noodles, and they continued to hunt. Over the years, Jack got crazier. He was a good shot, and from his upstairs bedroom window he would aim at squirrels, rabbits and the rare visitor who came by. It was all the same to him: buck or man. "Steady, steady," he yelled. "Gotta get that one." And then it went bang, and bullets whistled past the old cottonwood trees. Lucky he never killed anybody.

The sheriff went out more than once to talk to Dan, who promised to keep an eye on his brother. Eight years ago Dan died. They only found out about it because Jack didn't stop shooting. For two days he was firing into the air and at everything that moved until the sheriff and his men stormed the house. The house looked and smelled like a pigsty, they said. Dan was lying on his bed, stiff and bloated. They only managed to capture Jack when he ran out of bullets. They kept him locked up in jail and pumped him full of pills that knocked him out. The next thing people heard was that some relatives had come and taken him away. The sheriff wouldn't say if one of them was Mabel. But he told them that they put Jack into an asylum. Then the house was boarded up and offered for sale. Two years ago Jack had died. It was rumored that he had gotten hold of his hunting rifle and killed himself, but nobody knew for sure.

Casey wasn't interested in the Nielsen house as such. He knew all about it and considered it a pile of worthless lumber. Broken windows, leaking roof, peeling walls.

"That's what I don't understand. Nobody in his right mind would buy a place like that," he said.

Marty shook his head. "It don't make sense."

"What's that guy look like?" Casey wanted to know.

"Tall, fortyish, brown hair," Ed said, and all of a sudden he took a real strong dislike to the man. There was something grand about him, something fine and smart, even though he wore plain clothes. He looked different from the people in Junction City. Proud, distant. And the little girl was sure obnoxious with those blond curls around her clean, well-fed face. The kids here didn't look like that. They were rough and dirty, like country kids ought to be.

Casey kept probing. Did he wear glasses? Was his hair really short? Did he have a small scar by his right eye?

"Why you wanna know all this?" Ed asked.

Casey looked at him without saying a word. Then he whispered in a low voice, "It could be FBI. There was this agent. He's still after me. I was in a group once, several years ago. We got chemicals, lots of chemicals, to make a bomb. I bought most of them. We were going to blow up the office of the county treasurer in this small town in Kentucky. He was a Democrat, the only elected Democrat in the county. It was before Election Day. We had the pickup, we had the bomb, but somehow the cops found out. They arrested several of us, but I got away, barely. They're still looking."

A bomb? Ed swallowed nervously.

"That man ain't no FBI man," Marty said. "He got this li'l girl with 'im."

Ed explained to Casey that the man, Michael Barron, was traveling with a child. Casey nodded his head and murmured, "I've been hard to catch. That could be a cover. They use her as a cover. Maybe I'm right, maybe I ain't. You two boys keep an eye on that fellow."

When Ed left with Marty at two in the morning, he felt that they had had a great time. Ed had given valuable news to Casey and had been able to feast his eyes on Grace. People could say about her what they wanted: she was a prize to go after. Too bad Tif didn't look more like her. Grace was round and soft and voluptuous, and all he could

22

think about was sex when he saw her. In comparison, Tif was boring. Small and thin with straight, dark hair that she tied in a ponytail. She always wore big, shapeless T-shirts, and you couldn't tell what was underneath. But she was all he had at the moment.

Chapter 4

When Michael woke up, he felt rested for the first time in several weeks. Emma was still sleeping, her body small and vulnerable in the big bed. Her round cheeks, the little nose, the pink mouth—as usual, he was surprised and awed that he had produced such a perfect being. He sighed because with the surprise came the old anxiety.

It wasn't long before Emma woke up. While she was watching TV, she clamored for breakfast. He'd have to get her used to a regular life now, less TV and no junk food. He had more or less let her do what she wanted on the trip, but now he would have to be stern. He was not sure that he knew how to be a stern father. Emma was used to getting her way, and she was remarkably independent. She got up, took a bath, brushed her teeth and dressed herself competently. Michael was proud of her. He didn't know if all six year-olds could do that.

"I'm ready, Daddy. Let's go," she said briskly. "They have donuts here. That's what Tiffany said."

Tiffany, yes, the girl from last night. An odd name for a girl in this god-forsaken place where everybody else was probably named Margaret or Mary. She was pretty in a quiet, unremarkable way. He had been through enough of these small towns to know that this was rare.

"Honey, tell me, what happened last night? I was very sleepy." He sat down next to her on the bed. Giggling, Emma explained the events of last night. She found it funny that he couldn't remember much. He listened to her attentively. A little girl's fright, innocent enough, but he would have to be careful. He didn't want to attract any attention.

When they stepped out of the musty motel room, he breathed in deeply and cool air filled his lungs. So this was the end of their journey: a small, raw town like so many others he had seen. He fought back a surge of panic. He had been told that the house was outside of town, in the country. Surely, the countryside was different from this desolate place. They would make their home there and enjoy peace and quiet, the simple pleasures, nature, the seasons. He'd get back to his work, and life would be good again. His work—it seemed ages since he had been able to sit in front of a computer writing words, moving them around on virtual pages until they fit. He lifted his head. Above him, white, feathery clouds were drifting across the blue sky, and the sun was throwing its golden light over the odd assembly of flimsy houses.

A large, platinum blond woman stood behind the counter in the office smoking a cigarette, watching TV. There were a few donuts left, but she'd have to make a new pot of coffee, she said. Reluctantly she put her cigarette into an overflowing ashtray and busied herself with the coffee pot, all the while glancing at the television. Once or twice she stopped altogether, coffee pot in hand, to watch a particularly interesting segment of the morning show. When he asked her where the Nielsen house was, the woman scrutinized him briefly before her face slipped back into sullen boredom. It was obvious that she found the TV show more interesting than her customers, and that was all right with Michael. With eyes moving back and forth between him and the small screen, she explained that the house was two miles north of town, then three miles west on a dirt road.

"You can't miss it. It's a big house." Once more, her eyes lingered on his face. "It's empty. Nobody lives there."

The donuts were stale, and the coffee was a tasteless brew. Michael couldn't wait to get out of this shabby place. As they drove away from the town, Emma leaned back against the plush brown upholstery of the car, a happy smile on her face.

"The house is big and white with a white picket fence around it. There is a lawn and beautiful flowers grow everywhere. Every day I'll pick some for us, Daddy, and then there is the lake. It's our lake, and we can swim in it whenever we want to. I can invite all my friends, and we can have a party by the lake."

Michael realized that Emma was recounting to him what he had told her about the house. She had embraced his suggestions eagerly, maybe too eagerly. "You know, I've never seen the house, honey. I think it's big and pretty. I am not sure if there are flowers. Maybe we have to plant them."

Their frantic trip was over, round two was about to begin, and he was uneasy. All he had done for the past two weeks was drive from one place to the other trying to shake off his pursuers. Had there been any? He didn't know. He had been scared all the time, and he was still scared. The towns, the motels they had stayed in hadn't mattered. They had always left them behind. But now he had to make a home for Emma, and he had never done that before. Emma had the highest expectations because he had built them up. She imagined the house like the place she had lived in before, the mansion in the suburbs with its manicured lawn, shrubs and flowerbeds. There had also been a lake for swimming in the summer and rowing in the winter. He had spent many desperate nights gazing at the shimmering blackness of the water, wondering what to do. Could he have avoided this mess if he had been a better father to Emma?

He came to a dirt road and turned west. Cows grazed lazily in fenced pastures; a cowboy boot was stuck on a post; tumbleweeds hung in barbed wire fences. A look at the dashboard told him that they had nearly gone three miles, and then he saw it. To the right of them, a large, gray house came into view. It stood all by itself on the grassy plain, lonely and austere. There was no picket fence, no flowers. Only a few scraggly bushes hunkered down in the wind. An old trail with faint tire tracks meandered through the weeds past two gigantic cottonwood trees which looked as much out of place on this empty land as the dwelling. For a brief second Michael wished he were back in the predictable and temporary dreariness of the motel. He slowed down the car and steered it cautiously onto the bumpy trail.

"Is that our house?" Emma asked. "But it's not white."

He swallowed, but the lump that had formed in his throat did not disappear. "Honey, I thought the house was white because most houses are white, right? But we can paint it white. What do you think?"

She'll think I'm a liar, he thought desperately. But Emma clapped her hands. White or not, she was ready for her new home.

He knew that the house was old and had been vacant for eight years. It needed a few repairs, he had been told, but it was basically in good condition. The house had not been cheap, and he had paid cash for it because Vincent, his lawyer, had assured him that it was a good deal. The location had struck Michael as ideal. Out of town, away from the prying eyes of nosy neighbors, but close to Junction City, where Emma would go to school. And once they were settled, he would be able to do his work again, the way he used to when he managed to turn out page after page without effort.

When he stepped out of the car, a strong breeze touched his face and ruffled his hair. The high grass was bent; the leaves of the cottonwood trees were shaking nervously. The wind had a physical quality, at once startling and invigorating, more real than the house in front of him.

Windows stared at them, dirty and empty. A balcony had lost its railing. Gray paint was flaking off the wooden siding. To his surprise, Emma's face was glowing.

"Come on, Daddy." Limply holding her hand he let her pull him, but Emma couldn't wait. She let go of him and rushed ahead, her blond hair fluttering in the wind.

Something made a clanking noise, and he wondered how many loose boards were dangling in the breeze. The first two steps that led up to the spacious porch were broken. The wooden railing and intricately carved columns looked brittle. Piles of sawdust surrounded their base. Termites? Cracks and small holes marred several window panes. BB guns. There was no doubt about it: this once stately Victorian house was falling apart. It was not what he had expected.

He cautiously approached the front door. With relief, he noticed that it was of solid wood and new. Somebody had installed it not too long ago. But his relief gave way to alarm when Emma opened the door and walked in. Whoever had been here last had not bothered to lock it.

A whiff of dry, musty rot struck him as he entered the house. It was the kind of rot that turns wood into dust. Emma wrinkled her nose. And there was another odor that he couldn't identify. Maybe it was the way a house smelled when its windows had not been opened for eight years. Michael stared at the cracked linoleum. For a brief moment he saw old people, farmers in faded overalls and wasted women in worn cotton dresses, shuffle through the house, and he smelled their unwashed clothes and unwashed bodies. A feeling of hopelessness overcame him. Vincent hadn't told him about this. He hadn't told him that he would have to live with the smell of other people's lives. Instead, Vincent had extolled the beauty of a tasteful Victorian house, ideally located, perfect for him. It would give him space and solitude, large vistas for his eyes to feast on. But the house the lawyer had described had little resemblance to this one. Vincent had probably never seen it. He had invented a Disney-type story for Michael. It was all bullshit, and he should have known it.

"Daddy, come here!"

He followed Emma's voice through an arched doorway and found himself in a bright, airy room. Emma was standing in a large bay window impatiently waving her arms. Sunlight streamed through the window and silvery dust particles were dancing around her. "Look, there's the lake, our lake."

Maybe Vincent was right about one thing: there were large, empty vistas here, grass, grass and more grass, and a sparkling, steel-gray patch of water behind which stood a grove of cypress trees, and above it all hung the huge, never-ending sky.

"It's a big world out there, isn't it? And it's pretty empty." As soon as he had said it, he cursed himself. It was lucky that Emma took it all in stride. But he was feeling very lonely.

Emma looked at him, puzzled. "It's nice, Daddy." He realized she was reprimanding him gently, and he wondered if she knew more than he did.

Chapter 5

When Tiffany arrived at the motel in the early afternoon, Ed was waiting for her. Michael Barron had bought the old Nielsen house, he told her, and Casey was interested in the man. When she wanted to know why, he mumbled something about the FBI and surveillance. It didn't make any sense to her, and she wished that Ed wouldn't go to Casey's. She didn't like the man, and she didn't like his parties and the gambling. She had only gone there once. Ed had had too much to drink and had started fondling her as if she were his girlfriend. But she was nobody's girlfriend. And what was worse, she knew that Ed wasn't interested in her that way. She had pushed him away and told him to stop. But he had pressed himself against her and said in a loud voice that he'd show her a good time. Casey had overheard them. She could tell from the way he smiled at her. She never went there again, and she was embarrassed every time she ran into him. Her sister Grace often went to his place. She didn't gamble, but most of her boyfriends did.

"Some fishy business about that guy, Tif." Ed grinned maliciously when he left.

It was a slow day at the motel, as usual. The insurance man checked out. The Indian treasure hunter was still here, and somebody's distant relative checked in. She muted the TV and was watching the silent gesticulations of the soap opera actors. She sometimes did that when the shows were too boring and predictable. Then she would guess what the current problem was: divorce, pregnancy—wanted or unwanted, husband cheating on wife, wife cheating on husband. Once in a while, she'd turn on the sound to check if she had guessed right.

The door opened, but she didn't bother to look up. The beautiful woman on TV was just starting to cry, and the mean but handsome man was glaring at her angrily.

"They don't seem happy, do they?"

Tiffany turned and looked into the mocking eyes of Michael Barron. Emma stood next to him smiling at her.

"Why don't you have the sound on? The TV isn't working? You are probably missing a lot." He was teasing her, not unfriendly, but there was an edge in his voice. She quickly switched the television off.

"It's working. It's a game," she murmured, her eyes on the counter.

"I guess it kills time, right? Not much happening here."

He reminded her of her teachers, and they had never been very nice, always ready to criticize her. Last night at the motel, he had been tired and worn out, less sure of himself. It was different now. His face wasn't quite so pale and haggard, and he wasn't jumpy anymore.

"Look, I'm sorry I upset you. I didn't mean to. My phone isn't connected yet. I'm looking for a public phone, but the one by the supermarket is out of order, and there's no phone book."

Tiffany told him that the telephone by the supermarket hadn't worked in a long time. He could use the telephone in the office if he wanted. While he made various phone calls to utility companies, Emma pulled her over to the breakfast corner. She settled into one of the cheap plastic chairs, waiting for Tiffany to do the same. After she did so, Emma shoved one of the children's books that she had brought along at her, and a hot wave of anxiety turned Tiffany's face dark red. Books always did that to her. She tried to get away, but Emma insisted that they read one of the books together. Luckily the little girl started reading, and she did it far better than Tiffany could. With one ear, she followed Emma's slow, methodical voice as she read about the adventures of a mole, with the other, she listened to Michael Barron,

31

fervently hoping that he would be done soon and relieve her of this unbearable situation.

"Tiffany, read this to me," Emma said suddenly.

She protested, claiming that Emma could read so well, she wasn't needed. Just then, the door opened and Marty walked in.

"Hey, Tif, ya know where Ed is?"

Tiffany got up quickly and walked to the desk. When Marty recognized the newcomers, a sly grin spread over his round face. "Ah, you're them new people."

Michael Barron had put down the receiver and was writing in a notebook. Now he looked up and turned toward him.

"Who are you?" Emma asked. She put the book on the table and was scrutinizing Marty curiously.

"I'm Marty. What's your name?"

"Emma." She frowned. "Tiffany is going to read to me now." The little girl wasn't pleased by his interruption.

Marty guffawed. "She can't read." His face glowed as Tiffany looked on helplessly. Shame, like the pain from a festering wound, gripped her.

"All grown-ups can read. My daddy reads all the time, and Tiffany is a grown-up," Emma explained patiently.

Marty shook his head and laughed maliciously. "I'm right, Tif, ain't I?"

She was silent, then said with a shaking voice, "I don't know where Ed is."

Marty smiled, well satisfied, as he turned around and ambled through the door.

Nobody spoke, until finally Tiffany mustered all her strength and without looking at Michael or Emma whispered, "I can read." She knew they wouldn't understand. Nobody who could read understood. Suddenly she felt a warm hand under her chin. She let Michael lift up her face and through her tears, looked at his blurred face.

"It's okay," he said softly. Then he turned back to his notebook

32

and leafed through its pages. "There are two roofers in town. Which one is better? Do you know? What about a good electrician?"

Simple questions, simple answers. Slowly her tears faded.

"The house is really old, Tiffany." Emma stood on her tiptoes and held on to the counter trying to get Tiffany's attention. "Daddy said it'll take a long time before it is nice."

"She is right," Michael Barron said, "the house is a mess. I could use some help." His gray eyes, so dull when she had first seen him, suddenly lit up. "Would you be able to help out? Cleaning, get things organized, you know, the household. I am not very good at that."

Tiffany was taken by surprise. The man who had just witnessed her embarrassment needed her help?

Emma jumped up and down clapping her hands. "Yes, yes, Tiffany, come to our house. I'll show you the lake, and we can have a picnic there. Oh, please, say yes."

"I don't know," she murmured. A part of her wanted to agree at once, but she had other commitments, at home.

"I am sure we can agree on an hourly wage. I'll pay you well."

"It's not that. I only have a few hours in the afternoon. I usually work at the motel in the mornings and at night. Today is an exception. I switched shifts."

"That's fine. Agreed. Come tomorrow afternoon, or as soon as you can. The old Nielsen house." His warm, dry hand enclosed hers and shook it gently.

When she told her father late that night that she maybe had a cleaning job, the old man nodded his head weakly. He wasn't really old, but when the emphysema had begun to ravage his body, he had aged quickly. He was only fifty-three. Of course, it didn't help that he sat indoors in a smoky room day after day. It had made his skin look pale, nearly translucent. She had tried to convince her mother to stop smoking in the house and let in fresh air, but it was useless. Her mother said that he was getting plenty of fresh air through the oxygen tube.

While Tiffany fixed his medicine and made sure that the tube was fastened properly to the oxygen compressor, she told him about the newcomers for whom she would be working. She also mentioned Marty and that the man knew she couldn't read very well and how painful it had been. It was only during these late night hours, when she came home from work that she could talk about her fears. In the depth of night, the world outside didn't seem to be so threatening. Things could be spoken of in the dark room that were best kept quiet during the day. Sometimes she thought she ought not do this. She should make her father happy and not burden him with her problems. But it was like when she was a little girl and had told him everything that had happened to her during the day, the good and the bad, and he had listened.

She had seen the pain on his face when she had told him many, many years ago that the children in school were making fun of her and didn't like her. She had been so confused, and he had comforted her. He had been young and strong then and had made her forget the hurt and the isolation she felt. He had joked and laughed with her and made her feel happy because he loved her so much. Every day, when the school bell rang at three o'clock, she had dashed home, so anxious for his love and comfort. The next morning, the old fear and hate of school was back, but his consoling words were still fresh in her mind. They helped her face the constant small torments of the children and the indifference of the teachers.

When the teachers told her father that she had a severe reading disability, he did not believe them at first. He was convinced that she was smart, smarter than all the other children in her class. But her poor grades proved him wrong, and he became impatient with her. He told her to try harder. She wanted to try harder, but she didn't know how. Her father didn't tell her what she had to do; neither did her teachers. They ignored her, and the other children said she was dumb. Eventually she meekly accepted their verdict, and so did her father. He gave up on her, just as he gave up on himself when his sickness struck.

He was no fighter. But his love for her was still there. It was a helpless, quiet love now. He asked fewer questions. He listened mostly, and there were no jokes, no laughter anymore. He frowned when she told him about Ed and Marty. She knew he didn't like them, but he never said anything. Poor Dad, he didn't have much luck with his family. Tiffany, his favorite, would never make anything of herself. He now seemed content that she was staying at home, doing odd jobs in town. And he came to depend on her because he was a sick man. She sometimes told him that his emphysema would get better. Then he nodded his head and smiled at her. She knew he didn't believe her. He had long accepted that he would not get better. But she couldn't accept that death would take him away from her. He would get well again, laugh and make jokes, and they would help each other forget the sadness of their lives.

After he had taken his medicine, she tucked the blankets around him. Imperceptibly, he drifted off to sleep, the way he did every night. She was always surprised how quickly it went. He didn't shift his body; he didn't move his head. Only his eyes told her. When his eyelids started to flutter and slowly closed over the pallid, watery eyes as if pulled by the earth's gravity, she knew he was falling asleep. Wakefulness and sleep, her father wandered so effortlessly from one to the other, and death sometimes seemed so near.

Chapter 6

Ed had been pleased when he found out that Tif was working for Michael Barron. She cleaned the house, did some cooking and shopping, and watched that little girl occasionally. He had told Casey that he had managed to get his girl into Barron's house. Of course, it wasn't exactly true, but it sounded good, and he had surely impressed Casey with his prompt action. But Ed's pleasure had soon turned to frustration when Tif didn't cooperate. He wanted to know things about the new guy, and so far, she hadn't told him anything. She said there was nothing to tell, but he knew she was keeping things back. It infuriated him.

Michael Barron was a writer, she said. Well, he knew that was a lie. From the moment Ed set eyes on that man, he was convinced he was a fraud. Why would a writer come to Junction City of all places? When he asked Tif what he wrote, she didn't know. Of course, she didn't because she couldn't read. Barron had probably figured that out and for that reason alone he posed as a fake writer. It was the best cover. He told Casey about his suspicions, and Casey had agreed with him.

"You and me, Ed," he said, "we can smell when something isn't right. We can tell if a man is what he says he is because we know deceit firsthand. If you tell me this guy is a fraud, then he is a fraud. I believe you. Keep an eye on him. It's important for all of us. The FBI is everywhere, Ed, watching us. Something is not right, I am sure of that.

We have to be watchful."

Ed didn't care if the guy was an FBI man or not. Nobody was after him as far as he knew. But he certainly felt honored that Casey trusted him, and now he had to deliver. That's where Tif came in. He had been at the motel earlier in the day, trying to get her to talk. He knew she went to Barron's place every afternoon. At first he had tried to be nice. He talked casually, asked about her father to soften her up a bit. But she had been sullen. He had tried to put his arm around her shoulder, and she had shaken it off right away. It made him furious when she was so obstinate. But then, she had always been funny about touching. In any case, when it came to women, he had another body in his mind. Grace, her sister. Looking at her was a feast. What would it be like to touch her? Maybe with Casey's help, he might get something going there.

Quite a few workmen had been out to Barron's place, and Ed had tried to talk to them, but they had brushed him off like an annoying fly. At some time or another, he had worked for all of them, the roofer, the painter, the plumber, and for one reason or another they didn't appreciate him. True, there had been a few problems. Sometimes he didn't show up for work, but he always had a good enough reason. The plumber had accused him of filching some equipment, but he had only taken discarded stuff that nobody wanted. It was he who should be upset at them for being so stuck up.

Of late, his nights had been long and idle, full of empty talk, and he was itching to do something. After trying to squeeze something out of Tif and a few beers at the tavern, he and Marty set out for the Nielsen house. He had no clear idea what he was going to do there, but afterwards he'd go to Casey's place and tell him that he had checked on Barron himself. Maybe Grace would be there.

It was a clear night. The stars sparkled, and the full moon bathed the land in a milky-white light. When he turned onto the dirt road, he switched off the headlights. Ahead of them to the right was the Nielsen house. The windows on the first floor were lit; the upstairs was dark. Ed parked the pickup on a patch of grass behind an old, twisted cottonwood tree whose branches were creaking softly in the night breeze. Silently, they set out across the dry rangeland. He held a dim flashlight, and Marty followed closely behind. When his friend stumbled, Ed cursed at him under his breath, and for a few minutes, they briskly walked next to each other, sharing the faint beam of light.

Marty was gasping when they reached a shallow ditch not far from the house.

"Stop snorting like that. Close your trap," Ed snarled while scrutinizing the two cars that were parked by the front door, an old, rusty Ford and Barron's Buick.

"Looks like Tif's car," Marty whispered. "What she doin' here so late? Ain't she at the motel?"

"Shut up! Stay here!"

Cautiously, Ed made his way across the grassland. It was hers all right. She hadn't told him that she would be coming out here that late. Crouching next to Tif's car he gazed at the house. Everything was still. With bent back, he crept closer, feeling with his worn cowboy boots for gopher holes. Then, in a quick dash, he covered the last few yards. He pressed his body against the wall underneath a brightly lit, open window and tried to get his heavy breathing under control. The damn cigarettes! But all was quiet, and he slowly raised his head. The kitchen, empty. A stack of clean dishes was on a rack by the sink, two cups on the table. Disgustingly tidy. Cautiously he scurried along the wall. He had nearly reached the next window when he heard a voice and froze in his tracks. The voice was faint. Then it stopped and music set in. He remained crouched underneath the window until he was sure that no other sounds disrupted the soft music from a radio and the monotonous babble of the announcer.

His mouth was dry and his heart was beating rapidly against his ribs as he made his way back to Marty, who was lying comfortably on his back in the shallow hollow, eyes closed, breathing deeply. Cursing, Ed punched the big, fat man in the stomach, not much, just enough to make him feel some pain. He was ticked off that Marty had fallen asleep while they were out on an important mission. Reconnaissance, that's what it was called. Ed was the leader, and he had every right to pound some discipline into Marty.

"They ain't in the house, but they're someplace around here."

"Why ya think they ain't in there? Maybe they're upstairs in one of them bedrooms." Marty glanced at him, smirking.

For a second Ed was stunned. Then he dismissed the thought. That old geezer and Tif? Tif in a bedroom with a man? Only somebody as stupid as Marty could think that up. Anyway, Tif was his girl. Anger stirred in him at the man who was hanging out with his girl. He had to do something about it. He'd go in and check the place out.

"I dunno, Ed. That ain't a smart idea," Marty protested when he told him. "Let's go home."

But Ed didn't care. If need be, he could always say he was looking for Tif. Her father had taken a turn for the worse. Yeah, that would work well. Marty would stand guard by the open window from where he could hear and see anybody who approached the house, and Ed would slip in through the front door. Tif had told him that the back door didn't open, but he already knew that. Dan had nailed it shut so that old Jack couldn't run away with his gun and shoot up the neighborhood.

They both crawled to the house, Marty heaving and panting, Ed urging him on in a breathless whisper. He positioned Marty by the window and told him to be watchful. If he messed up . . . Ed raised his fist. Then for a short moment he stepped into the glare of the single light bulb that illuminated the porch. Swiftly Ed opened the screen door and slipped into the house. As he noiselessly walked through the hallway, the last vapors of the beer drunk earlier lifted from his brain. Idly, he touched the jackets that hung on wooden pegs on the wall. He felt in the pockets, but found nothing of interest. He proceeded to the living room and stopped in surprise. The room was decorated for party, maybe a birthday party. There were presents on the table, all kid's things. Ed picked up a stuffed monkey, turned it this way and that, then dropped it scornfully. He hated birthday parties. Against the wall stood an old-fashioned sideboard. Cautiously he pulled out one of the drawers and winced at the soft clank of the metal handle. A Los Angeles phone book, an address book, a pocket calendar, folders with typed and handwritten papers, some receipts, and something that looked like insurance papers. He opened the address book and read the names of unknown people, most of whom lived in big cities, Los Angeles, New York, Chicago.

"Hurry," Marty whispered through the open window, "I seen somethin' move down there by them trees."

Hastily Ed returned the address book and closed the drawer. Everything looked undisturbed. As he sneaked out of the room he saw Tif's blue denim jacket draped over the back of a chair. It was a man's jacket with a pink rose stitched in the corner of the collar.

"I seen them, two people down by the lake between them trees. Maybe they're behind them now. I swear, Ed, I seen them." Marty was agitated, and Ed had some trouble calming him down and stopping him from running heedlessly into the night. Back in the shallow, they both listened, but everything was quiet. The dark silhouette of the house, surrounded by a pale, white circle of light, loomed large against the black sky. The leaves of the cottonwood trees whispered softly in the stillness.

Ed berated Marty. He called him an old woman who was scared of her own shadow, who couldn't tell the difference between a mouse scurrying through the grass and the footsteps of a real person. Just when he was ready to knock Marty around a bit to get the anger out of his system, he heard a sound. It was a sound that didn't belong here, that rose above the rustle of the cottonwood trees. Ed pushed Marty down and pressed his hand over his mouth when his friend wanted to protest. Breathlessly they listened into the night.

"Did ya hear that?"

Marty didn't answer. He couldn't, but Ed didn't want to loosen his grip on his face, not until he knew what was going on. Ed heard the soft purring of an approaching car, the snapping of twigs as it turned onto the track that led to the house. It came closer and closer, and then it stopped not far from them. They heard a door open and softly close. And then it was quiet again until very close to them, a shape suddenly materialized out of the night. A man of medium height walked by them stealthily. At one point he stumbled and fell down on his knees. Probably a gopher hole. He cursed under his breath, brushed off his pants and continued slowly toward the house. Ed focused his eyes on the front porch, expecting the man to appear in the circle of light. But the night had swallowed him up.

"Who's that?" Marty twisted his face free. Ed knocked him in the stomach with his elbow.

This was promising, very promising. There was no question now that they had to stay and watch, even though Ed didn't feel exactly comfortable with an invisible prowler around when he thought he and Marty were the only ones. Casey would be interested in the secret doings here. He'd expect him to find out what was going on. While Ed was wondering what to do next, two figures emerged from the darkness. They were about halfway between the lake and the house, too far to hear them but clearly visible.

"Didn't I tell ya?" Marty whispered in his ear.

The two people were walking side by side, slowly, unhurried. One was tall and thin, the other about a head shorter and of a slight build. It had to be Tif and Barron. Why was she walking around with this man in the middle of the night without letting Ed know about it? Housekeeping, babysitting? Ha! This didn't look like work. She should have told him about such a get-together. She owed him. It was understood. He understood it, and she ought to.

The nightly wanderers stopped by the cars, barely within the circle of light that radiated from the porch, two dark shapes opposite each other, silent and motionless. Ed thought they looked ridiculous as they stood there, mute, staring at each other. Then he heard a soft, deep laugh. The larger figure moved and leaned against Tif's car. And again they stood there silently.

41

"What're they doin'? Let's go home, Ed," Marty pleaded. Ed punched him, hard.

He thought he saw a movement by the front porch, but when he looked again, nothing stirred. The prowler was still out there. Ed was sure of that, and he was glad the stranger wasn't after him. He glanced back at Tif and Michael, wondering whether they would take that much time if they knew a man was hiding by the house. Michael Barron had moved away from the car now and opened the door for Tif. There was a hesitation about his movements and a slowness about hers that made Ed impatient. They lingered over the door until finally she was in the car, and Barron slammed it shut. Tif backed up and drove away. Even that was painfully slow. Barron watched the car disappear, and only when the taillights weren't visible anymore did he turn around. As he slowly walked into the whitish light that spilled from the porch he looked very much alone and unprotected. Safely hidden in the shallow, Ed sensed his vulnerability and waited gleefully for the second installment.

Before Barron reached the steps of the porch he lifted his head and scanned the windows upstairs. Was his little girl sleeping up there? Suddenly, the man stepped out of the black shadow of the wall. This time it was Marty who boxed Ed in the side. From his hiding place Ed sensed the shock that paralyzed Barron's movements. He knew instantly that Barron was afraid. The new man leaned against the railing of the porch, at ease. The two men talked in low voices. Now the stranger put his hand in his coat pocket.

"He's gonna get his gun," Marty whispered with delight. But the man only pulled out a pack of cigarettes, which he offered to Barron who shook his head. The stranger lit a cigarette, inhaled slowly and said something in a hushed murmur. In response Barron raised his voice, but the other quickly interrupted him pointing with his cigarette to the windows on the second floor. Then the two men walked up the stairs, Barron with heavy steps, the other lithe and fast.

Chapter 7

He didn't know how it had happened. He didn't want to have somebody in the house. It made no sense, not at the present time. As soon as he had left the motel he regretted the offer to the young woman. He needed to keep a low profile to blend in, and the last thing he wanted was a local girl who worked in his house unsupervised and might prattle about him and Emma to anyone who would listen. He decided to return to the motel and call the deal off. He'd find some excuse. When he told Emma that he had changed his mind, she protested loudly. It was embarrassing. The more he insisted, the louder she got. She stopped in the street, stomped her little feet and started crying. With dismay, he realized that he given in too often when she had behaved like that. But this time he had to be firm, for her sake.

After they had finished their errands, he drove back to the motel. He walked into the small office and realized too late that Tiffany wasn't alone. A woman was sitting in the breakfast nook smoking a cigarette, talking to Tiffany. They both looked up, and for several long seconds the man and the women stared at each other silently. It was Emma who rescued the situation, in a way. She told Tiffany that she'd show her around the house when she came tomorrow. Then she turned to her father and smiled. He looked down at her and knew that she had managed to override his decision, like a scheming adult. He was quite unable to argue with her in front of these two women.

"So, you're the man who hired my little sister." The woman

stumped out her cigarette and got up slowly. "She'll do a good job for you. Tif can work." She laughed. Languorously she lifted her well-rounded arm and touched the mass of blond curls that framed her face. She was beautiful, in an old-fashioned way. Her blond hair complemented a face that reminded Michael of a dainty porcelain doll, while her heavy bosom, barely contained in a tight blouse, revealed a mature woman. She charged the small room with a sensuality he found difficult to ignore. At the same time, he thought there was something repulsive about her. Maybe it had to do with the laziness of her movements, or perhaps it was the sullen expression on her face that disturbed the beauty of her immaculate alabaster skin.

"Yes," he mumbled. He looked across the room at Tiffany who was talking with Emma now. They didn't look like sisters, one so pale and voluptuous, the other slender and dark. There was something childlike about Tiffany in her oversized, shapeless clothes.

"I'm Grace." The woman smiled and parted her lips just wide enough to show a row of perfect, white teeth. "How do you like your new house?" She got up and leaned against the desk, letting her large breasts rest on the surface.

Michael wondered if she knew how provocative her movements were. Probably every man she talked to got that treatment. He wanted to get out of the office, away from this woman who stirred his senses even though he didn't find her attractive.

"It's a good house, but a lot needs to be done." He turned to Tiffany. "So tomorrow then, right?"

Tiffany briefly glanced at him, then lowered her eyes and smiled at Emma. "I can come a few hours in the afternoon before I start here at the motel at night."

"It's the old man, you know. Why don't you tell him," Grace said to her sister. "He's giving you a job and, by God, you need it. But he needs to know about your special circumstances."

Tiffany shook her head. Grace shrugged her shoulders, and her breasts moved under the thin blouse. "Our father is real sick. Actually he's dying. He's been dying for a while, but it's coming to an end. Lung cancer."

"It's emphysema. He's not dying." Tiffany's voice was so low he could hardly hear it.

"Tif refuses to take a job that interferes with taking care of him. There aren't many jobs she could get anyway. She isn't exactly qualified for anything." Grace laughed lightly. "She takes care of Dad, cooks his meals, checks his medicine, she can even give him a bath. If you ever get sick, mister, she'll do all right."

"Grace, stop it," Tiffany pleaded.

"He's got to know, baby."

Michael looked at the unlikely sisters and wondered again how they had grown up under the same roof and turned out so differently. He assured Tiffany that she could pick her own schedule. He'd probably only need her occasionally, but right now her help was appreciated. The house wasn't fully furnished yet. They didn't have enough dishes. There were no curtains on the windows, and there was a lot of cleaning that had to be done. While he was speaking, he knew it was all wrong. The words came out of his mouth, and his brain was screaming to stop. But it was too late now. When they left, Grace called after him that she worked at the beauty parlor. He should stop by some time. She'd give him and his daughter an expert haircut. As he drove past the office, he saw the two sisters talking animatedly behind the window. They could be arguing.

Grace was right. Tiffany proved to be a big help, and he was pleased with her. The house took on a more pleasant appearance. But he was still worried. He had to be; he couldn't be too cautious. Secretly, he watched her. He told himself that it was essential for his and Emma's safety to observe her, to make sure she didn't snoop. But when he discovered that he actually enjoyed it, he felt like a voyeur.

Sometimes he tried to talk to her, but she never said much and most of the time avoided looking at him. Emma was luckier. He heard them laugh and talk together, and he wondered if he could ever join in their conversations. He had tried it once or twice, but it hadn't worked. Tiffany had clammed up, and Emma had ignored him. Maybe in time, they'd allow him into their little circle. He could do with some friendly, innocent banter.

Tiffany usually came in an old, rusty car. This afternoon, when he was upstairs in one of the bedrooms that he had converted into his study, he saw a pickup drive toward the house. He didn't expect any workmen. Then Tiffany slipped out on the passenger side and lifted her hand in goodbye to somebody in the car whom he couldn't see. Slowly, too slowly for his taste, the pickup made a circle and drove away. When he asked her why she hadn't come in her car, she told him that it wouldn't start. He had a good idea who had brought her, probably one of those sinister looking young men who liked to hang out at the motel. One face in particular he remembered, a thin, sharp-nosed, sallow face with curious, restless eyes. He thought he had seen the same pickup in town with that face behind the dirty windshield. He didn't want strangers on his property, he told her gruffly. She ought to have called him, and he could have picked her up, or she shouldn't have come out at all. That's the way it would be in the future. Tiffany glanced at him briefly, one of those rare times when she actually looked at him. There was a trace of hostility in her eyes. Abruptly he turned around and walked away, angry at himself and at her.

Afterwards he was restless in his study and worried. He didn't want her to quit the job because he disliked her friends. When he went to the kitchen, she was standing by the sink scouring it vigorously. Her ponytail shook, and under the oversized T-shirt, her shoulders and arms moved back and forth furiously.

"Who was that in the car?" he asked.

Without looking up she answered, "A friend."

"A friend, hm." How could he tell her that her friend was an unsavory character?

"You're a nice girl, Tiffany. Why do you waste your time with that guy?"

"Ed is a good friend."

"Come on, a pretty girl like you and a guy like that?" He knew he sounded patronizing.

"You wouldn't understand. There was nobody else who would give me a ride."

Michael turned off the faucet and handed her a kitchen towel. Then he gently took her arm and led her to the table. "You have family here, your sister. Can they not help out?"

When she looked up at him, her eyes were brimming over with tears. Quickly, she turned away. "My family is busy, and Ed is there when I ask him."

He could barely hear the softly murmured words.

"It's my father, you see." She wiped a tear away. "He needs a lot of care, and I didn't have time to get my car fixed. But I want to keep this job. I like it and . . . ."

It was very still in the kitchen. The faucet dripped steadily into the sink. A gust of wind rattled the window pane as if it wanted to remind Michael why he was here in this old, drafty house. He leaned back on the chair and folded his arms over his chest. No, he would not take her hands in his, no matter how much he wanted to. This was not the time nor the place.

"I understand, Tiffany. But remember, the next time you need a ride, let me know. I'll pick you up. There is still a lot to do here, and Emma likes you."

"They are done with my car tomorrow. Just the spark plugs," she murmured. "I don't need Ed to bring me anymore."

"If I can do anything, let me know."

They both stood up. She looked forlorn and frail, lost in her misery. For one brief second, before he could think, he put the back of his hand against her cheek. Later, he wasn't sure that it had happened at all.

From then on, she always came alone. Sometimes they exchanged a few sentences. He told her he was a writer. After all, that part of his life was true. She didn't ask any questions like what do you write, why

47

did you come here to write? What would he have told her? I write for a newspaper, an agricultural magazine? That's what people in Junction City might understand. She might spread the news, and that was all right with him. The people here would want to know how he earned his money. Occasionally, he asked about her father, and she told him that he was doing better lately. She was still shy, but the ice had been broken.

It was Emma's birthday, and she had invited Tiffany. He wanted his daughter to have a real party with other children, but they had only been here for a few weeks, and Emma hadn't made any friends yet. It wasn't easy to be the only newcomer among children who had grown up together. But Emma didn't seem to mind; on the contrary, she had told him that she preferred to be by herself. Then the other children didn't ask so many questions. She wanted to reassure him that she would never talk about the mother who had vanished from her life, or the people who had moved into the house in the suburbs by the lake. In time, he hoped, the curiosity of the children would fade, and Emma would be one of them. So it was a small party with paper streamers and balloons, hot chocolate and cake.

Tiffany gave Emma a pretty blouse, and Michael surprised her with three large stuffed animals, a dog, a bear and a monkey. But the highlight was the fire by the lake. It was Tiffany's idea to burn all the rubbish they had collected in the house. And there was plenty of it: old chairs, broken crates, torn burlap sacks. Most of it they had found in the attic. It was a haven for insects and mice, dead and alive, and the smell was awful. He was glad to get rid of the foul remnants of the former owners. Emma and Tiffany had collected dead branches and twigs by the lake, and he had stacked them in a tidy pile. When they caught fire, Michael began throwing bits and pieces of furniture into the blaze. As he watched the trash burst into hot flares and dissolve into ashes, a soothing calmness came over him. The possessions of the Nielsens were going up in flames, and with it any remembrance of them. Maybe it was possible to put the past behind and start over. He would try his best.

The night got cool after the bonfire burnt down, but close to the red embers it was still warm and comfortable. They sat on the sandy ground, watching the last of the fire's glow. Once in a while, he threw a piece of dry wood on the cinders. Then a flame shot up and spread its soft light. Michael had wrapped his jacket around Emma, who had fallen asleep with her head lying on his leg. Her face was flushed, and she looked as if she was dreaming a happy dream. Tiffany crouched next to them, her legs pulled up to her chest, her head resting on her knees. She had lost the rubber band that held her hair together, and it was now flowing freely over her shoulders. The light of the flickering flames danced on her cheeks, and when she blinked, her eyelashes appeared unnaturally long.

When he carried Emma to the house and put her to bed, she didn't wake up. The fun and late hour had exhausted her. She would sleep well, protected by her menagerie of stuffed animals. As he walked back to the lake, he made out the dark contour of Tiffany, still sitting by the fire, seemingly lost in her own thoughts, in her world that was so unfamiliar to him. She stood up when she heard him, her face hidden in darkness. Every fiber in his body was suddenly aware of her presence. Slowly he walked up to her, lifted his hand and touched her cheeks, her forehead and her mouth, like a blind man. She held still and let his hand come to rest against her throat where he could feel her blood pulsating. He heard her breathing softly and felt the shiver that ran through her body. How he yearned to press her against him, but he did not dare. For a brief moment he felt the soft touch of her fingers on his hand. They walked back to the house in silence. He wanted to put his arm around her, but the circle of light ahead of them by the porch stopped him. Whatever had happened in the darkness by the lake, he wanted to keep it hidden.

There were times in his life when everything seemed right. These moments didn't come too often, and they didn't last. When he was younger, he often ignored them, waiting for bigger, greater things to happen. But life had humbled him and taught him to be grateful for a moment of happiness made bittersweet by the knowledge that this brief sense of delight would soon be swallowed up by the unpredictable distortions of life. They said good-bye slowly and hesitantly without looking at each other.

When he walked to the house, he sighed softly. He had been lonely for so long. He had accepted it as punishment for his past mistakes.

He had nearly reached the porch when a figure stepped out of the darkness.

"Hello, Mr. Barron."

Michael's first thought was that he was taller and stronger than the other man, who was in his mid-thirties, well-groomed and expensively dressed, not unlike the people Michael used to associate with. There was a guarded, unpleasant look in his otherwise handsome face as his eyes darted warily from Michael to the house to the black emptiness behind them.

"Sorry, to bother you like this, Mr. Barron," the man continued, "but I didn't know you had company."

"Who are you?"

"My name is Coe, Jim Coe but that won't mean anything to you. I'm a friend of Vincent's." His voice was smooth, his eyes probing slits.

"What do you want?"

"That's a delicate business." The man smiled. "And it'll take some time to explain. Why don't we go into the house and talk it over?"

"I don't know you."

"You'll get to know me, Mr. Barron. Let's go in. Your daughter is sleeping. We don't want to wake her. That's her room up there, isn't it?" With his cigarette he pointed to Emma's bedroom window.

Michael didn't answer. He walked up the steps, and the man followed him.

Chapter 8

When Tiffany drove home that night, she did not notice the black silhouettes of fence posts and cottonwood trees under the sparkling sky. Agitated and bewildered, she touched her throat and felt the blood burn under her skin. What was happening to her? She had never felt like that before. Feeling desire was something that belonged to Grace, and she found her sister's promiscuity loathsome. Tiffany remembered with shame Ed's half-hearted fumbling when he was drunk. They were just friends, and she had found his groping offensive and disgusting. Grace, who thought of nothing but men and sex, laughed at her and called her a saint, a nun, an ice queen. She didn't want to be like Grace.

Michael Barron was different from the people she knew. Most of the time he was serious and melancholy. She didn't know the source of his pain, but she thought it was not unlike what she experienced so often. When he was quiet and dejected, she felt close to him.

The nearer she got to Junction City, the more unreal the events by the lake became. When she parked the car in the driveway, she had nearly convinced herself that it was a fantasy or an episode from one of her soap operas.

It was only then that she noticed that all the windows of the small wood-frame house were lit. She glanced at her watch. It was a few minutes past eleven. When Grace came home late, if she came home at all, she never turned on any lights. She just flopped into bed. And her mother rarely stayed up beyond ten o'clock.

A sudden fear wiped out all other thoughts, and she hastened into the house. When she opened the door, she saw her father sitting in his recliner as he always did. His eyes were closed, and his breathing labored. Her mother and Grace stood by him. Her mother, who normally slept through her husband's worst attacks, was wrapped in a threadbare, pink bathrobe. Her dyed blond hair was disheveled, and her face was bloated. In her hand she held a glass with a brown liquid, and Tiffany knew that it wasn't ice tea. Grace wore tight, flashy clothes; her face was carefully made up. Both women were staring impassively at the sick man who was struggling for breath. Tiffany rushed to her father.

"What's wrong? What happened?" A cold hand was clutching her throat.

Her mother turned to her and said in a subdued voice, "Thank God you're finally here. Where were you? We called the motel but you weren't there."

"I think he's dying," Grace said.

"No, he's not." There was no reason why her father should be worse tonight than on any other night. Tiffany knelt down next to the recliner and looked into his face. It was ashen and drawn, the way it had been for months. He struggled for breath, and the muscles of his shoulders and chest contracted in a spasm. Then his breathing became shallow again. She took his hands into hers. They were so thin, skin and bones, cold and lifeless, colder than they had ever been. She rubbed them gently trying to put some warmth back into them, but they didn't respond. It was as if ice water rather than blood was flowing through his veins. Her father had given up the fight.

"He's been like that for hours. I don't think the medicine is helping anymore. We've called the ambulance. They'll be here any time now." There was no emotion in her mother's voice. When Tiffany glanced at her, she could see relief in her face, relief that she wouldn't have to deal with a dying man in her house anymore after the ambulance took him away.

When her father got sick four months ago, he told them that he didn't want to go to the hospital nor to a nursing home, not then, not at the end. He had talked it over with his doctor who had said that it was all right for him to stay at home. A nurse would come several times a week to check on him. Her father had assured them with a pathetically worried face that he wouldn't be a burden, but neither her mother nor Grace liked the idea. They tried to convince him that he would be better off in a facility, and they were furious at Tiffany when she pointed out that the care facility was forty miles away and that it would be difficult to visit him often. Her father had smiled at her and said, "That's my Tiffany." He moved out of the bedroom and took up his place in the recliner in the living room. Again and again her mother complained that it was inconvenient. She couldn't bring her friends home; she couldn't watch TV without disturbing him, and they couldn't have big family dinners anymore because the living room had become a sickroom. It was ridiculous. Tiffany knew it, and so did her father. They never had family dinners except at Christmas, and her mother had her own TV in the bedroom. As far as her friends were concerned, she met them at the bar or the beauty parlor and liked that much better anyway. Her father smiled and ignored his wife's tirades. He relied on her, Tiffany, who arranged her work schedule around his needs. The motel wasn't far away, and she could sometimes dash home and check on him. She took care of his meals, watched over his medication and at night she made sure that he was comfortable.

In the kitchen, her mother and sister sometimes talked about him dying. They talked about his railroad pension, his life insurance and the cost of the funeral. Occasionally, their friends from the beauty parlor stopped by and advanced their own opinions about the sick man. When Tiffany listened to them, it seemed to her as if they were trying to solve a crossword puzzle together. Everybody was busy filling in the blank squares and contributing words. And when the squares were all filled in, she thought, her father's life would be over.

Tiffany loved her father and avoided examining too deeply how she felt about her mother. Her mother was loud and shrill and totally absorbed with herself. She didn't know how to take care of a husband and two children. The reason she got along so well with Grace was that they were very similar in looks and tastes. Both had stunning blond hair with a touch of copper, which matched the rosy hue of their cheeks. Both liked to dress in bright, garish clothes. Both had been beautiful, in a way Grace still was. Tiffany remembered a hot summer day, Sunday, when she first noticed how different she was from both of them. Her mother was dressed for church in an especially lovely dress and elegant, high-heeled shoes. Grace looked equally gorgeous in her pink summer dress and matching Mary Janes. They carried small, white handbags, and when her mother opened hers, a sweet fragrance escaped from it. Elizabeth Arden, she said. Tiffany was seven then, thin, with dark hair and deeply tanned skin. She felt like the ugly duckling, even though she was dressed as nicely as Grace. But she didn't mind, she loved and admired her older sister. When they all stood in the sunlight outside the church, her father took her by the hand and joked about the two pretty females in the family who were floating through the crowd like magnificent butterflies. "We're the dark horses, Tiffany," he said. She could tell he was proud of her mother and Grace. He forgave them their foolishness until there was no forgiveness left in him, just resignation. With Tiffany he talked and laughed. He told her about his work, and sometimes they were quiet together. She was sure of his love which was gentle and constant. They were good company for each other.

Things changed as they got older. Grace turned out to be wild. All the boys were after her, and she wasn't clever enough to protect her reputation. There was a rumor that she had had an abortion or two. It could well be true. The nice boys, of whom there weren't many to begin with, soon turned away from her, and Grace fell back on the others. They didn't mind that she was an unsteady woman who drank too much and slept around.

Over the years, the ready laughter of her father died down. He went to work with a quiet dignity that made Tiffany proud of him. He was doing real work, not like her mother and Grace, who lounged around in the beauty parlor snipping away at hair, and not like her, who never learned any skills. Her father liked working for the railroad. Everybody respected him, but he had no close friends. He went to work and then came home, ate, slept, and went to work again.

When they diagnosed her reading problem, she felt she had let him down. It was in fourth grade, when she was struggling worse than ever and her grades were very bad. She told him she was sorry that she couldn't learn to read like the other children. He had smiled at her, affectionate, resigned. "It wasn't supposed to be, little Tiffany," he said. He sounded so hopeless that she gave up her efforts in school altogether. Life became easier then, but also sadder. There was little she expected for herself.

Grace opened the refrigerator and poured a bottle of wine cooler into a glass. She drank in small, hasty gulps, her eyes darting around nervously. Tiffany knew that her sister wanted to be done with it all. Their father's sickness was nothing more than an inconvenience in her frantic life.

"Dad doesn't want to go to the hospital," Tiffany said.

"Tif, he's dying," Grace insisted. Her alcoholic breath mingled with the odor of the sick room. "Everybody dies in a hospital. Mom and I don't want him to die in the living room. We'll never be able to forget it. How can we sit and have coffee here, when he's died in this room? I mean it's spooky."

"That's right," her mother added. "He's put me through so much. I can't take anymore." She fumbled in her bathrobe pocket and pulled out a pack of cigarettes.

"Don't smoke." Tiffany glared at her. "Not in the house! Don't you understand?" She could hear the siren of the ambulance.

"Tiffany." Her father's voice was faint, his breathing was shallow. Restlessly he moved his hand over the blanket which covered his thin legs.

55

She put her head close to his and whispered, "Daddy, it's all right. You won't go to the hospital. I'll take care of you." Their cheeks touched, and she felt his eyelashes flutter against her skin. When she looked at him again, his eyes were wide open. There was an expression of surprise in them. His mouth moved but no words came out. Then he gave a little gasp.

She threw her arms around him and moaned. "No, no, no." She had never seen anybody die. It couldn't be that simple. It couldn't just be a little gasp that divided the dead from the living. If she'd hold him and rock him, he'd be warm and comfortable, and he'd wake up and smile at her and talk to her. The tubes in his nose, she had to be careful about the tubes. He needed the oxygen.

Then she heard the front door slam and suddenly loud voices filled the living room. People were everywhere, switching on lights and pushing furniture out of the way. One man in a blue uniform talked to her, but she didn't understand what he said. When he grabbed her arm and pulled her away, she tried to resist, but he was stronger. He pried her off her father. She heard her mother say, "Tif, it's over. Let go." And then she stood back and stared at them. If he was dead, why were they working on him so frantically with an oxygen mask?

A policeman entered the house and surveyed the scene calmly from the door. Tiffany watched him walk over to her mother and talk to her. Her mother nodded her head, and he left again. Through the confusion of voices, she heard Grace give instructions to the ambulance people who had put her father on a stretcher and were ready now to carry him out of the house. When they passed her, she put out her hand and stopped them.

"He isn't dead, is he?" Her voice was barely audible.

The man at the head of the stretcher shrugged his shoulders. "You talk to the doctor. He'll tell you." Then they were gone.

The living room looked like a battlefield. The old, shabby furniture had been pushed to the wall. Her father's medicine bottles, his magazines and books were scattered on the floor. His recliner with its frayed armrests stood in the middle of the room, empty. She could still see the imprints of his legs on the seat, the dent his head had made in the cushion. When she walked to the armchair, Grace and her mother left the room. She could hear them in the kitchen, talking, pouring water into the coffee machine.

Her father's smell clung to the faded brown velvet of the upholstery. It was not a pleasant smell; it was the smell of a sick man. She didn't mind. She had gotten used to it. It was the smell of a sick man who was alive. Thin, fine brown hairs clung to the worn headrest. He wasn't even old enough to have gray hair. She, who cried so easily, stood next to the chair with dry eyes. Slowly, she began picking up the medicine bottles, the magazines and books, and arranged them on the small table the way he liked it. Then she sat down on the sofa and stared at the old recliner, unable to grasp the unfathomable.

She didn't know how long she had sat there when her mother told her that they were ready to go to the hospital and asked if she wanted to come along.

"He's dead, Tif," her mother said. "They told me so. He wasn't breathing at all."

Tiffany shook her head. An eerie silence descended upon the house after they left. Without her father, her home was a desolate place, and she wondered how she could live here without him. Slowly the tears gathered in her eyes and spilled over on her cheeks. She didn't know if she was crying for her father or for herself. She didn't know how long she sat there giving herself up to a steady stream of gentle, silent tears. It was toward morning when the pain and anguish receded, and a drowsy desire for healing raised its head, cautiously, hesitantly, but insistently. She saw her father sitting in his chair smiling at her.

Chapter 9

Ed told Marty to stay in the ditch. He would make his way back to the house. If the two men had gone into the living room, as he assumed, he'd be able to eavesdrop. When he reached the brightly lit window, he heard their voices. Slowly, his heart beating in his throat, he raised his head. There they stood in the middle of the room, Michael Barron staring at the newcomer with hostile eyes, the other man looking around curiously, a mocking smile on his face.

"So that's what it looks like," the new guy said. "May I sit down?" He walked to a rocking chair by the window. Michael Barron's eyes followed him, and for a split second he looked straight at the window through which Ed was peering. Ed quickly lowered his head and held his breath. Nothing happened. Then he heard the sound of wooden floorboards creaking under the rhythmic movement of the rocker. Cautiously he moved to the next window from where he had a better view of the two men without being seen himself.

"I'm sure, Mr. Barron, you are used to grander accommodations than this. But I imagine, under the circumstances, the house meets your needs," the man said.

"You are not here to talk to me about my house, Mr. Coe."

"In a way, I am." The man laughed softly. Michael Barron was staring at the stranger with single-minded hatred, and Ed felt a delicious shiver run down his spine. But it was the newcomer who gripped his attention. It was the way he talked, the way he leaned back, rocking calmly, his hands flat on the wooden armrests, his knees moving easily with the chair, hardly disturbing the sharp creases in his expensive, gray pants. A tiger, Ed thought, ready to jump.

"It was me who sold the house to Vincent," the man continued. "My grandparents lived here, they built it. They were dirt farmers, but they weren't poor. They had lots of land and enough money, but they lived like poor people." He smiled contemptuously. "They were poor for so long, they couldn't get used to being rich. They never enjoyed their money, just scrimped and saved, stashed it away and worked like animals. The kids at school used to make fun of my mother and the twins Dan and Jack. They always wore old rags, never had any money, never went out. Mother couldn't stand it. She ran away when she was seventeen. Wasn't done with school yet. That was all right. I would have done the same. You've got to move on in life. The only bad thing was that she got stuck with other madmen, probably a worse kind than the ones she had left behind." Jim Coe took his eyes off Michael Barron and let them wander through the room again. He wasn't smiling anymore. He had stopped rocking and his fingertips were tapping nervously on the armrests.

"Why am I telling you all this?" He turned his face to Michael again and laughed. "Never mind, we all have skeletons in the closet, don't we, Mr. Barron? I don't think I would have liked to grow up here. This is a lousy house, and Junction City isn't much better."

"I don't know what you want from me. If you want to look at the house where your mother grew up, you could have come during the day. It's late. Not exactly the time for a social call."

"Don't rush me, Mr. Barron. I've come a long way. In a way, it's like a homecoming for me, and I've got to enjoy it, right? Mother never came back here except to bury Uncle Dan and put Uncle Jack in the nuthouse. She tried to sell the place, but nobody wanted it, and then she lost interest. I think she couldn't face coming back here anymore. Too many bad memories. I know what that's about. There are places where

I don't like to go. Places where we lived when I was young. Mother always hooked up with the wrong guys. One after the other, and they didn't particularly like me. One shabby apartment after another. Not like the place where you used to live, Mr. Barron. A big house by the lake with a fence and a security gate that keeps out unwanted elements like myself."

Ed's mind was working feverishly. So this was Mabel Nielsen's son, and he had obviously done better than his mother. He was well dressed, and there was a certain air about him. He was a force, nobody's fool.

"Tell me what you want, and then get out."

Ed smiled with malicious glee. It was a pleasant feeling to see Michael Barron on the defensive. Even though Ed hadn't figured out what the game was all about, he was on the side of the new guy.

"Well, Mr. Barron—you see, I don't mind calling you Mr. Barron because I'm not interested in blowing your cover. I understand that you have a very good reason to assume a fake name. Why am I here? I need money. It's as simple as that. Don't misunderstand me. I got a lot of money for this old house, too much, really. When Vincent bought the place for that ridiculously high price, I got suspicious. It wasn't difficult to find out that he was working for you. I just had to put a bit of pressure on him. I think all lawyers have something to hide, don't you? Anyway, now I have a problem, Mr. Barron. All that money is gone. I don't believe in living like a poor dirt farmer, and I went through it a bit faster than I thought. That and a few bad deals. It's not unusual in my line of work." He laughed as if the thought of some past business failure amused him.

Michael Barron briefly covered his eyes with his hand. "You seem to know a lot, Mr. Coe. Then you should also know that I don't have much money left." His voice sounded strained.

"I know it's not quite that bad. There's your agent. You get royalties from the last two successful movie scripts you wrote. I am quite an admirer of your work. And there's some property in your name.

Vincent could liquidate that. We can come up with a solution together."

Michael Barron didn't answer. He was staring at the floor. Jim Coe continued to rock back and forth.

"How does Emma like it here?"

Barron shot him a furious glance. "Leave her out of it."

"But that's what it's all about, isn't it? Her mother is quite upset."

"Why don't you ask her for money? After all, you found us. She'd be happy to pay you and get Emma back."

"She has notified the authorities. Not a smart move in her situation, but she was desperate. I guess she loves her daughter. Don't all mothers love their children? Anyway, I never work with people who are in with the police. Too dangerous. Besides, the only money she has is what you give her. It's plenty, but the way she spends it, she'll never have any left over. You, on the other hand, can make more money. You're the better bet." He paused as if waiting for a response, but none came. "I know you have to think about all of this. I'm not an unreasonable man, Mr. Barron, and I'm not in a particular rush. I need a bit of peace and quiet myself, and Junction City seems a good place to stay for a while. I've checked into the motel. I told them that I'm in business looking for investments. People love that kind of thing." He got up and smoothed his dark-blue blazer with his hands. "I think you realize that you'll lose Emma as soon as I tip off the police. She'll be back with her mother in no time, and you'll be in jail." Coe smiled. "I'll find my way out."

Ed lowered himself to the ground and listened to the soft, unhurried footsteps of Coe as he walked down the porch stairs. At the bottom, he stopped and lit a cigarette. The flame briefly illuminated the stranger's face. He was no longer smiling. Silently he disappeared into the darkness.

Marty sat in the ditch, his arms wrapped around himself. "What happened? I'm cold."

"We're on to somethin' big. Let's go to Casey's."

"Yeah, let's go. I wanna drink somethin' and warm up a bit."

61

The two men waited until the soft purring of Coe's car grew fainter, and the silent night closed in on them. As they walked back to the pickup, Marty stumbled a few times and cursed, but this time Ed didn't get mad. He was sure Barron would not be listening into the night for suspicious sounds. The guy had other problems.

It was nearly one in the morning when they got to Casey's. The last card players were getting ready to leave, and Casey was switching off the front light. Ed saw the frown on his round face, but he wasn't worried. He walked up to the rotund man and whispered urgently that he had something important to tell him.

"Ya wanna know, Casey. Ya need to know."

"It better be good, boys. I'm tired. It's been a lousy night. No big winners. Come on in then." He waved them inside.

Ed had warned Marty to be quiet and leave all the talking to him.

"You want to drink something? You think your news is worth a beer?" Casey laughed softly and his stomach shook like pudding.

"Ya got some of that Mexican beer, Casey? Ya know, the one with them Xs on it? It's real good." A big smile spread over Marty's face.

Ed boxed him in the side, and told at him to shut up. He could never trust Marty to follow his command to be quiet, say nothing, just sit there and listen. Here he was, blabbering because he forgot, misunderstood things, or was too dumb to understand Ed in the first place.

"Sure, Marty, can't say I like Mexicans, but I'm with you. Their beer is good." Casey walked to the refrigerator with a grace and speed that Ed didn't expect in a man so heavy. He wondered briefly if there was real strength underneath the folds of flesh. "What did you find out?"

Ed told himself to be calm and cool, like this man Coe. Slowly he recounted what he had learned this night, that Michael Barron was not his real name, that he was probably from Los Angeles, and that he had a wife there. He didn't know exactly why he was here with his daughter. Most likely, he was hiding from something or someone. When he described what clearly looked like blackmail, Casey shook his head and sighed.

"I doubt Coe is his real name. We got to find out what this is all about," he murmured.

"He's the son of Mabel Nielsen, but I ain't never seen him here in Junction City. Hell, I ain't never seen Mabel Nielsen here. He checked into the motel. I figure he's gonna stay a while."

"You did a good job tonight, Ed, a real good job. But this is just the beginning. We need to know the whole story, don't we? Barron, Coe, we got to find out all there is. We don't want strangers messing around here."

"I'm gonna find out about him, Casey. It's easy. My girlfriend, Tif, she works at the motel. She'll find out things for me."

"This girlfriend of yours, Tif, isn't she Grace's sister?"

"Yeah, they are sisters, don't look alike at all. Well, me and Tif, we ain't really together. We're friends from school. She ain't very smart. I look after her a bit. Now Grace, that's a different story."

Before he had a chance to mention that he had his eyes on Grace, and that maybe Casey could lend a helping hand in this matter, Casey interrupted him. "Her father died tonight. Just heard it from one of the boys who was here earlier. He wasn't very old." Casey shook his massive head sorrowfully as he got up from his chair.

Randy—could it be true? It was over then, really over. In a brief flash Ed saw Randy's face in his mind, handsome, always smiling, even though he had little to smile about. Ed put down his beer. He should go and see Tif. What time was it? Two?

"Gotta go now, Casey. Too bad about Tif's father. Me and Marty, we better hit the road now."

As his truck rattled through the dark night, his stomach was queasy. He would go home and take some antacids. No use bothering Tif and her family now.

Chapter 10

Michael didn't know how long he sat in the living room after Jim Coe had left. He was stunned, unable to form a clear thought. His brain was a whirlwind of confusion, one dazed thought chasing the other, one chaotic picture crowding out the next. He had to calm down and think, and the longer he sat on the shabby couch, the more fantastic the nightly encounter appeared to him. Michael looked at the rocking chair in front of the large window. Had somebody really sat there, his elegantly clad legs moving the chair in a gentle rhythm, a man with a pleasant face who didn't hide the fact that he was a crook? Maybe this man was a figment of his imagination, a phantom of his dreams. No, he was real, an ugly reminder of what he and Emma had left behind.

Michael tried to rouse himself, but it was as if his blood had turned to lead, paralyzing his body while his brain was on fire. He rubbed his eyes, covered them with his hands, but the darkness he saw frightened him. Aimlessly, he glanced around the room, but saw nothing until he noticed the denim jacket that hung over one of the dining chairs. A small, pink rose was artlessly stitched in the corner of the collar. The faded blue cloth was puckered, but the pink rose shone brilliantly, perfect in its simplicity. He stared at it for a long time. Gradually his mind stopped racing.

He'd have to call Vincent. The lawyer was the only person who could help him. Vincent had brought him into this mess; he had to get him out of it. At the time, it had seemed like a good idea to work with him. He was equally at home in Michael's world as in the shady world of half-truths and borderline legalities. In a way, he liked Vincent and had come to trust him, partly out of necessity and partly because he appeared so competent and self-assured. But what did he really know about this man who operated in the gray areas of the law? As a writer Michael only knew about movies, working with agents, producers, actors. He knew nothing about the law and its subterfuges, until now. Tomorrow he would call him. Vincent had to help him get rid of this man Jim Coe.

Michael didn't feel rested when he woke up the next morning. He had dreamt wildly, and remnants of his dream were still floating through his brain. Tiffany with a bunch of pink roses in her hand, her face half-hidden behind the flowers. She said something to him, but he couldn't understand it. He was trying to talk to her, but couldn't get any words out. His dream was like a silent movie without the text.

Emma brought reality back into his life. They had breakfast together, and she reminded him to ask Tiffany if she could return her library books. He wondered if he had remembered the due dates of his library books when he was her age. Emma was so competent, like a little mother. Did he bring this out in her? He was clumsy in the kitchen, clueless about the household. Who was taking care of whom? The events of last night proved that it was he, the adult, who was incompetent. He had been so sure that he had done the right thing, that it was best for all of them, for Emma, himself and even for Marcia. Of course, Marcia wouldn't see it this way, but things couldn't go on the way they had. She would realize it someday because she too loved Emma, because every mother loved her child. But he hadn't foreseen somebody like Jim Coe.

At first, Vincent was of no help. He insisted that he had never heard of Jim Coe. Only when Michael described him, it clicked. Yes, the lawyer told him, that was the guy who sold the house to him, but he had a different name then. Not unusual in certain circles, Vincent added. What did he propose to do to get the man out of his hair? There was silence on the other end. In his mind Michael saw the beefy lawyer sitting behind his desk squinting his small eyes, his free hand ruffling the thick, black hair. Vincent was a middle-aged, overweight, pleasant-looking man. He had gentle manners and smiled most of the time. But his appearance was deceptive, Michael realized once again when he heard his cold, clear voice.

"I'll take care of it, Michael. Don't worry. I need to do some checking. I'll let you know."

When Michael put down the receiver, a feeling of bitterness overcame him. He and Emma were at the mercy of people like Vincent and Coe, one a blackmailer, the other a shady lawyer whose business was the desperation of people like him. Should he have gone to the authorities instead of Vincent? By the time he had thought about it, it was too late. He and Emma were heading east, away from California. The law would not forgive him for that.

Until last night, he had thought Vincent had done a good enough job. He had supplied him with a new identity, he had handled his finances, and he had suggested the escape route. However, one crook had sniffed out the other crook. Vincent had not been cautious enough, and now he would have to come up with something because lawyers like him were always resourceful. Michael had paid him well, and Vincent knew that he would continue to pay him well.

During the past few weeks, his life had taken on a semblance of normalcy after years of turmoil. Emma had started school and was doing well. She had stopped being temperamental and difficult. She had adjusted to her new life. He knew that some credit went to Tiffany because Emma wanted to please her. He himself had enjoyed the practical challenges of their existence. They had cleaned up the house, and with Tiffany's help, had bought furniture and household goods. Workmen had come and done the necessary repairs. They were straightforward, matter-of-fact, never asked any personal questions. Sometimes he shared a beer with them after they were done. It was a simple, agreeable world.

Had his dream of a peaceful life been an illusion? Was it possible to run away from one's past? Was that not the preposterous idea of an imaginative writer who had lost touch with reality? Instead of writing a play or a movie script, he was trying to live one: his escape with Emma, their house in the country complete with a budding romance, the appearance of Jim Coe. Their bungled situation had become the play he would never be able to write. He had fallen into his own trap by using his imagination in real life. But now reality had overtaken him, and he was losing control. There was no new start because the past had stretched its claws and hooked them into his flesh, tearing him apart, pulling him back. He could accept this fate for himself because he had made many mistakes; he had much to atone for. Never would he forgive himself for the way he reacted when Marcia first told him about the pregnancy. But Emma was without guilt. For her sake, he could not give up. To protect her, to give her back her childhood, that was the only goal he had.

He loved Emma. He loved their life together. He loved the gentle pleasures of being a family man. When he was with Marcia, he was shy with his daughter. Marcia had never given him a chance to be a father. She and the nanny were in charge of Emma. Whenever he tried to act like a father, Marcia quickly reminded him that he had not wanted this child and that she didn't care for his intrusion. He had accepted this because he did not want to fight with his wife. He had lost his rights when he had suggested an abortion.

When he left them two years ago, he thought it was best for all of them. Marcia was doing better without him, at least that's what he had told himself at the time. And he believed that Emma was happier. He knew she suffered when he and Marcia quarreled. Every argument flared into a screaming match that frightened his child and left him exhausted and ashamed. And Marcia was acting crazier all the time, running from one guru to another, heaping toys and clothes on Emma, crying uncontrollably when he tried to interfere. The only way out was to leave. She promised him to go into rehab, and he believed her.

Marcia kept the house, and he gave her a generous settlement and a good monthly allowance. He wanted to make sure that Emma was well provided for. The nanny was a competent person and would make up for Marcia's inadequacies. Emma had a dog and a cat; she took piano and ballet lessons. Whenever he saw her, she seemed fine. He thought he had done right by them.

That all changed the night he made a surprise visit. Marcia had to sign some papers, and he had been unable to get hold of her even though he had called her numerous times and left countless messages. It was after nine when he finally drove over to her house. The windows were brightly lit, but nobody answered the doorbell. To his surprise, the door was unlocked. He was wary as he entered the large hallway with its black and white tiled floor, the opulent mirrors on the walls and the enormous vases that filled the corners. The old feeling of sadness and despondency overcame him. He had been unhappy here, unable to work. Every creative impulse had been killed in an atmosphere of distrust and anger.

He walked through the rooms on the ground floor but found nobody. The elegant living room was a mess with pillows and magazines scattered over the carpet, dirty glasses on the table and discarded clothing on the white Italian leather sofa. He went upstairs to check the bedrooms and found the beds untouched, including Emma's bed. He went downstairs again and waited with mounting apprehension in the vast, silent house. When he finally heard them, his worst fears were justified. The loud clatter of Marcia's high heels stumbling across the floor was all too familiar as was sluggish incoherence of her high-pitched voice. Emma looked confused and scared when she walked in trailing her mother and a thin young man with untidy hair. She clutched her doll in her arms. The two adults were high. They threw themselves on the sofa, staring into space, ignoring him. Maybe they didn't even see him. There was a veil over Marcia's eyes. Her blond hair was disheveled, and lipstick smeared the corner of her mouth. He saw a fresh, red swelling in her left arm. In a way, he wasn't surprised.

It was his daughter who tore out his heart. She stood there, lost in the middle of the palatial room, the doll pressed against her, watching her mother with bewildered eyes. This was his child, the princess of this house. She didn't even look at him. She looked at her mother, the only parent she knew. Michael had never felt such pain in his life before. Too concerned with himself and his work, he hadn't much thought about her. Marcia, the nanny, and his money were supposed to take care of her. And now he didn't count.

He told Marcia that he would take Emma to bed. His wife looked at him with blank eyes and tried to smile, but the smile collapsed into a grimace. Her boyfriend burst out in a shrill laugh as he stumbled toward the cabinet that held the liquor bottles. Michael took Emma by the hand, and she followed him passively. Upstairs in her room, he hastily went through her closet and indiscriminately grabbed some clothes while his daughter watched silently. He told her that they would go on a vacation. That's why he had come tonight. They'd go away for a while to some nice place. Emma gazed at him with puzzled eyes, but never uttered a word. When he was ready to leave, he put a few stuffed animals under the blanket of her bed. It might fool Marcia at least until tomorrow morning. Then he took Emma's hand, and she went with him silently. The lively child he knew had little resemblance to the mute child who moved like a robot, asked no questions, uttered no protest. Later, he told himself, he would explain, and she would understand. They left the house through the back door. Nobody stopped them. Probably Marcia and her friend had already forgotten about them.

When they drove away, and the gate of the beautiful estate closed behind them, Emma turned her head back and asked, "Does Mommy know we're going away?"

He didn't know how he forced the words out. Yes, Mommy knew. Mommy was sick. She would go to a hospital, and when she was better, Emma would go back home. They never talked about Mommy again.

The sun shone through the window in his upstairs study; the wind rustled in the old cottonwood trees. It promised to be an ordinary day.

After he had taken Emma to school, Michael spent the day thinking and waiting. Waiting for a phone call from Vincent that did not come, waiting for the sun to warm the air, waiting for the wind to pick up the dry leaves from the ground, waiting for Tiffany to arrive. He listened for the sputtering sound of her car, but there was only silence outside. It wasn't like her not to come. She was punctual. She'd let him know if her car didn't work, if something kept her in town. Had he offended her? He tried to go through last night's events, but his memory was vague, overshadowed by the threat that lurked behind the pleasant face of the stranger. That man was so much more real and immediate. The blackmailer had already succeeded in destroying much that was good in his life.

Vincent called him the next morning. "Michael, I have a lead on this guy, Jim Coe. Don't worry. I'll be able to take care of him. Just sit tight."

"What do you mean? Sit tight. The guy is here, knows who I am and wants money." His voice was shrill, and he tried in vain to control his desperation.

"Calm down," Vincent purred soothingly. "I can't change things overnight, but I'm working on it. What you need to do, Michael, is string him along. Tell him you're ready to liquidate your assets and pay him off. I need a bit of time, and things will be all right again."

Vincent refused to tell him more, and Michael wanted to believe him.

When Tiffany didn't show up for the third day, Emma complained and insisted that he do something about it. On their way home from school, they stopped at the motel. An old, thin man, dressed in worn overalls, stood behind the counter in the office. Mumbling to himself, he was sorting through bits and pieces of paper and didn't pay any attention to them. When Michael repeated his greeting, the man finally looked up and told him that the motel was closed for a few days.

"If anybody thinks that I'm making any money with this place, he's mistaken." The old man pounded with his hand on the counter and some scraps of paper fell to the floor. "Did anybody tell me there was a problem? 'Course not. And now two rooms are flooded. I've got to replace everything, the pipes, the floors, the carpets. And the pipes in the other rooms need to be checked." He stared at Michael angrily, as if he were the culprit who was responsible for his misfortune. "This is not the Hilton. It's an old place. I've told the girls to keep an eye on the bathrooms. But do you think they'd do it? Liz, that dumb gal, she's too lazy. And Tif, well, I guess, she has other problems. Didn't think about bathrooms. Can't blame her." His head with the sparse gray hair bopped up and down. "They think I'm making money with this place. They don't know. It all goes to salaries, repairs and taxes. I'm going to be a poor man. Where the hell is Lester's phone number?" He furiously sifted through the papers, then stopped abruptly and squinted at Michael. "I need a plumber right now."

Michael pulled the plumber's business card out of his wallet and pushed it across the counter. A satisfied smile spread across the man's face creating a network of wrinkles on his fine, smooth skin.

"Thank you, mister, thank you very much. That's what I need. Must have lost his card." He sighed. "This office is a mess. Can't find anything because the girls don't put things in the right place. No wonder. One is a slob, the other can't read. I told them, the registration forms here, the bills there, everything else in this little box. But no, they stuff everything in this drawer here."

Emma was pulling at Michael's hand.

"I'm looking for Tiffany. I am wondering—," he said.

"Al Wiederspan," the man interrupted him. "I've owned this motel for three years and I've had nothing but trouble with it. Of course, Junction City isn't the hub of the world, but we get a fair number of people in the fishing and hunting season. It's been slow this year, and I told the girls I might not be able to keep them both. And now this plumbing business . . . ."

"Tiffany," Emma piped up, "where is she? She hasn't been to our house for three days."

Mr. Wiederspan looked down at her and frowned. "Tif? Yeah, she works here. Nice girl." He paused. "Don't you know? Her father died a few days ago. Poor Randy, didn't deserve to go so early. A good man. Didn't have much luck with his family, but a good man for sure. They are busy with the burial right now." He shook his head.

When Michael asked when the funeral would take place, Mr. Wiederspan told him he wasn't sure. His wife always kept track of those things. He should go to the beauty parlor and ask there. "Audrey and Grace, they work there. They'll tell you. If they aren't there, the other gals will know." Holding the plumber's card close to his eyes, he dialed the number.

That was the day Emma got her first haircut in Junction City. When he suggested it, she nodded knowingly. She had done this before, Michael thought, as he watched her in the barber's chair covered by a wide cape that completely hid her small body. With the self-confident grace of a grown up, she told the hairdresser her name, asked for the woman's name and told her that the salon looked very nice, when in reality it was a rather seedy place. "Cut off half an inch, please. I think that's right. That's what Mommy always said." Startled, Michael glanced up from his magazine. When their eyes met in the mirror Emma smiled at him reassuringly, and he understood. It was her turn now. Indifferently, he turned the pages of the hunting magazine. It was all he could find other than women's housekeeping magazines.

The hairdresser was snipping away at Emma's hair silently. "Do you know Tiffany?" Emma asked.

"Tiffany Keiser?"

"I don't know her last name. Are there any other Tiffanys here?"

"I think she's the only one. It's an odd name."

"Do you know her?"

"Yeah, we went to school together. Her sister works here, her mother too. But they aren't here today."

"Why not?"

"There's a funeral tomorrow. Tif's father died, real young, just over fifty. I'll go to the wake tonight."

"What's a wake?"

"It's in the funeral home. You see the dead body. And kinda say good-bye. Randy, that's Tif's father, he used to come here and get his hair cut. We all knew him, and then with Grace and Audrey working here, we owe it to them to go there."

"Could I go to the wake too? We know Tiffany."

"Yeah, I guess so. Anybody can go. She works for you, doesn't she?" The girl glanced at Michael with a timid smile. "Tif will be there, and lots of other people. Have you ever seen a dead body?"

Before Emma could tell her that she had never set eyes on a corpse, the glass door of the beauty parlor swung open, and Grace walked in. Her high heels clattered on the linoleum floor. She wore a black, tailored suit, the skirt ending above her knees.

"What do you think? I bought it in Munster. I tell you, I was lucky. They hardly had anything nice in black."

Grace spread out her arms and whirled around the room. Emma's hairdresser stopped snipping and stared at her with admiring eyes. The suit was gorgeous, a perfect fit for Grace, she exclaimed, but Grace wasn't listening. She had noticed Michael and came to a stop in front of him.

When she dropped in the seat next to him and slowly crossed her legs, he found himself assailed by her overpowering sensuality. It was as if vibrations emanated from her body and stirred up his blood, but the sweet, heavy smell of her cheap perfume brought him back to his senses. He looked at her with cold eyes, and his lips froze into a thin line.

"I'm so glad I ran into you." She smiled at him. "You know, don't you? The old man died. He hung in there for a long time, just sitting in the recliner in the living room. You could never tell if he was awake, asleep, or dead. He sat there, day after day after day. The funeral is tomorrow at eleven, at St. Rita's. Did Tif tell you?"

He shook his head. "No, we just heard about it now."

Grace glanced indifferently at Emma's image in the mirror. "Tif's

73

taking it quite hard. He died three days ago, just when she got home at midnight from who knows where. I'm sure she'd be glad if you'd come to the funeral."

Emma was done and walked over to them. Calmly she scrutinized Grace and said in a dispassionate voice, "You are Tiffany's sister, aren't you? You don't look alike."

Grace raised her eyebrows. "Of course not. We're very different." She turned to Michael as she rose. "We'd love to have you. At eleven." It sounded like an invitation to a lunch party.

Her heels clattered on the floor again, and he watched her shapely figure vanish through the glass door into the soft light of the warm fall day.

Chapter 11

Her sister and mother had taken over. They had arranged the wake, planned the funeral, and notified all the relatives. Most of them lived in Junction City or in the vicinity, but not Uncle Carlton, who lived in another town, in another state. He was one of Dad's brothers. It was one of the great mysteries of life that he had left Junction City, gone to college and was now a well-respected, prosperous dentist. He was the only real success in the family. Her father and his three other brothers had started working right after high school, and they had stayed close to home. Uncle Carlton and his wife couldn't make it to the wake, but they would be there for the funeral.

The wake was a dignified affair. Those who were related to the family were present, the uncles and aunts, the cousins. And then there were Dad's railroad buddies, neighbors and friends. Tiffany knew them all. The director, Mr. Beasley, was standing in the hallway, his pear-shaped body slightly bent forward, greeting everybody with a subservient smile, as if he wanted to apologize that his parlor wasn't quite as splendid as the deceased deserved. But of course, it was extremely magnificent, at least for Junction City. The walls of the entrance hall were painted light blue, and tiny silver dots sparkled on the ceiling. Chairs, upholstered in blue velvet, lined the hallway. Tiffany's feet sank into a thick carpet, the same light blue color as the walls, with little pink roses sprinkled over it. Did angels tread on clouds like this? Did Mr. Beasley's baby-blue carpet serve as a path to heaven?

Tiffany walked on, uneasy in this lavish dreamland.

The room where her father was laid out was carpeted in the same blue color, minus the roses, with the same blue walls and the same starry, glittering ceiling above. A celestial realm. Some people were sitting in rows on brown metal chairs that were strangely at odds with the blue decor; others were filing past the open casket. The smell of perfumed candles hung heavily in the air. French vanilla, her mother's favorite scent. Hushed whispers and the low, oily voice of Mr. Beasley kept up a steady hum in the splendid room.

She hadn't seen her father since he died. When she had arrived at the hospital in Munster late that night, he had been declared dead and was already transported back to Junction City. It had been her mother's wish. Warily Tiffany glanced at the coffin. It was made of dark wood and padded with a white, silky fabric that spilled opulently over the edge. Two candles were flickering at the head, a bouquet of pink and white flowers stood on the floor at the other end. Why did a dead person receive so much more attention than the living? Slowly Tiffany joined the line of people who passed by the coffin. It was unreal, the sweet smell, the blue room, the whispers of people who were normally loud, who had dirty fingernails, who smelled of work. And now they were sitting in this make-believe heaven with Mr. Beasley as the smiling gatekeeper who was pleased with himself and his clever funeral arrangement. None of this had anything to do with her father.

When she reached the coffin, she stopped and stared at the dead body. Her father looked thin and small. Even in his recliner he had appeared bigger than in the coffin. He wore his best suit, but the padded shoulders were too big, and his shirt collar was loose around his shrunken throat. His brown hair was combed back in a stylish, fluffy fashion, not at all the way he wore it. Tiffany knew that Grace worked on corpses and often gave them elaborate hairstyles that had little resemblance to the living persons. Grace had explained to her that the families wanted their deceased to look better in death than in real life. Mr. Beasley had said so and encouraged her to give the dead a fancy makeover. "Think about this person as going to a great ball or a fabulous reception. Is going to heaven any less? No, this is the greatest reception ever, and you want them to look their best." Tiffany wondered if Grace had worked on their father.

His face looked pasty and pale, but there was a red blush on his cheeks. Makeup. His eyes were closed, his mouth compressed into a thin line. He could be sleeping, but his chest was so still. It should be heaving, up and down. Sometimes he was breathing in small, shallow gasps, sometimes in painful convulsions. During his sickness, she had learned to read the movements of his chest. They told her how he felt. And now there was nothing. It was odd. She stared at his chest waiting for the small, barely perceptible movement that always reassured her that he was all right. Nothing.

Tiffany turned away from the coffin. People were staring at her. Some were whispering into their neighbors' ears. Her family sat in the first row. There was her mother in an elegant black dress with a ridiculous small hat on her blond hair. Next to her sat Grace, who was talking animatedly with Uncle Rich, one of Dad's brothers. Her mother motioned impatiently for her to sit on the empty chair beside her. As soon as Tiffany took her seat, she felt a heavy hand on her shoulder, and a moist mouth whispered into her ear, "Be strong, girl, we all need to be strong now."

Uncle Bert. They said he had wanted to be a preacher, but the family didn't have enough money to send him to the seminary. Instead he had become the assistant manager at the lumberyard, and in his free time, he was the family's conscience. At every wedding, baptism and funeral he gave a speech. He always thundered against the evils of the world and offered everybody his help in finding the right path to God. He and Dad didn't get along very well. Uncle Bert had visited him once when the sickness was starting, and nobody knew how bad it was. He had admonished Randy to control Grace, so she wouldn't bring shame on the family. Dad had laughed, but when Uncle Bert went on and on, he finally got up, took him by the arm and shoved him out of the house.

Afterwards, her father was shaking and didn't speak for a long time.

Tiffany turned around and smiled weakly at her uncle. She despised his platitudes. With a slight twist, she moved her shoulder forward and his hand fell off.

She didn't see or hear much of what happened during the wake. Once she lifted her head and looked at the coffin. The thought that her father was lying in this fancy box was preposterous, as absurd as the atmosphere of heavenly bliss in Mr. Beasley's funeral parlor. After a while, people got up and walked toward the door. Mechanically she got up with them, filed past Mr. Beasley's assistant, a dark-haired young man with a big, fleshy mouth and a fake grin, and then she was outside in the street in the middle of her untidy hometown. She was in a dark mood, and it occurred to her that if Mr. Beasley's funeral home was heaven, Junction City might as well be hell.

It was late. People quickly got into their cars and drove home. Soon she found herself alone in the street. A cold gust made her shiver in her thin dress. Through her new shoes she felt the jagged pieces of gravel on the sidewalk. She would have liked to sit down on Mr. Beasley's porch for a while. Since her father's death, she had hardly been alone. Her mother, her sister, the family, they were constantly at the house. Friends and neighbors were always coming over with flowers, cards, and home-cooked meals, and Tiffany was running from one thing to the next to keep from thinking, from grieving. In the back of her head she felt a pain that was ready to overwhelm her as soon as she gave in. The desire to let it come on was strong at times, but she couldn't allow it because she didn't know how she would stop it again. Now, alone in the street, near her father's strange and wondrous resting place, the urge to despair was strong, more powerful than ever.

The next morning she put on the black dress that Grace had bought for her. It didn't fit very well, and she thought it was too childish for her age. It was a simple black dress with a white lace collar and white lace cuffs. Something wasn't right with the shoulders. She stood in front of the mirror and pulled the right sleeve, then the left sleeve. But the dress hung down on her like a sack. She didn't care.

She dreaded the funeral and kept reminding herself that it was the last installment of the show that Grace and her mother put on, with her father as a minor participant. They had organized the funeral like a big party where people had to be entertained and fed. After that, Tiffany hoped, she would have her father to herself again.

They left for church in plenty of time to greet the mourners. Her mother expected twice as many people as for the wake. This time it wouldn't just be family and those who had been close to Randy. Nearly all of Junction City would be there to pay their last respects to a man who had grown up here, who had been liked and respected.

The hallway of the church was still empty when they arrived. In the corner by the swinging doors that opened into the church, stood the coffin. Next to it was a table with pictures of her father and the family. Her father as a five-year old at the lake by the Nielsen house. In those days everybody went swimming there. It was only later that the Nielsens chased the local kids away. They claimed that they had cut a barbed-wire fence and some of their cattle had strayed through it. Then there was a picture of her father on the high school football team. He looked so strong and handsome in the photo, kneeling in the first row laughing cheerfully, his hair untidy. Next to it was the wedding picture, two beautiful people who seemed made for each other. Her father with a happy smile on his face and her mother, stylish and gorgeous. Tiffany searched her mother's face for the familiar self-absorbed, vain expression that she had known from her earliest childhood, but she only saw a jubilant, beautiful bride. She wondered if maybe there had been a time when her parents were happy with each other, before she and Grace were born. She sighed. It didn't matter anymore. Another photo showed all four of them, mother, father, Grace and Tiffany. She looked small and insignificant, with her head turned slightly to the side, clutching the hand of her father as if she wanted to pull him away from the others, out of the picture.

"That's you, isn't it?"

Tiffany turned around and blushed. She hadn't expected Michael Barron to come to the funeral. She had thought about him now and then wondering if he knew why she didn't come to work. News spread fast in Junction City, but he was a newcomer. She had not called him. The night of her father's death had become a shadowy recollection that receded farther and farther into the fog of memory, and soon she didn't know what was true and what was imagined. She had banished him from her thoughts, but she couldn't banish the live person next to her.

She nodded her head and stared at the floor, at his black, polished shoes and the sharp creases of his pants. Tall and thin like Uncle Carlton, he was dressed in an expensive suit that told everybody that he too had made it in the world. Until now, she had not realized how big the gulf was that separated them. He didn't fit here, and she didn't want him to meet her family. He must have already walked past her mother and Grace who had positioned themselves close to the entrance so they could greet everybody who walked in. When she lifted her head, she saw that Grace was looking at them.

Mourners began to fill the hallway. They walked past the coffin and stopped by the photos. She overheard them talking about Randy, the football player, Randy and Audrey, the handsome couple, Randy, the family man, Randy, the hard worker. This was the time to reminisce about the dead and observe how the living were doing. Tiffany had been to enough funerals to know how cheerful those funeral conversations could be. The living were glad that death hadn't knocked on their door yet. It was not unpleasant to lament another family's loss.

"I am sorry about your father." His voice was low and soft; his words were only meant for her to hear.

She felt tears gathering in her eyes and fought against them with all her might. Not here, she told herself, not among all these people. When she glanced at him, she was taken aback at how sad and tired he looked, as if he hadn't slept for several days. He tried to smile and lifted his arm awkwardly, but quickly it fell against his body and hung down limply.

Tiffany turned her head away, and let her eyes wander through the crowd that filled the entrance hall. Men in dark, ill-fitting suits, women in tight dresses. All these people had been part of her father's life. They had played football together, had attended his wedding with the most dazzling girl in town and had been there when his little girls were baptized. Some children in their Sunday best were playing hide and seek among the soberly talking adults. They laughed and screamed. For them it was definitely a party. Uncle Carleton, tall, thin, dignified, was talking to her mother right now. Aunt Susan was standing behind him, impeccably dressed in a black suit. Her mother and Grace always found fault with them, but they also liked to show off with the relative who had done so well for himself.

Suddenly she felt a warm hand around hers, a soft, fleeting pressure, and then her hand was free again. It was an intimate touch, not observed by anyone. When she looked at Michael, his eyes weren't tired anymore but anxious. For a short moment he appeared very young. She blinked her tears away and tried to smile, casually. In a small town there was always gossip.

"My father died the night that I got back from Emma's birthday party."

"I know." His mouth was twitching nervously.

"I didn't expect it. Nobody expected it. When I left him in the evening, he was all right." She wanted to tell him about her father, that he had been a good man, a good father. But this was not the right place. Some other time. "How's Emma?"

"Oh, she's fine. She wanted to come here, but I convinced her to go to school. She misses you."

"I had to help at home. There was a lot of work with the funeral. I meant to call, but I never got around to it."

He coughed and cleared his throat. "Do you think you'll come back soon?"

Of course she wanted to come back soon. What was there for her at home now? Nobody would be waiting for her, nobody would ask how her day was, nobody would need his blanket tucked in. Michael's tired face reminded her of her father. Sometimes her father had looked the same way, vulnerable, embarrassed.

"Maybe in a few days. There's still a lot to do at home."

People began going into the church. Her mother and Grace passed her and motioned for her to come along. Uncle Carlton briefly put his arm around her as he walked by. Aunt Susan did the same and whispered in her ear, "Sit with us, Tiffany."

Tiffany drifted away from Michael and followed her relatives. As she walked through the swinging doors, she turned around and saw that he was staying behind, watching her. He was one of the last to enter the church.

Chapter 12

Ed and Marty kept in the background. Ed never felt comfortable in crowds because he was always worried that he would stick out. He'd dressed well enough for the occasion in the dark-blue suit that had once belonged to his father. It was a suit that the old man had inherited from his brother, Uncle Ted. Now it was common property in the family. His cousin Joey had been the last to wear it at his court appearance when the cops had nailed him for DUI. The suit was okay, but definitely not great; the arms a bit too long and the pants too wide and also too long, but he had hitched them up. If he squared his shoulders, buttoned the jacket over the pants, and took long steps it nearly looked right. In a way, Ed felt smart in the suit. "Like your father," his mother had mumbled. He didn't know if he should take that as a compliment. His father had been a gruff, bad-tempered man. It was a good thing that he couldn't recall him ever wearing this suit. It wasn't the old man's best. That one, they had buried him in three years ago.

Ed had gone through quite a bit of effort with his wispy hair. He had plastered it down with gel, and now it clung to his head like a tight cap. Thin strands hung over the white collar of his shirt. He regretted that he hadn't gone to the barbershop. He had thought about it, but then found out that Grace wasn't there, and it didn't seem worth the effort without her.

He and Marty stayed by themselves. They caught a quick glimpse of Randy, but that was frightening. It was Randy all right, but then it wasn't. His face was like wax, despite some red stuff on his cheeks. They had done the same with his father, fixed him up. Ed hated looking at dead people.

Marty whispered into his ear, "It's that smokin'. That's what killed 'im."

Of course it was the smoking. He wanted to box Marty in the face where that big oaf would feel it, but he couldn't do it with all the people around. Everybody knew what had killed Randy, and Marty wasn't supposed to rub it in. It's not what you tell another smoker, though he didn't smoke as much as Randy, definitely not, and he was trying to cut down. Well, Marty was just dumb. He looked stupid. It was embarrassing being seen with him, but he couldn't very well tell him to stay home when he, Ed, went to the funeral. They were both friends of Tif's, and everybody knew that. However, it would have been better if Marty had been able to dig up a suit. Ed had sent him to the Goodwill store, but they had nothing in his size. So here he was in a pair of black pants, a gray shirt, and a brown wool jacket. God only knew where he had found that awful jacket.

They moved to the door of the church to talk to Grace and Audrey, but the two women were gabbing forever with a tall man who looked like he was in business. Ed hadn't seen Tif yet, and he wondered if she was here at all. Maybe she couldn't handle the funeral. It would be hard for her. Then Marty tapped him on the shoulder.

"That's Michael Barron over there," he whispered. "See 'im with Tif by the table with them old pictures? What's he doin' here?"

Yeah, there he was, and there was Tif. Ed hardly recognized her in that ridiculous black dress. She looked as pale as a ghost. Barron just stood there. He didn't speak, just stood there and stared at her. Now Tif raised her head and said something. She even smiled, which surprised Ed and made him a bit angry. She was supposed to mourn. That guy in his fancy suit, Michael Barron, he didn't belong here, and he definitely had no business staring at Tif like that. In a way, Tif was his girl. They went back a long time. When the whole funeral business was over, he'd have a talk with her and tell her she'd have to find things out about Barron. And if the guy got chummy with her, it would happen for Ed's benefit.

He wished he could have a smoke. A cigarette always helped him relax, but then he thought of Randy, whose life had been snuffed out because of a pack a day. Or was it two? He didn't think he could smoke in the entrance hall of the church anyway. Probably wasn't very Christian. He looked at the people mulling about. A few of the men were heavy smokers, he knew that, but even they held out. They looked a bit stressed and fidgeted with their hands, but they didn't clinch the usual cigarette between their lips. Maybe looking at Grace would dispel his craving. But before he could do so, the crowd began to move into the church.

Audrey and Grace were walking past him with the tall businessman, paying no attention to him at all. Ed found himself at the end of the crowd that filed into the church, with Marty close at his heels. And there, only a few steps from him, stood Michael Barron, watching the mourners disappear through the swinging doors.

"Let's hurry," Marty said, and pulled on Ed's sleeve. "We ain't gonna get a seat."

There were few people left in the hall, and Michael Barron must have heard him. He turned his head to look at them, and Ed saw a wave of contempt wash over the other man's face. Anger flared up in his stomach like a hard, fiery ball. He hated the guy.

He didn't listen much to the sermon because he couldn't get Michael Barron's face out of his mind, the way he had looked at him, the way he had looked at Tif. He had money; he thought he was better than Ed. Surely, even that little girl thought she was better than him. Ed twisted in his seat, turned his head here and there, scratched his neck. It was hard to sit still with so much anger churning in his gut. Briefly he glanced behind him, and his eyes met Barron's who was sitting not far from him in the last row. Ed did not try to hide his loathing, and for an instant he felt naked. He knew that the other man had seen his disgust.

85

With a jittery hand he fumbled in his pocket to make sure he had his cigarettes.

After the service, Ed joined a few other men for a smoke outside the church. He didn't feel like going to the lunch in the church basement. It wasn't only the encounter with Michael Barron that had put him in a bad mood. He didn't like small talk, and that's what people did on such occasions. The only person he wanted to talk to was Grace, and she was always surrounded by a bunch of people. They left quickly. When Marty started whining about the lunch they were missing, Ed told him to shut up.

For a while, they drove around aimlessly. Then they headed to Casey's place. Ed heard the dogs before he could see them. The fence shook under their weight as they threw their massive bodies against it, vicious, snarling, foaming with rage. It was a solid, new fence, and Ed didn't worry. For a short moment he even felt like teasing the brutes, the way he had done as a kid when he was sure that the dog was properly chained. But he decided against it. Those mad eyes and sharp teeth were nothing to joke about.

Carrying a bucket and shovel, Casey rounded the corner of the trailer and called to the dogs. At the tone of his voice, they reluctantly stopped their barking. Silent, quivering, they remained at the fence, their front paws leaning against it, their huge bodies nearly upright. They were as tall, if not taller, than Ed.

"Just cleaning up after these beauties." Casey laughed. He bent down and scooped up a huge pile of dog shit.

Ed was sure the dogs could easily kill a man and devour him in a matter of minutes. The huge mass of shit showed that their digestive system could handle it. If they got their teeth into him, they would happily grind him into pulp. It wasn't difficult to imagine how they'd crunch his bones between their jaws and how their stomachs would knead a piece of him into slop.

"Come on in, boys."

"What about them dogs?" Marty asked.

"They won't do a thing as long as I'm here. Don't worry. Come in."

Casey turned to the dogs and spoke to them. Their ears pricked up; slowly they lowered themselves to the ground and sat down, trembling. Ed hoped that Casey's magic words would keep him safe.

"Don't be a chicken." Ed boxed Marty in the back. He lurched forward. The dogs growled at them but didn't move. Ed made sure to stay close to Marty as they passed through the gate.

When they were inside the trailer, the barking began again, loud and vicious, followed by a plaintive whimper. Then Ed heard the dogs scratching at the door.

"They are like spoiled children," Casey explained. "They like to come in and keep me company." He chuckled. "But with you boys, that might not be safe." He poured them a cup of coffee. "I'm glad you came. I found out some things, and I think you'll be interested." He cleared his throat and looked at them solemnly. "You know that I once belonged to a group of people who fought the good fight. Me and my buddies are good people, decent citizens. We don't like the government because it isn't what it used to be. Many of my friends are still fighting. I'm not. I had to give up for reasons I can't explain." He paused and his eyes wandered to a spot someplace above Ed's head.

"I dunno what ya mean, Casey," Ed said, "me and Marty, we ain't interested in the government." Marty nodded his head.

Casey focused his eyes on them again. "I know that, boys. Just hold on, I'm getting to the point, which is that I've got to be vigilant. The FBI isn't sleeping, and this story here is getting unpleasant. You said Jim Coe is a blackmailer. That's a criminal activity. So I did some checking." He added two teaspoons of sugar to his coffee mug and stirred it slowly. "Mabel Nielsen had custody of her crazy brother Jack, and she inherited the house when he died. Well, she died about eight months ago, and her son got the place. And that's our guy. His name is Jonathan Coburn, at least that's what the records say."

"How ya find out all that? Ya know the police? Ya ask them?"

Marty asked.

"No, not the police. You never ask the police, Marty. There are other ways. I ask the right people, I listen. Melanie, the realtor, she made a handsome profit from the sale of the house and chatters about it all the time. She never expected to sell that pile of lumber at all. And I got a few clever friends. Didn't take them long to find a Jonathan Coburn from Chicago. He has a police record and a pretty long one. Pimping, extortion, taking money from little old ladies who trusted him and his investment schemes. The last time police questioned him, it had to do with drugs. It's possible he is connected to some of the big cartels. He might be into some serious stuff."

"Ya think he's a real heavyweight?" Ed wasn't surprised.

"A criminal, boys, a real criminal. And then there is Barron. He looks harmless enough, but he is hiding out here with the little girl. That much we know. And the mother told the police. None of that is good. Next thing, the FBI will come here looking for Barron or Coe. Well, we don't want that, do we?"

"I ain't seen nobody lookin'," Marty said.

"Not yet. The point is, boys, we got to be careful, very careful. Drugs is a dirty business, so is blackmail and taking little girls from their mothers. If the FBI comes here, I don't want them setting eyes on me. I would advise you guys to watch Coe and Barron, see what they are up to, but don't get involved. And always let me know if you find out something."

"How d' ya know your friends are right?" Ed asked. Was Casey afraid?

"They know. They are reliable. Their word is good enough for me." Casey got up and took their half-empty coffee cups. It was time to go.

The pickup rattled and lurched as Ed drove carelessly through several potholes. He told Marty to shut up and be quiet because he had to think, make plans. "Important stuff is happening and I'm gonna be part of it."

Ed had never met a real criminal. Small crooks, he knew those. He was one himself on occasion, but always smart enough to cover his tracks. Sometimes people suspected him, but they could never prove anything. But whatever he did never amounted to much in terms of money. Junction City wasn't big enough for that. Jim Coe was quite another caliber. His clothes, his looks, the way he talked to Barron. There was the smell of power around him.

All of a sudden, Ed didn't feel comfortable in his father's suit any longer. They drove to his place, and he changed back into his old, grubby jeans and a flannel shirt. His mother asked about the funeral, but he threw the suit at her and told her to get rid of it. He'd never wear such an old rag again. Marty wanted to put his regular clothes on too, but Ed didn't feel like driving to his house.

"Your rags look old enough. What ya want to change 'em for," he snapped at his friend.

While Marty was sulking, Ed was cursing under his breath, feeding the slow burning flame of anger as they cruised down Main Street. With an abrupt turn to the right, he pulled up in front of the motel.

"What we doin' here? Liz is workin' now," Marty said. He was distantly related to Liz and knew her shifts. Ed was aware that Marty dropped in often at the motel when she was working. Liz was always nice to him, he claimed. She gave him as much coffee as he wanted, and he liked talking to her. Ed didn't like her much because she mostly ignored him. He only went to the motel when Tif was there, but today it didn't matter. There was a new guest staying there, Jim Coe. Maybe Liz could tell them something. He would even try to be nice to her.

Liz stood behind the counter, watching TV, a cup of coffee in one hand, a cigarette in the other.

"Hi, Liz," Ed hollered, "why aren't you at the funeral? I'm sure Tif missed ya."

With indifferent eyes, the buxom woman glanced at him. Then she looked at Marty, who was trailing behind, and smiled.

"Al didn't want me to go. Somebody has to be here. How are you,

Marty?"

"We were at the funeral, Liz, big, fine funeral. Everybody's still there. Now they're eatin' lunch, but Ed didn't wanna stay. We gotta do important things. We couldn't stay."

"What do you have to do?"

Like a flash Ed turned around and pierced Marty with his angry eyes. He knew Marty was upset because he hadn't let him stay for lunch, and then he didn't let him change his clothes, but Marty better watch it and not talk, not to Liz or anybody.

"I dunno," Marty said in a low voice. "Ya got some coffee, Liz, or maybe a Coke?"

Liz raised her eyebrows and motioned with her head toward the breakfast nook, which was partially hidden behind a wooden trellis with plastic greenery that had never been dusted. Ed saw Al Wiederspan and Jim Coe sitting at the table with an older man, drinking coffee. "Who's that old guy?" he asked in a whisper.

"Indian treasure hunter, been staying here off and on for several weeks."

Leaning against the counter, his back to Liz, Ed observed them. The treasure hunter was a small, delicate man. He had a thin face with a carefully trimmed, gray beard. His eyelids were fluttering nervously, and his thin hands were moving up and down in a gentle, wavy movement as he talked to Jim Coe. It was a sissy way of talking, and Ed wondered why a man like Coe bothered with such a ridiculous guy. The little man was speaking in a soft voice, and he couldn't understand him except once in a while when he slowly articulated a word with great care, such as "river" and "field." Then his lips pulled away from his teeth and he stared expectantly at Coe as if such unimportant words carried a special meaning. It was all about some Indian treasure by the river. Coe listened, smiled and smoked.

This was as good an opportunity as any. Ed stretched his body and straightened his shoulders.

Chapter 13

Michael Barron was staring at the thin line in the distance where land and sky met. The wind was blowing from the north, as usual, shaking the old cottonwood trees, bending the grass to the ground. Was there anything out there except land and sky and utter bleakness?

Leaning against his desk, he wondered when Tiffany would come back. Maybe tomorrow or the day after? When she was in the house, he didn't feel the emptiness quite so much. It was comforting to hear her move around in the kitchen, to see her play with Emma. But his pleasure was mixed with a certain unease. He had enough problems and didn't need to add another, a young woman with a pretty face. Had it been a mistake, a weakness on his part, to bring her here and ask her to work for him? He had not looked for a woman, not back home and not here, in this forlorn town on the prairie. He had been faithful to Marcia, even after he moved out. Marcia had been enough for him, and after it was over, he was tired of women and love.

He sat down in the swivel chair and tried to banish that oval face with the large, dark eyes from his mind, only to have it replaced by another image, that of a man with a crooked smile and a dangerous glint in his eyes. Michael hadn't seen Jim Coe since the night when he had waited for him outside his house. Their encounter had shaken his confidence, the little bit he possessed. During the day he was anxious, and at night bad dreams hounded him. They were like the nightmares he had when he and Emma were driving through the country to get away from Marcia. In them he was always trying to escape from obscure dangers. When he woke up in the morning, wet with sweat, exhausted, the fear of his dreams lingered, and he had to remind himself that it was only another nightmare. Was Jim Coe a figment of his imagination? As a writer, he was able blot out reality. He could invent people, as real as those he could touch with his hands.

He saw a car turn off the county road and drive toward his house. It swerved to the right and left as it tried to avoid the potholes and ruts that marred the track. He should have the path fixed. Was it still worth it?

The car was new and white, and he had never seen it before. He didn't expect any workmen, and they drove pickups anyway. It had to be Coe. How fitting, at the very moment when he tried to lure himself into believing that the man didn't exist, he showed up

The car came to a stop in front of the house. Its door opened and a foot emerged, then a leg whose calf was partly covered by a black skirt. Panic flooded through him. Marcia—she had finally found them, and now she would take Emma away. He got up and went to the window. Anxiously he searched for the familiar characteristics of his ex-wife when a woman emerged, dressed in a long, black skirt and a loose, light-blue sweater. Her dark hair was tied in a ponytail and hung across her shoulder. It wasn't Marcia. Tiffany. But why was she here? She hadn't mentioned at the funeral that she would be coming today.

He watched as she lifted her face and scrutinized the house until her eyes came to a stop at his window. She had told him that she was twenty-four, yet she looked so much younger. Even the elegant clothes she was wearing didn't change that. She must think him an old man. Forty-one, it surely must seem ancient to her. He lifted his hand in a silent greeting, and she started walking toward the porch. When he opened the door, she was already there. Uncertain what to say, Michael stared at her bent head.

"Can I come in?" She smoothed an invisible crease in her skirt.

"Of course." He stepped aside, confused. Was it her appearance, so different in these clothes? Was it the shock of expecting Marcia?

Slowly they walked into the living room. The jacket that she had left the night of Emma's party was lying on the armrest of the sofa, carefully folded, with the pink rose shining brightly on the collar. She picked it up and pressed it against her.

"You forgot the jacket." He couldn't think of anything else to say.

"Yes, I know."

"Emma will be glad that you are here. I'll pick her up from school in a little while." He coughed to clear his throat. "I didn't expect you so soon. You said you'd be busy with the funeral and your family, but now you came."

"There are so many people at our house. They talk about my father and what a great funeral it was. I don't really have to be there." He was surprised when she looked into his face, a rare occurrence. Her eyes were calm, and there was an expression of shy resolve in them.

"Thank you for coming to the funeral today. I didn't expect it," she continued. Her lips curved in a small smile, and her eyes darkened. "You would have liked my father. I wish you could have met him in his better days."

"You look like him, don't you? I am sure I would have liked him. Do you feel like telling me about him?" He walked to the armchair and motioned for her to sit on the sofa.

"I didn't come to talk about my father," she replied. "I have to tell you something about me that you should know. I was afraid to talk about it earlier. It has to do with my work here. It's not the cleaning. It's about Emma. I might not be the right person for her." Tiffany's voice trailed off in a whisper as if her courage had left her.

My God, what was she trying to tell him? She didn't like her work anymore? Surely, she was fond of Emma. He had seen it. And then it dawned on him. It was Coe. She had met him at the motel and Coe had told her that Michael was a fraud, a man who lived under a false name, a father who had abducted his daughter. Tiffany wanted nothing to do with his mess, and who could blame her.

"What do you mean?"

"I can't read." She breathed the words so quietly that he thought he hadn't quite understood them.

"What?" He bent forward eagerly.

"I can't read."

Michael felt like a drowning man who had been tossed about in stormy waters when a wave caught him, lifted him up and carried him safely to the beach. With eyes closed he threw himself back into the armchair.

"It's always been like that. I mix up letters. The words, the sentences, they don't make any sense. You remember the time in the motel when Marty said I couldn't read? It is true. You are a writer, an educated man. Emma reads better than most children her age. She reads far better than me. You and she are superior to the people in Junction City, and I am the last person you should have in your household." This was the longest that Tiffany had ever spoken to him.

"It makes no difference to me, Tiffany, whether you can read or not."

Ignoring his words, she continued. "I've never met anybody like you. You belong to one world, and I belong to another. I could see it at the funeral. You looked so different from anybody else, like my Uncle Carlton, and he is ashamed of my family."

"What are you talking about? My world!" He laughed scornfully. "Do you think my world is so great? You know very little about me. Have you ever wondered why I am here, in this shabby house in the middle of nowhere? It's not you. I am the problem. You are young and beautiful. I have no right to expect anything."

"No, no, that's not the way it is." She blushed. "You might like me a little. But it's not possible."

"What is not possible?"

"I don't know. All I know is that I am so different from you. Even my father never accepted the way I am. I disappointed him, and in a way he was ashamed of me. People made fun of me in school. Now it doesn't matter much any longer. I don't need to know how to read to do my job at the motel or clean houses. There is a place for me in Junction City. But I know that out there where you are from, people read books and they talk about them. They read articles in newspapers. It's another world. You would be ashamed of me too."

The wooden floor sighed when he walked around the table and sat down on the sofa next to her. "Why would I be ashamed of you? I think you know me better than that. You have a reading problem. Dyslexia, that's what it's called. Lots of people have it, and there are ways to overcome it. I can help you with it. It's not a great problem, Tiffany. Compared to my problem it's a simple one."

"I've tried to work on it, on my own," she went on stubbornly. "It's too hard. The teachers gave up on me, and so did my father."

"Nonsense. Nobody ever worked with you properly. I'll try to find some books about it, and then we'll start."

Michael took her hands. He meant to be encouraging, fatherly, but he knew he held them too long. Vaguely, he registered a noise coming from the hallway. It sounded like footsteps, but before he could try to understand who would be walking into his house, the living room door flew open.

"Sorry, Michael, I knocked but nobody answered. I should have guessed you have company. Nice car outside, nice visitor too." Jim Coe smiled at both of them, his uneven teeth showing between his parted lips.

Michael jumped up and rushed toward him, his fists clenched, his eyes burning with anger. For a brief second, Coe's face lost the mask of good humor, and Michael saw the cunning features of a man who was used to the game of hunter and hunted. It was clear that Coe intended to be the hunter in this encounter.

"Michael!"

He halted and turned around. Tiffany was staring at the two men anxiously.

A smile spread over Coe's face, and he gazed at her appreciatively.

"What a coincidence! We met at the motel a little while ago. We could have come out here together, couldn't we? I wouldn't have minded such pleasant company, not at all."

"I hope you like it at the motel," she mumbled. Clearly, Tiffany wanted to calm the situation, and Michael tried to quash his fury for her sake.

"Of course, I do. Clean place, quiet and cheap. Don't tell your boss. He might raise the price." Coe laughed. "I had a nice chat with him today and with that Indian treasure hunter. What's his name? Heitman, isn't it? Quite a character." Tiffany got up and started walking toward the door. "I hope I didn't cut your visit short, but then I do have some business to discuss with Mr. Barron here."

Michael's anger rose again, anger at the man, at his unwelcome intrusion, anger at the way he stared at Tiffany. She was already on the porch when he caught up with her. He reached for her hand and pulled her back toward him. As his lips brushed her cheek, he felt the beating of her heart against his chest.

"Tiffany, I have to sort some things out with this man." He tried to smile. "Never mind about the reading. We can work on it together. Come back soon. Emma misses you."

When Michael returned, Jim Coe turned away from the window through which he had been watching Tiffany depart. "Good looker, but a bit young for you, isn't she?" He grinned and sat down on the rocking chair.

"What do you want?"

"Money, Michael, it's always money. It's the story of my life. We talked about this before. I don't have a regular income, you know, but I have bills like everybody. It's time now to be a bit more specific. I'm sure you want to know where we stand. Don't worry, I'm not intending to make you my regular income. One flat sum of, say, $500,000, and you're off the hook."

"I told you I don't have that kind of money. My writing career isn't exactly flourishing, as you are well aware."

"I know, I know. But you'll write again . . . with that young beauty as your inspiration. Romance isn't really your strength, though, is it? You see I have done my research about you. You are more into drama in your writing and in your real life. But now you need to relax, Michael. You're too excitable." Coe rocked back and forth and gazed at him thoughtfully. "Let's get down to business. I've decided that I can't wait for your next movie script. Who knows when and if you'll be able to sell it? It could be months, years. Movies, it's an unpredictable thing. I'm thinking about that house of yours in France, a more tangible asset. Vincent can sell it for you."

Indeed, Jim Coe had done his research well. Many years ago Michael had bought the house for less than half the sum the other man had quoted. Was it worth half a million dollars now? It was the only asset left to him besides his house in Junction City. Everything else he had given to Marcia.

"That'll take time," he said.

"I can wait a bit. Not too long though. Get the process going. I'm sure your lawyer will be able to sell it in a reasonable amount of time for a good price. A little real estate transaction, what could be easier? I don't mind staying here for a while. I have roots here, right? I might as well get a good taste of what life in the heartland is like. I won't be homesick then when I leave. In the meantime, I intend to enjoy myself. I talked to a few people in town and managed to convince them that I'm an important businessman and investor. They want me to do something for the economic development of Junction City. My word, they need it. What a pitiful place. I think I can help them."

"I thought you had your hands full as a blackmailer."

"I never pass up a good opportunity, and the people here are too gullible. I could tell them I'm the king of Greenland, and they would believe me. You could never pull that off in L.A. or New York—maybe in a nursing home." He laughed. "I'll give you some time to get the money. But, as I said, don't let me wait too long. Let's say two, three weeks? As soon as I have the dough, I'm gone forever."

"How do I know that?"

"Only amateurs try to milk a cow too often. I need some money now to get on my feet, and then I'll pursue other projects. They call that a diverse portfolio. It confuses the authorities and safeguards me. By the way, don't do anything stupid. Don't pack up and leave. The police will get an anonymous call and you know what happens to kidnappers in prison. It's not pretty. Play along, Michael, it's for the best. You talk, you go to jail, and Emma? Who knows?" Jim Coe got up and buttoned his blazer. "I'll be back to check on the progress of our project. But remember, no money, no safe haven for you or your precious daughter. You get me the money, and I'm gone. Otherwise, I'll be back. I'll trail you for however long it takes."

At the door, he turned around. "Before I forget it, that girl, she has a boyfriend. Little fellow from town. I just talked to him at the motel. Ed is his name. He told me she's his girl. I don't know what Ed would think about you and her holding hands. Maybe she's not the right one for you. You have enough problems, Michael. Don't add to them."

The front door closed softly. Michael heard the floorboards of the porch creak under Coe's steps. Then a car started, and he listened until the engine noise had faded away. His head was spinning; his heart was pounding; his mind was racing from Jim Coe to Tiffany to Ed. And Emma, she was his first responsibility. Soon he would have to pick her up from school. With long strides he walked back and forth in the living room, unable to form a clear thought. Coe's face appeared before him, the way he had smirked, insinuated things, and a surge of hatred and anxiety overcame him. Why had Coe talked to Ed? Was he Tiffany's boyfriend? Was the relationship as innocent as Tiffany had told him? Michael dropped on the armchair and buried his face in his hands. What had he gotten himself into?

Chapter 14

Exasperated, Tiffany watched her mother and sister revel in the status of the grieving bereaved. During the days after the funeral, they talked about Randy to everybody who would lend an ear. The relatives soon had enough of it. They had gone to the wake; they had gone to the funeral; life went on. It wasn't healthy to indulge in anybody's death for too long; it could lead to despair, but nobody worried that this would be the case with Audrey and Grace.

As usual, Uncle Carlton and Aunt Susan were quickly disgusted with the family. It all started when they were gathered in the basement of the church after the funeral, eating the lunch prepared by the church ladies. Several bowls of Jell-O, dark-blue with blackberries, stood between sandwiches and coleslaw. There was no social get-together in town without Jell-O, Tiffany was well aware of that, and dark-blue with blackberries was as close as the church ladies could come to black, the color of mourning. Only the punch was red. The children drank it incessantly, and their lips were smeared with red food coloring. They were soon on a sugar high and chased each other around tables and chairs.

Uncle Bert was talking to his brother Carlton and repeated for the umpteenth time, in a solemn voice, what a tragedy it was that poor Randy was taken from his family in the prime of his life, a life well lived, so sad for his widow and the two beautiful daughters. Tiffany and everybody else knew that Uncle Bert didn't care for Audrey and had no liking for Grace. Aunt Susan smiled a pinched smile, and Uncle Carlton shot angry glances at his brother.

"Eat your chicken, Bert, and spare us the sermons. Randy didn't have a great life. He was a good-natured fool, and you know it." Uncle Carlton spoke in a low voice, pointedly looking down at his shoes rather than at his brother. Poor Uncle Carlton. He wasn't one of them anymore. He had forgotten how people lived and talked and conducted themselves in Junction City. They didn't speak the truth, especially not at a funeral.

"Well, Carlton, you're getting grumpy for no reason. We are here to honor the deceased in a dignified way, and your tone is not appropriate," Uncle Bert replied. "And what is more important—"

Carlton cut him off sharply. "Randy threw his life away, for her." With his head he pointed in Audrey's direction. "You know that as well as I do. He was not a happy man."

Uncle Bert looked annoyed and shrugged his shoulders. "One must not talk about the dead in this way, Carlton. This is the time to speak well of poor Randy. It is not right to do otherwise."

"Randy had more going for him than any of us," Carlton continued in a low voice. "The university offered him a football scholarship, and he was all set to go. He would have been the first of us to go to college. We were proud of him. But then Audrey told him she was pregnant."

Aunt Susan tugged on his sleeve and whispered into his ear. Tiffany could imagine what she said: *stop, dear, it's no use bringing the past up again.* But Uncle Carlton was not in a mood to listen to her.

"And Randy, he married her, the fool." His voice was getting louder. A fat woman with tight brown curls turned around and looked at him curiously. "And you know what? He never knew if Grace was really his child. He didn't care. He didn't want to know. There were rumors, but Randy ignored them. He thought it was the honorable thing to do."

Tiffany put her hand on his arm. This was an old story, useless then and pointless now. In his anger her uncle didn't notice her.

"It's what he wanted." Uncle Bert smiled piously.

"Audrey was the death of him. If it hadn't been for Audrey . . . ." Carlton didn't finish because his wife forcefully pulled him away.

When Tiffany caught up with them at the motel where she had reserved a room for them, Aunt Susan scrutinized her with critical eyes and wanted to know why she was wearing such an ill-fitting dress. Tiffany shrugged her shoulders. Shaking her head angrily, Susan unpacked her suitcase and spread her clothes on the bed. It was lucky, she said, that she didn't have any children because that way she had kept her figure which was nearly as trim and slim as Tiffany's.

Tiffany knew that her uncle and aunt felt sorry for her. They gave her clothes and took her out for meals and movies whenever they came to visit. It seemed to appease Susan's dismay about leaving her favorite niece in a dysfunctional family. It had been like that throughout Tiffany's childhood. At some point they would have liked to take her with them. They tried to convince her father that in the big city, where they lived, somebody could help her with her learning problems. But her father didn't want to let her go. Tiffany suspected that it wasn't only because he wanted to have her close to him. They both knew that her mother would never have agreed. She didn't like Susan, and that was reason enough to deny her wish. Susan had achieved success where Audrey had failed. Carlton's wife lived in a big city, had a beautiful house; her husband was a well-off, respected man. There was only one thing that Audrey had and Susan didn't: her daughters. More than once, Tiffany had overheard her say to her father that she certainly wasn't going to let Susan have one of her children, no matter what she promised to do for Tiffany.

When she was younger, Tiffany didn't understand her mother's envy. She always looked forward to the visits of her uncle and aunt, but as she got older, she began to dread them because these visits so often turned sour. The two brothers got along well enough, but there was always friction between Susan and her mother. As time went on, they came less often. It had been three years now.

Aunt Susan held a white blouse with small mother of pearl buttons against Tiffany. "Who was that good-looking man in church, the tall, thin guy?"

"I work for him, keep house, take care of his daughter. They moved here a little while ago."

"I could see right away that he is not from here." Her aunt picked up another blouse made from gray silk. "And, my dear girl, he is obviously not just an employer. The way he looked at you . . . ."

Tiffany quickly interrupted her. "I'll have to see him this afternoon. We have to discuss some things."

"Well, if that's the case, you've got to get out of this terrible dress. Here, put this on." She thrust a black skirt and a light-blue sweater at her. "You've got to show him how beautiful, how precious you are, sweetheart. And then you take our car. This old clunker of yours, it's so Junction City, and you are better than that."

Meekly, Tiffany took the clothes. It made no difference to her what she wore. She didn't tell Aunt Susan why she was going to Michael's place. Her aunt would not have approved that she wanted to tell him the truth about herself. That would be the end of it, no matter what her aunt was thinking. Michael would realize that he had failed to see her for what she was, a loser, a disappointment to everybody. It was as simple as that. Then she would change back into her old jeans and T-shirts. Life would continue as before. She would work at the motel, hang out with Ed, try to be nice to Marty. She might even go to Casey's with them. Of course, she would miss Emma, but it was better to quit now when Michael might pity her, rather than later when he would despise her.

As it turned out, her confession had changed nothing. It wasn't even important to him, and she was confused. Somehow the conversation had taken a different turn, and then this stranger from the motel had appeared. He was Michael's business partner, that's what they said about him at the motel. But Tiffany could tell that Michael didn't like him. The stranger had a menacing presence, and she had never seen Michael so angry.

After the relatives left, Tiffany folded Aunt Susan's skirt and sweater, put them in the dresser, and started wearing her old clothes again. She tried to slip back into the life she knew and not fantasize about a life she did not know. Everybody in Junction City had a place, and she was assured of hers. Even Grace, wild as she was, had her place here. Yet, deep down she knew that things weren't the same.

About a week after the funeral, her mother insisted that the house had to be cleared of her father's things. She called it taking care of Randy's estate. They would have a big garage sale, and then they would redecorate the house. Audrey called on friends and neighbors who came and carried the furniture into the garage. Then the hairdressers from the beauty parlor stopped by to give advice about colors and designs. Carpet and wallpaper samples were everywhere.

Tiffany watched silently as they packed up her father's clothes. She took the few books that he had owned and added them to the cardboard box she had found in the attic. It contained the remnants of his childhood and youth: a football jersey, wrestling shoes and a few school medals. These items seemed so insignificant for a man's life. What would be left of her if she died now? She had no school medals, no sport's trophies. She wouldn't even need a shoebox. The few photos that existed of her would fit into a small envelope. She'd have a moment of glory as a dead body in Mr. Beasley's funeral parlor, but people wouldn't know what to say about her because she had never done anything noteworthy in her life. Throughout her twenty-four years, she had been locked into a kind of non-existence. Was it her inability to read that lay at the heart of it? It had paralyzed her. For as long as she could remember, it had made her want to hide because she was so afraid that people would find her out.

Her father had never made an effort to help her. The beautiful Audrey dominated his life, sapped his strength, broke his spirit. And then came the sickness. Tiffany missed him terribly, his quiet presence, his kindness, and his unspoken love for her. She yearned for that love more than anything.

While her mother enjoyed a new lease on life with her decorating schemes, Grace indulged in nightly excesses. Since her father's death, she was wilder than ever. Often she came home early in the morning and then slept all day. Her mother complained that she didn't show up for work regularly, but Grace shrugged her off. If her mother enjoyed herself by spending Dad's life insurance on new carpeting, Grace snapped, she would have fun her way.

Ever since the funeral, Ed had been coming to the house nearly every day. While her father had been alive, he had kept his distance because Randy didn't care for him. At first, Tiffany assumed Ed came to visit her, but it didn't take her long to figure out that his real reason was Grace. When her sister wasn't home, he sat in the kitchen, drank countless cups of coffee and waited for her. When she didn't show up, he left in a foul mood.

Grace paid little attention to him until the evening when he told them that he was working for a new guy in town. Jim Coe was his name, an investor from back east.

Grace looked at him curiously. "I know who you mean. He eats at Dub's sometimes. I've seen him there with that funny little guy from the motel, the Indian treasure hunter. What's an investor doing in this dump of a town?"

"I ain't tellin', but it's big things." Ed grinned knowingly. "How 'bout it, Grace? Ya wanna go to Dub's? It's Saturday. They gonna have some band playing."

Tiffany was surprised when Grace consented immediately. She knew that her sister didn't like Ed, and she had never gone out with him before.

"Why not? Give me an hour, Ed. A girl has to look good, right? And Tif, let's take her along. She needs to have a bit of fun. She spends all her time in the house. It's not good for her." Grace squeezed Ed's arm and gave Tiffany a stern look, the kind of look that Tiffany never dared to challenge.

When they were children, Grace had employed the same look to make Tiffany do chores for her, and Tiffany had learned to comply. If she didn't, Grace's fury would make the whole household suffer, but it was Tiffany who bore the brunt. Slaps for the little sister, ridicule and nasty gossip later. Yet when Grace had her way, she would be the sweet and charming big sister, and Tiffany would love her again.

Punctually, Ed returned an hour later. He was dressed in a brightly striped cowboy shirt that looked brand-new. So did his cowboy boots, brown, with pointed black tips. He limped slightly. When Tiffany asked him if he had hurt himself, he shook his head and rocked back and forth in his new boots. He had never taken such care with his appearance before.

When Grace walked into the room, Ed jumped up from the chair and stammered something about Grace looking real nice. Her sister smiled at him as she moved her head back in that languid, slow motion of hers and shook her curls. She wore tight jeans and an even tighter T-shirt with a low neckline. A fake gold necklace glittered on her white skin, golden bangles jingled when she moved her arms. Tiffany could never understand how her sister managed to transform herself from the untidy, bleary-eyed person who stumbled out of her bedroom after one of her wild nights, into this flawless creature.

Tiffany had spent the last hour cleaning up the kitchen. She hadn't even combed her hair.

"Why haven't you changed?" Grace's thin eyebrows pulled together in a frown, and Tiffany worried that the familiar stern look would come back, but her sister was far too pleased with herself to bother much about her.

They squeezed into the pickup, close together, Grace in the middle. After her initial eagerness, Grace became moody and didn't pay much attention to Ed. She leaned back, her soft body gently swaying between them. Did her sister notice that Ed touched her thigh every time he shifted gears? The air in the cab was oppressive.

When they reached Dub's, Tiffany jumped out of the truck,

relieved to get away from Ed and Grace. Country music floated through the open door of the bar. People stood around talking, smoking. A live band played in the back and some couples were dancing. They sat down at one of the empty tables, and Ed ordered a beer for himself and a mixed drink for Grace. "A Coke for me," Tiffany mumbled before the waitress disappeared. Ed drank his beer in small, hasty gulps, his eyes glued to Grace. Every time her sister took a sip of her drink, she ran the tip of her tongue around her lips, and Ed eagerly followed its slow course from one corner of her mouth to the other. He was getting more and more agitated, swallowing hard, his Adam's apple quivering in his thin throat. Tiffany sipped her Coke and watched her companions warily.

She was surprised when she noticed Marty lumbering through the dance-hall with his unmistakable awkward gait. Usually he didn't go to Dub's alone. At the bar, he clumsily lifted his body onto a small stool. She wasn't sure that Ed had noticed his friend. When the band started anew, Ed asked Grace to dance.

She laughed. "You want to dance? I didn't think you were the dancing kind, Ed." Her sultry eyes, half hidden under long, artificial eyelashes, wandered through the room. Lazily she waved to people, sent a kiss here, a smile there. Grace didn't pay attention to Ed's disappointment. When Tiffany tried to talk to him, he scowled at her.

Suddenly her sister's demeanor changed. She had been sitting on the wooden chair, limply slumped against its back. Now she straightened her shoulders, leaned forward and lifted her chin. Her eyes sparkled, and she pursed her lips in a sensuous smile. Clearly, her full breasts, the round shoulders, the waist with its hint of a few extra pounds were inviting somebody. A hot wave of embarrassment surged through Tiffany. How she wished she was someplace else, far away from her sister who strutted her sexuality so publicly. She was sure that Grace hadn't gone through this metamorphosis for the sake of Ed, even though Ed seemed to think so. He jumped up and grabbed her arm while his eyes were devouring her hungrily, but Grace quickly shook him off.

"Leave me alone," she snapped. Confused, Ed let go of her. He sat down again and fumbled for a cigarette.

Tiffany glanced around and saw Marty talk to a man who was sitting next to him at the bar. She hadn't noticed him earlier. They were both looking in their direction with their backs to the bar, but in the dim light Tiffany couldn't make out the other man's face. Now Marty was pointing toward their table, his pudgy finger stabbing the smoke-filled air. When the stranger lit a cigarette, Tiffany recognized him. It was Jim Coe.

"Ed, over there, at the bar, isn't that the man you're working for? Marty is talking to him," Tiffany whispered into Ed's ear. He looked up squinting. When he recognized Coe, a smile spread over his face. He raised his hand and waved. With a mixture of interest and misgiving, Tiffany watched as Jim Coe laughed and lifted his beer glass toward them. Who was this man? What did he have to do with Michael?

"Ed, why don't you introduce us to the new guy in town?" Grace's voice was soft and silky, and Ed nodded his head eagerly. He would be only too happy to forget her brusque behavior. "Ask him over here, will you? I can't imagine that he wants to spend the evening with Marty." Her silvery laughter worked like honey on Ed. He jumped up so quickly that he nearly pushed over his beer.

Bow-legged, his feet turned inside, Ed stumbled to the bar. It must be the new cowboy boots, Tiffany mused. She watched apprehensively as Jim Coe slipped from his bar stool and followed Ed to their table, with Marty ambling after them. For the first time ever, Tiffany welcomed Marty's presence. Jim Coe smiled when his eyes met hers, but it was Grace who attracted his attention. His bold gaze lingered on her brazenly. It was the gaze of a pleased connoisseur, and he seemed in no hurry to look away, taking in her sister's heart-shaped face, her voluptuous body. Grace turned to Tiffany and began a silly conversation about lipstick, red or pink. All of a sudden, it became clear to Tiffany: Grace had come here hoping to meet Jim Coe. Tiffany and Ed were the extras in this little charade.

She remained quiet when Coe bent down and said something to her about having met before and that it was a pleasure. Then the music started up with a new, popular song, and suddenly everybody was in motion. Coe turned to Grace who tossed back her curls and slowly got up. Marty shouted that Grace was a real good dancer and that Jim Coe was lucky to be the first one to dance with her tonight. Ed hadn't even noticed what was happening because he was trying to get the waitress's attention. Surprised, he stared at Grace's empty chair.

When Coe and Grace came back to the table, they looked more like old friends than new acquaintances. It wasn't that they touched or smiled at each other. On the contrary, it was the way they ignored each other that convinced Tiffany that they had established some kind of rapport. When the next round of music started, Ed got his chance to dance with Grace. As they walked to the dance floor, her sister turned around and made a grimace, then laughed and let her hips swing. Tiffany was afraid that Coe would ask her to dance, but he didn't.

"Nice place, this bar." He smiled at her. "I'm enjoying myself tonight. Your sister is a charming person, so full of fun. But you look a bit sad, Tiffany. I hope it has nothing to do with a certain person?" There was a glint in his eyes, insincere, mocking. "Don't worry, I have the highest regard for Mr. Barron. We have a business deal going, and we are anxious to finalize it. On the other hand, I have become quite fond of Junction City. A pleasant, little town. I am used to cities. This is a welcome break. Who knows, I might stay a little longer than planned. There's another business venture taking shape, with Al Wiederspan. I think I can be of some assistance to him and this delightful town."

"Yessir, Junction City is a great place. I've lived here all my life, and there's no better town." Marty's face glowed. Little pearls of perspiration had formed on his nose and forehead. He was happy to talk, and Ed wasn't there to shut him up. "Old Al's a good man, mister, real smart businessman. Me and Ed, we often do jobs for 'im. He owns the motel and the gas station, but ya know, he used to run a little store in town, a long time ago, when I was small. That's gone now, but we got the supermarket. Lots of towns ain't got no supermarket. We're lucky that we got one." Marty's voice trailed off, and he slumped forward as if his rambling speech had suddenly exhausted him. Coe had listened quietly, a faint smile on his lips.

It was a long evening in the loud, smoke-filled bar. Tiffany didn't know how it came about that she and Marty were in Ed's car when they left at one in the morning and Grace wasn't. Full of apprehension, she watched Jim Coe's Lincoln Continental disappear with her sister inside. Ed was not in a good mood. Marty didn't improve it when he said, "Just like always, you an' me an' Tif."

She sat squeezed between them. Ed pushed the gearshift roughly and sometimes accidentally hit her thigh with his bony fist. It hurt her, but he wasn't even aware of it. There was an angry scowl on his face. Nervously, he grabbed a pack of cigarettes, then threw it out of the window.

Without a word, he dropped Tiffany off at her house and raced away, motor howling, gravel spraying against her legs. During the night she woke up several times, and once she sneaked into Grace's room to see if she was there. But it was empty, and her bed was untouched. As she dozed off again, her sister's flushed face and Jim Coe's trim silhouette flitted through her tired mind. Then they disappeared, and for a brief moment another face appeared, Michael Barron, too faint to stir her into wakefulness, too real to let her drift off into a restful sleep.

Chapter 15

Ed didn't know what to make of it. He had wanted to impress Grace with his connection to Jim Coe, and at Dub's he thought it had worked. Jim Coe had enjoyed himself, and so had Grace, and they all owed it to him. He had danced with her several times. It had felt good to put his arms around her soft body. He had smelled her perfume and touched the thin layer of sweat on her arm. They blended into a sweet odor that nearly drove him crazy. Once he managed to pull her close to him, and she had molded herself against his body so easily, it took his breath away, but then she had slipped out of his embrace. When he tried again to press himself against her, she had only laughed and pushed him away. It had annoyed him a bit, but he was going to be patient. After all, he had now been closer to her than ever before.

He wanted to take her to his room that night, but then it all had happened so fast outside Dub's. Clearly, it was Marty's fault. He messed up everything. Marty had heaved himself into his truck before he could tell him to get lost. And Tif? Couldn't she have hitched a ride with somebody? Instead, there she stood, waiting for him to give her a ride home. He was cursed with these two. And Grace was nowhere to be seen.

After he dropped off Tif and Marty, he drove into the country, parked the car and just sat there. He didn't feel well, and a small, bitter flame of anger was burning in his belly. Why had he thrown his cigarettes away? He rummaged in the glove compartment and found a lonely, broken cigarette. Greedy and jittery from too much beer on an empty stomach, his hands shaking, he dropped the first match. When he watched the end of the cigarette burst into a brilliant glimmer at the second try and finally tasted the acrid smoke in his mouth, his anger began to subside. Soon the cab was filled with the fumes of his Marlboro that mixed pleasantly with the smell of spilled beer and discarded food. The night was pitch-black, no moon, no stars. It was as if a thick cloak covered everything around him.

Smoking slowly and with relish, he let his mind wander over the last few days. He didn't actually work for Jim Coe, as he had told Tif and Grace, not yet. But things were moving along. On the day of Randy's funeral, when Ed had walked up to Wiederspan, Coe and that strange fellow Heitman, who were sitting together in the breakfast nook, he had started the ball rolling. It had taken some guts to introduce himself. "Hi, my name is Ed. I heard about ya, Mr. Coe. I know this town. If ya need anything, let me know. I can help and show ya around." Ed didn't know why Marty giggled and old Wiederspan guffawed. Well, maybe he hadn't said it so smoothly, but that was no reason to laugh at him. What else did one say? Coe had smiled politely and shaken his hand.

He could tell that Wiederspan didn't like him to butt in. The old man shot him angry glances, but Ed stayed. He had just overheard enough to be curious, and old Wiederspan wasn't going to push him aside as usual. The three men had been talking about some new business scheme, something to do with old bones and spearheads. Wiederspan seemed to be cooking up something with Heitman, and Coe was in on it. But Ed knew things they didn't. Coe, he reckoned, hadn't introduced himself as the son of Mabel Nielsen and hadn't told them that he was after Barron. Ed would play his cards carefully. He had thought of going to Casey, but then dismissed the idea. What could he tell the fat man? All Casey was interested in was some FBI agent who was looking for survivalists. This here was going to be Ed's chance to move up in the world. He'd show Wiederspan and all the others in Junction City

111

that he could do what Coe was doing, and then Grace would be his.

Ed turned on the radio, the oldies station. A soft voice purred a song that filled him with yearning, and he thought of how he had held her in his arms ever so briefly, her face flushed, her eyes glowing. God, she was a beauty. Mechanically he started the car and slowly steered it along the dirt road paying little attention to where he was going. He knew this country inside out, every fence post, tree and windmill, and before he saw it, he sensed the big, square house on the barren rise to the right of road. The house was completely dark except for a small window on the first floor. On the dashboard, the clock said 1:30. He parked the pickup behind the cottonwood trees and noiselessly slipped out of the cab. Cautiously he started walking toward the house. It wasn't easy because of his new boots. Every step sent a sharp pain through his feet up his shins. When he had danced with Grace, he hadn't even noticed it, but now the pain made him clumsy. Under his breath he cursed the dark night that obscured everything, and he cursed the fact that he didn't have a flashlight. He couldn't see the damn gopher holes that pockmarked the ground and made him stumble.

He didn't know why he went to the Nielsen house. Was it curiosity, idleness or frustration? He staggered on until he reached the house. There he kept close to the wall and crept to the brightly lit kitchen window. He had to stretch himself and stand on his tiptoes to peek in. His feet felt as if an iron clasp was pressing them together, and he suppressed a groan. The kitchen was empty, but a half filled glass of milk stood on the table that was covered with papers. And then he saw the strongbox. It was open and full of dollar bills. He had never seen so much ready cash in his life. Ed strained to see what the denomination was. It looked like one hundred dollar bills. Yes, he was sure, that's what it was. He dropped down and crouched against the wall. He had to be careful and keep his wits about him. Barron wasn't in the kitchen, but he was somewhere; that was sure. Ed thought about Jim Coe, how he had gone into the house full of self-assurance. That's how he wanted to move about, but he couldn't do it yet, not tonight.

All of a sudden, he felt weak, sick. He knew the feeling. His stomach was in upheaval. It was always the same. Fresh air was a shock to his system when his brain was befuddled after a night of boozing. If others went out to sober up in the cold night air, it didn't work for him. He felt better in the stale, smoke-filled air of the bar, his bedroom or his pickup and rarely found it necessary to open a window. Ed pressed his lips together wondering if he would have to throw up. Mercifully, his stomach calmed down after a while, but an overwhelming weariness took hold of him as he slumped against the wall. He had better call it quits for the night. If Marty was here, he would help him back to the truck. Strangely, he always felt better with his daft friend around. The thought of crawling through the darkness over the uneven prairie with thorny weeds everywhere brought on another wave of nausea.

After a few deep breaths, he slowly got up and listened into the night. He had just taken a few steps when he felt something hard and thin jabbing into his back. For an instant it didn't seem real, and he asked himself if his brain was playing tricks on him, but then he heard a voice very close to his head. "Put up your hands." The hard thing pushed against his bony spine as he stumbled forward, his arms lifted above his head. Somebody shoved him toward the porch, up the steps, into the house. Every time he tried to slow his pace, the muzzle of the pistol pressed harder into him and forced him forward. No sound, no word came from the person behind him. It had to be Barron, but it didn't seem right. He wasn't the type to run around with a gun and threaten innocent people like him. Ed cursed his bad luck and wondered if Barron even knew how to handle a weapon. There was a nervousness in the abrupt movement of the hand that held the pistol. Ed didn't want to be shot accidentally. So he stumbled forward trying to think up a story that would get him off the hook, but fear muddled his thoughts.

"Sit down, but keep your hands up," a voice said in a hoarse whisper, and Ed dropped heavily on a kitchen chair. He was relieved that the gun wasn't digging into him any longer. Michael Barron stood in front of him now, the pistol in his hand, pointed at him. Ed's stomach was in turmoil, and his mouth felt as dry as paper. He needed something to drink.

"Look, Mister. I ain't done nothin'. It's all a misunderstanding. I'm not feelin' so good. I need a glass of water or coffee. Do ya have a cuppa coffee?"

Barron's face was pale and impassive, but his eyes, narrowed to small slits, sent out sparks of fury. A desperate man, weak from anger and fear. Ed knew that feeling. The gun didn't seem quite so threatening any longer, and he tried to smile to reassure that twitchy man in front of him. But Barron didn't pay attention. He motioned for him to get up and felt along his body. Ed cooperated gladly, feeling more sure of himself by the second as his head cleared and the sick feeling receded. An innocent man would have yelled, talked about trespassing, been real furious, but Barron was silent, on edge. Ed didn't think he had ever held a gun in his hands before.

Barron motioned for him to sit down again and stepped back. "Don't tell me you are coming to my house at two in the morning to ask for a glass of water. What do you want?"

"I swear it's nothing. I know it sounds strange. I was drivin' around, and I got sick, real sick." Ed grinned. "Too much beer at Dub's. I had to get outta the car and walk around a bit. When I saw your house I thought maybe there's a hose outside and I could get a sip of water." He paused. "Ya know, I went out with Tif tonight and had too much to drink." Was there a change in the man's face when he mentioned Tif's name?

"Where's Tiffany?"

"Oh, I brought 'er home quite a while ago. She ain't drinkin'. She's pooped, ya know, with the funeral and all them people. But she needed a good time. Take her mind off things. I gave 'er a good time."

Barron stepped further back and leaned against the kitchen counter, his steel-gray eyes boring holes into Ed, his mouth twitching nervously. "I don't believe you. Why did you come here?"

"Ya know, I'm a real good friend of Tif's. I've known her for

114

years. She likes to hang out with me because I help 'er a lot. She does a good job for ya, right? Anyways, it's late. Sorry, I bothered ya. No harm meant. I'm feelin' better already." Ed knew he babbled, but maybe that would soften Barron up, and he would let him go without a fuss.

Michael Barron cut him off sternly. "You tell me why you came here. You tell me the truth, or I hand you over to the sheriff for attempted burglary."

"I wouldn't do that, Mr. Barron. I wasn't tryin' to break in. I was in need. I never took nothin'. And the sheriff? I dunno. Ya don't wanna get involved with 'im."

Barron looked at him full of hatred. Ed could see his jaws working under the taut skin.

"It ain't a smart idea to get the sheriff. Ya got nothin' against me. All I wanted was some water from your hose. That ain't no crime. I'm no burglar. People know me here; they don't know you. The sheriff is a cousin of my mother's. He ain't gonna believe ya." It wasn't true about the sheriff being a relation, but how would the newcomer know?

Michael Barron took a step toward Ed. "I'm not going to waste my time with you. If I ever catch you again trespassing on my property, day or night, I'll shoot you." His voice was hoarse with fury. "You stay away from my family and my property or I'll shoot you," he repeated. His face was drawn, and there were sharp creases around his mouth. He looked old and worn out. With a wave of his pistol he motioned for Ed to leave.

Later, Ed could barely remember how he got out of the house and to his pickup. He could only recall being in a hurry as he stumbled through the darkness, his heart beating rapidly, aware of the man behind him who might still be pointing a gun at him. With shaking legs he climbed into his truck. His fingers trembled when he inserted the key into the ignition. When he backed out onto the dirt road, the familiar rumble of the motor reassured him, and he let the engine howl and rocks and dirt flew from the tires. He meant it to be a signal for the man back there that he wasn't scared. As he was driving away, he turned around. He had been afraid of this place as a kid because of the Nielsen brothers. Crazy Jack and gruff old Dan. Sometimes Ed and a few boys from town would dare each other to sneak close to the house. They did it once or twice, and each time Jack fired at them. At least that's what they thought. Maybe he had fired into the sky because the moon was too bright. They made up stories about the brothers, one wilder than the other, and frightened the younger kids and girls with them.

The clock on the dashboard showed three. Time to turn in. Tomorrow he had to work at the motel. Wiederspan had hired him for some odd jobs. With distaste he recalled how Al always ordered him around, demanded that he crouch next to stinking toilets and get his hands into the sewage pipes. No, he wasn't really interested in Wiederspan's type of work any longer, not after seeing a box full of hundred dollar bills sitting on Barron's kitchen table. But Ed had agreed to work at the motel because that's where Coe was, and he had to talk to him, let him know that he could be his partner. And then he'd have to get a gun. His old hunting rifle was of no use in this business. He needed a real good gun so Jim Coe would see he was no fool. And Barron would understand that he could not threaten him, not ever again. Casey, he'd talk to Casey. Casey could help him get a real gun.

Chapter 16

When Michael called Vincent about the house in southern France, his lawyer was not helpful.

"What are you thinking, Michael? I have no expertise in international business transactions."

"Come on, Vincent, what's so difficult about selling a house? I can give you the address of the French real estate agent I bought it from. He can sell it again, and you're the contact person. That's all I'm asking."

"I don't speak French. Those people over there don't speak English. I know that. I've been there on vacation."

"My agent speaks perfect English." Michael tried to keep his voice down as he felt his anger rise. He waited for Vincent to respond, but the lawyer remained quiet. "Vincent?"

"How much is the house worth?"

"I need $500,000, no less than that."

"Don't forget, you need to pay me too. I can't operate on thin air, Michael."

This was Vincent, the savvy and greedy lawyer he knew. Was he concerned about his ability to pay? Maybe he had considered the house in France as his last security. Well, it was. When it was gone, there was only his work.

He had been in Junction City for two months now, but hadn't been able to write much. He missed the contact with other writers, directors and the studio bosses. Some royalties were still coming in, but it was a trickle. There was an outline of a movie script that he had sent to his agent shortly before he came to Junction City. It was a good idea, the agent wrote back. "Develop it, let me see more." Michael used to be able to sit in front of the empty computer screen and rapidly fill it with words. But now his creativity was slipping as fast as his bank account was thinning. The only plot he could think about was Jim Coe's devious scheme with Michael and Coe as the only characters in it. This was not the movie script he wanted to develop. Jim Coe's sudden appearance had delivered a deathblow to his imagination.

It had been a consolation to know that the house in France was his, paid off, beyond the grasp of Marcia. He had been reluctant to tell Vincent about it, but the lawyer insisted on knowing everything about his financial situation. He had even demanded that he show him photos of the house and give him an exact description of its location. At the time, he was too desperate to question why Vincent wanted this information. He needed his help when he and Emma disappeared from the radar screen. Vincent had given him a new identity, a new life hidden from those who could harm Emma. Michael knew he couldn't do without the lawyer.

When he thought about his property in France now, he felt it belonged to another person from another time, another life. It was a lovely old house of pastel colored stone with a reddish tile roof and high, narrow windows. Stone walls encircled the large garden and hid a sparkling blue swimming pool next to the terrace. He had built the pool for Emma. The house was supposed to be their retreat, their time away from Los Angeles, a break from the crazy world of movies, Marcia's hectic social life, and Emma's activity-filled days. Here they could lounge by the pool, sip cool drinks on the terrace, read and play. It hadn't turned out that way.

Several years ago he had impulsively bought the house when he was in Cannes for the Film Festival. On his only free day, he had rented a car and driven off into the mountains. It was love at first sight when he saw it with the "For Sale" sign at the gate. He called Marcia, and she was excited about it. The house, he told her, needed a few repairs, but it was solidly built. There was a quiet charm about it, and he felt a sense of peace within those walls that had survived so many centuries. When Marcia flew to France to inspect it, she insisted on major remodeling. It proved to be difficult. He couldn't be there to supervise the renovations, and the people he left in charge either didn't do it right or didn't do it at all. Marcia refused to go alone to check on the progress because she couldn't tolerate the dust and chaos that the workmen created. The house, it seemed, was never going to be finished.

A year later, after the swimming pool had been installed, they all went there together. Every morning after breakfast on the terrace he and Emma jumped into the pool. The air was still fresh, with the first hint of the midday heat lingering among the roses and the hibiscus bushes. Above them stretched the brilliant blue sky. He thought it was paradise and Emma loved it, but Marcia soon became restless. At first, she found fault with the lack of conveniences, no garbage disposal, no dryer. Then it was too hot, and finally she found the house too isolated. Her litany of complaints went on and on, day after day, until the swimming pool didn't appear tempting to Emma and him anymore, and they returned to Los Angeles.

He had been back twice alone after his separation from Marcia, but he didn't stay long. He hired a gardener who came several times a year to prune the trees, cut the hedges and roses, and make sure the heavy wooden shutters and doors remained firmly locked. When he was there the last time, he couldn't tell if the man had done any work on the property. The hedges hadn't been clipped, the terrace was covered with dry leaves, and the grass hadn't been mowed in a long time. The house and garden appeared to be in a state of blissful neglect which he found enchanting. So he continued to pay the gardener, hoping he would preserve the fairytale-like atmosphere until he could come back and reclaim his house properly.

In his weak moments, when he stared at the empty computer screen and the words didn't come, he indulged in the fantasy that he would go there with Emma and Tiffany. He could see them on the terrace, sitting under an umbrella, breathing in the intoxicating scent of lavender and thyme, with endless, sun-filled days stretching before them. Far away in Europe he'd be a free man again, free of worry, free of fear, free to start over again. Tiffany wouldn't think about what separated them. She would forget her harsh life in Junction City, and he would teach her to read. But the blank computer screen in front of him, the wind rattling the window panes, the empty expanse outside always brought him back to reality. Wasn't the house amid the roses and lavender just another scheme that would fail as miserably as the one that he had invented here?

When Michael offered Vincent ten percent of the sale price, the lawyer told him he'd see what he could do. It would take time. Time, Michael thought, to come up with a plan to get rid of Coe. When he asked the lawyer if he had found out anything about the man, Vincent wasn't forthcoming. He had a law practice to run, he told him, and of late things hadn't gone too smoothly. He didn't know anything about Jim Coe except that he had a lot of aliases and a police record in Chicago. As a matter of fact, they were looking for him right now about some drug business. If Michael needed more information about the man, he'd better hire a private detective. Vincent had agreed to help Michael with the abduction of his daughter because there were extenuating circumstances, but he didn't want to pry into the business of drug dealers.

Michael interrupted him angrily. "It wasn't an abduction. I removed my daughter from a harmful environment."

"Call it what you like. Some would say kidnapping. It doesn't matter. I'll try to sell the house in France, but that's all I can do. If you have a problem with this man, whatever his name is, you have to take care of it yourself. I have to watch out for myself, Michael. I'm sorry things aren't looking good right now. Maybe you should have gone to court and tried to get custody, but you didn't want to do that."

Michael went up to his study and sat down at the desk. It was covered with papers. He stared at the sentences that were written on them, but they didn't make sense. If there were writers who could work under pressure, he wasn't one of them. With his arm he swept the papers to the floor.

At three in the afternoon, he roused himself. It was time to drive to town and pick Emma up from school, but when he arrived he found out that she had to stay after. She had talked several times in class, he was told, and the punishment was half an hour of detention. It seemed a harsh verdict for his lively and at times precocious daughter, but there was little he could do about it. It had happened before and seemed to bother her less than it did him. Most of the problems stemmed from her effort to help those children who were slower than she was. She had attended a private school in Los Angeles and was ahead of her classmates in Junction City. He had asked if she could be moved to a higher grade. Impossible, he was told, the little girl would be confused. Her teacher and the principal were adamant. It would not be beneficial for her social development, they said. Besides, he shouldn't overlook the importance of fitting into the P.E. class. Emma did well in her first-grade P.E. class. She threw the ball as far as the others; she ran fast, and enjoyed the games. It would not be advisable to put her into a class with older children who would out-perform her. Couldn't one adjust her schedule, he suggested: P.E. in first grade, the other subjects in second grade? No, she had to stay in her grade and learn to restrain her vivacious nature. Michael suspected that behind their refusal was a hidden resentment that the newcomer's daughter was a better student than most of the local children.

He left his car at the school's visitor parking and walked several blocks to the donut shop on Main Street. It was empty, and this late in the afternoon there were more crumbs than donuts left. He examined the untidy scraps behind the glass counter and finally pointed to a crusty jelly-filled donut that appeared more intact than the others. When he asked for coffee, the sales girl pointed to a coffee pot on a hot plate. He filled a white Styrofoam cup with the scalding beverage and carried everything to a table by the large storefront window. The window had not been cleaned in a long time, but he didn't mind looking out on Main

Street through a film of gray dust. It muted the view and made the scene outside unreal, as if it were the background in an old black and white movie.

A number of cars were driving past the donut shop toward the school, parents picking up their children. Idly, he followed them with his eyes, wondering if he should envy them. Another life always looked simple to the observer. A simple life was all he ever wanted, a home, a wife he loved, and children. Yes, children. He bitterly blamed himself that he had suggested that Marcia have an abortion. When she had brought Emma home from the hospital and he saw his perfect little daughter, his world had changed.

Up to that point, he had been obsessed with his writing. He had hit it lucky with some TV movie scripts, and Hollywood had started taking notice of him. He had embraced the diversions that came with his budding fame. Beautiful women, expensive cars, fabulous parties, a flamboyant lifestyle. When he met Marcia, he was ready to give up this life which was sapping his energy and his talent. He thought that she was his angel, his muse, and she was for the first three or four years. She gave him the space to pour his energy into his writing and bring forth stories about human beings who were caught up in conflicts and drama.

Then things changed. At the time, he was working furiously and didn't notice what went on. When he did, it was too late. At first it was only alcohol; then it was drugs. He threw out her friends. Marcia assured him that she was getting help. A psychiatrist came to the house, then a nature healer. He caught her with drugs again and found her with the same old friends. She finally agreed to check into a detox center, and when she came home, he thought she was all right. But she hated him as if he had been responsible for her cravings and for the ordeal she had undergone. It was then that he decided to leave her. He had convinced himself that she would be better off without him. And Emma would be happy again because she wouldn't have to listen to their arguments any longer.

A blue, rusty pickup pulled into one of the parking spaces in front of Dub's Tavern, which was located across the street from the donut shop. Ed's truck. Michael knew it well enough by now. After a few minutes, the door opened, and Tiffany, dressed in the familiar old clothes, slid off the seat. Michael felt an ache in his chest as he observed her waving good bye to the man in the car and walking away in hurried steps. He wanted to run after her and tell her to stay away from this despicable guy, but all he could do was watch her disappear from sight. He despised her friend, with his haggard face, his vague grin, his scrawny body. What was his relationship with Tiffany? Ed, Tiffany, the townspeople, would he, the outsider, ever understand them? As he moved his legs against the table, the half-filled cup of coffee tipped over. He grabbed a handful of paper napkins and wiped up the liquid. Then he slumped down on the chair, his eyes glued to the pickup.

A mud-splattered four-wheel drive jeep with faded green and brown camouflage colors pulled up in the parking space next to Ed. When the door opened and a heavy-set bearded man in camouflage pants and jacket and an orange hunter's cap stepped out, a ferocious bark exploded in the interior of the car, and the jeep rocked back and forth. Behind the dirty back window Michael saw two huge brown heads, their snouts slobbering against the glass. Dogs, large dogs, straining against the confines of their prison. Slamming the driver's door shut, the man yelled something and the barking stopped immediately. The dogs stared out of the window now, silent, their huge, brown faces pressed against the glass. The man walked over to Ed's pickup, and Ed jumped out, grinning, rubbing his hands. The two talked together, then with a nod of his head, the bearded man pointed to his jeep. Ed slapped him on the shoulder and laughed. Then they disappeared into the tavern.

Michael looked at his watch. Emma wouldn't be out of school for another fifteen minutes. He got a refill of coffee and wondered if he should tell Tiffany about her friend's night-time visit to his house. Would she stay away from him then? But who was he to ask Tiffany for her loyalty?

When he was ready to leave the donut shop, the door of the tavern opened, and the two men reappeared. The bearded man had buried his hands in the jacket that stretched tightly over his balloon-shaped belly. Ed was talking. He was all smiles. Things must be going well for the loathsome louse. Michael couldn't shake the feeling that whatever these two were up to had something to do with Ed's nocturnal visit. Without being aware of it, he crushed the empty Styrofoam cup in his hand.

The two men stopped by the jeep, and Ed pointed to the dogs that had started barking again. The bearded man silenced them with two sharp commands before he opened the back-door a narrow crack. The jeep shook as the massive animals rushed forward. Ed jumped back, and the man laughed. He reached into the car, petted the dogs and spoke to them in a soothing voice. He waited until they sat down on their hind legs and then retrieved an oblong article wrapped in a piece of cloth. He handed it to Ed who was nervously jumping from one foot to the other.

When Ed started unwrapping the package, the other man's hand shot out and grabbed him by the wrist. He shook his head and spoke heatedly. Instantly the dogs jumped up and growled. Michael could see their bare fangs. The fat man quickly slammed the back door shut and, amazingly agile for his size, climbed into the driver's seat. Ed, meanwhile, had stopped unwrapping the package. Instead he now pulled the cloth tightly around the article, shoved it under his arm, and briskly walked over to his truck. Both cars pulled out of the parking spaces at the same time and drove away in different directions.

Chapter 17

Randy's life insurance, modest as it was, was spent in no time. The funeral had been expensive, and so was the ongoing redecoration of the house. When they told Tiffany's mother at the bank that she was in arrears and had been in arrears for many months, she flew into a rage. But the banker showed her the papers. Before Randy got sick, he had taken out a mortgage on the house to pay for repairs. The roof, the electrical system, the plumbing, all needed work; it was an old house. Her father had never told them about the mortgage. Did he think he'd have time to work, to save, to pay it off? Now it was too late. The bank would repossess the house if they didn't start making payments. Her mother had drowned her anger in wine and whiskey. Grace acted as if the whole business did not concern her.

Tiffany loathed the man with whom her sister was involved. There was something dishonest, false about him. And Michael had flinched at the sight of him. Yet, ever since that night at Dub's, Grace's behavior had changed. Tiffany suspected it had to do with her new boyfriend. It was as if her sister had finally found peace in her mind and body. The hectic activity of the days after the funeral had given way to unhurried hours in the beauty parlor, evenings at home devoted to beautifying herself, and nights away from home with Jim Coe. At least that's where Tiffany thought Grace spent her nights. Sometimes she met her sister in the morning when she walked into the kitchen, gulped down a cup of coffee before taking a long shower. She looked lovelier than ever now.

Her skin glowed, and there was an excited sparkle in her eyes. Even her mother noticed it.

Audrey was sitting at the kitchen table, her eyes still half shut from heavy sleep, the coffee mug steaming in front of her. It was close to noon, but her mother, who was only working part-time now, was staying up late every night, watching TV, drinking.

Tiffany sat down next to her. "Mom, I'm worried about Grace."

Her mother lifted her head, her eyes puzzled, not comprehending. "Why? What do you mean?"

"She's going out with this new guy in town. Jim Coe. There is something strange about him. I don't think he's right for her."

Audrey broke into a loud, guttural laugh. "What would you know about that, Tif? You of all people! Let her be. She knows what she's doing. She wants to settle down, and it's about time. This new guy, he can take her away from here to a big city, a big house, like Carlton's, and Grace will be happy. You'll see."

"Mom, we don't know anything about him." Tiffany wanted to tell her about the mistrust and anger that she had seen in Michael, but she didn't want to talk about him.

Audrey, who had been staring blankly at the new refrigerator as if Grace's blissful life was painted on its glossy door, focused her eyes on her daughter. Her voice was stern. "It's none of your business, and it's none of my business. Besides, I have other problems. Why don't you tell me how to get the bank off my back? Do you have any ideas? I have an idea, and that's the new guy. He's got money. He can help Grace's poor mother stay in her house. How's that for a plan?"

Her sister was standing in the cramped, cluttered bathroom, pulling her hairbrush through the mass of thick curls when Tiffany stopped by the door.

"Grace, I want to ask you something. This man, Jim Coe . . . ."

Her sister scrutinized her in the mirror, a mocking smile on her lips. Then she broke out in that throaty laugh of hers that was so seductive to men but alarmed Tiffany every time she heard it. Grace turned around and sat down on the edge of the bathtub. "You don't like him, right? Why? You normally don't concern yourself with my love life."

"He's different from the people here. He came from nowhere, and we know nothing about him."

"Sounds like your employer."

"Michael is living here now. He has a daughter. It's different."

"It's Michael now? Interesting." Her sister smiled derisively. "I watched the two of you at the funeral. I think there's more than an employer's interest. Don't act in that prissy way of yours, as if you didn't know. I don't understand why you are so dense. You would be dumb enough to let a guy like Barron off the hook and stick with Ed. God, I can't stand that scrawny little clown. I'm so tired of these people here." Grace's voice grew louder. "Don't tell me what to do. You're just scared, Tif, scared of men, scared of sex. Get a life."

"Please, stop it. I don't want to pester you. I'm just worried."

"Oh, you don't want to pester me? But you do. You think you are so good, don't you? You think it's virtuous to drive around in a pickup with two losers, while I am sleeping around. Don't you think I know what people are saying about me?"

Grace got up from the bathtub. One step brought her close enough that Tiffany could feel her sister's breath against her cheek. "I'm not half as bad as they think. I'm more honest than you, you pure little lamb. I give men what they want. What's so bad about that? Do you sleep with Barron?"

Shocked, Tiffany stepped back.

"Why not? It's what he wants. No, you play coy and pretend you don't know and get him all hot. You're Cinderella, and I'm one of the bad sisters. I've wasted years in this stupid town trying to find the right guy among these beer-guzzling bores. But they never came through. After Dad died, I was sad too. You weren't the only one who wept for him. Maybe you don't know, but I thought he was the only decent man in town. I felt very alone, and all I wanted was some comfort. For me that's men, but you wouldn't understand that, would you?" Hot anger

127

distorted Grace's carefully made up face.

Squirming under the furious stare of her sister, Tiffany stared at the scratched vinyl floor. In all these years, she had avoided interfering. Now she wished she could turn the time back a few minutes. Then she could have walked past the bathroom, remained silent, and would not have become the target of her sister's anger. Making fun of Tiffany, twisting reality in her own favor, had been Grace's preferred weapon against her since childhood, and she had employed it freely. Whenever they had an argument as children, Grace won, and Tiffany retreated in tears. It had set the stage for their adult lives: Grace got what she wanted; Grace did what she wanted, and Tiffany stayed away from her.

Now she wanted to leave, but Grace grabbed her wrist and pulled her back. Her sharp fingernails dug into her skin. "I finally met a man who can get me out of this dump of a house, away from this town. Jim is special. There is something between us that clicked, and it's not just in bed. He's right for me, and I'm right for him. I feel it. This time it's going to work. It has to work. So don't come again and pester me with stupid questions. I know what I'm doing."

Grace let go of her wrist and started brushing her hair again. The two sisters looked at each other in the mirror. "I'll give you some advice," Grace said. "Stop playing Miss Goody-Two-Shoes, and let Barron have what he wants. Get him before he finds somebody else."

Tiffany didn't go to Michael's place again. She worried about her mother, her sister, and the threat of losing the little bit of security they had, the house. How could she even think of him when they needed her so much? When she unexpectedly ran into him early one morning on the steps of the old town library, they were both caught off guard. He looked very pale, with his shoulders hunched over as if something was weighing him down. When she tried to walk past him, murmuring a greeting, he put his hand on her shoulder, and without saying a word turned her around and led her down the steps.

"Let's go for a drive," he finally said. His voice was hoarse.

Silently they walked to his car. Tiffany slipped into the seat next to him. The car was warm and comfortable. He drove through the empty town, past the false front buildings, past Dub's and the donut shop. At this time in the morning, Junction City always looked like a ghost town. She didn't know where they were going, and it didn't matter much to her. Shyly, she glanced at his profile. He looked as if he hadn't slept much. Once he searched for her hand, and when he found it, he crushed her fingers so hard that it hurt.

Soon, the town was behind them. To the right of them, behind empty pastures, stretched a long line of trees. Willows and cottonwoods. When Michael turned onto a dirt road heading for the trees, she knew where they were going. He was driving to the river. She had told him how to get there without trespassing on someone's property. After he parked the car at the edge of the road, she followed him down a narrow trail overgrown with brambles and shrubs. Small songbirds flew out of the thicket as they brushed against it. From the water came the sound of ducks and geese that rested here on their annual trip south. When she lagged behind, he took her hand and gently pulled her forward, holding branches away from her, guiding her over the uneven ground. At the riverbank, they stopped. He put his arm around her shoulder, and they silently gazed at the opaque, sluggish water that flowed past them.

The walk had livened up his face, and his shoulders seemed less stooped now. He took off his jacket and spread it out on the dry sand.

"Do you remember you told me about this place? I like to come here when Emma is in school and I am stuck with my writing. It's a peaceful place. The geese, the swallows . . . there is a benevolent indifference in nature." He sat down on the ground and motioned with his hand to the jacket next to him. "I like this river. It comforts me because it's so slow, so quiet. It just flows downstream, floods the banks, dries up, year after year, a predictable cycle. Life should be that well-ordered, but it isn't."

Michael lay down on his side, propping himself up on his elbow. She felt his eyes on her as she sat gingerly down on his jacket and pulled her knees up to her face. When he touched her cheek with his free hand, it brought a rush of color to her face. He smiled and threw himself on his back. She avoided looking at him but readily yielded to the pressure of his arm that reached for her. Nestled against him, she gazed at the sky, watching feathery clouds drift by, waiting for him to speak, but he remained silent. Sometimes he stroked her face and her hair, and once he breathed a kiss against her ear. She felt that he wanted to be close to her, yet there was a sadness in him that kept them apart. Her head was resting against his shoulder, a hard shoulder that remained rigid and tense. She didn't know how long they lay there, next to each other, immobile. She wanted it to last forever. A red-breasted finch flew up and started its song on the top of a nearby cypress tree.

Michael rolled on his side again and leaned over her. "Do you know that you are beautiful?"

Too shy to say anything, she turned her head away. She didn't find herself beautiful and wondered what he saw in her. But if he did see beauty in her, she wanted it to be so for him. When he got up, she closed her eyes trying to burn his image into her memory. He took her hand and pulled her toward him.

They spoke little on the way back to Junction City. At the town's first grain elevator, Michael suddenly swerved to the right and let the car come to a stop on the grassy shoulder. Silently he stared through the window, but she knew he neither saw the grain elevator nor noticed the passing cars. With his right hand, he massaged his face as if trying to chase away some cobwebs and get ready to face . . . reality, regret? That he was sorry about taking her to the river, running his fingers through her hair, holding her? Tiffany felt the burning heat of embarrassment rise from her throat to her face. The silence between seemed oppressive, and she wondered if she should get out of the car and walk home. It wasn't far. She could spare him the painful explanation.

But no explanation came forth. Instead he pulled her close to him, and she willingly leaned against his chest.

"I have to ask you something," Michael murmured into her hair.

"Be truthful. Is Ed more than just a friend?"

Tiffany sat up straight and looked at him in amazement. Why would he ask such a ridiculous question? It seemed nearly comical to her that he would worry about her and Ed.

She shook her head. "He's just an old friend. That's all. He's interested in my sister Grace, not me."

"I don't trust Ed, and I don't know what he's after. I'm not sure that you can be his friend and at the same time be with me." Michael tried to smile, but Tiffany saw only pain in his face. "I mean, if you want to be in my life. You have to know that there are things going on that are not right, maybe even dangerous. I shouldn't involve you in any of this. It's complicated."

"You don't have to tell me anything," Tiffany interrupted him. "It wouldn't make any difference to me. If you let me, I mean if you want me to, maybe I can help."

Michael lifted her head and softly kissed her on the mouth. "Promise me one thing. Stay away from Ed." She nodded her head. She would do anything for Michael.

Chapter 18

Ed knew that work wasn't much fun, but working for Al Wiederspan turned out to be worse than he expected. He and Marty had to tear out floors, dig up pipes and haul trash away. All the while, Al was nosing around, complaining about them: they didn't do it right, they didn't work fast enough. Then Ed got mad at Marty, who in turn started to sulk and work more slowly, which ticked Wiederspan off again.

Ed had only agreed to do this job at the motel because he wanted to find an opportunity to talk to Coe alone, but it hadn't happened yet. Either old Al or that funny, little guy Heitman were constantly around him, and they often drove into the countryside. He had considered looking him up in his room, but Al was watching his every move as if he suspected that Ed was up to something. That time, when Ed had joined Coe and Heitman in the breakfast booth, old Wiederspan had not been pleased, but he couldn't care less. Now Ed's anger was growing day by day, and there was only Marty to yell at.

The one thing that made him feel good was that he owned a rifle now, a semi-automatic with a thirty-round magazine. Sometimes at home he pulled it out from under his bed and positioned himself in front of the mirror, the rifle at his hip, ready to shoot, its handle smooth and cool in his hand. The weapon calmed his anger and excited him at the same time.

The day after he got it from Casey, he and Marty went to the old sandpit by the river. The sand business had folded years ago, and now some people used the place for target practice. Several barrels and canisters were propped up against a sandbank. Empty beer cans full of bullet holes littered the ground, along with rusty machine parts and construction trash.

Just to show off, Ed pointed the rifle at a beer can, his finger loosely at the trigger, and before he knew it, it came alive in his hand and was shooting wildly without stopping. The rifle, it seemed, had gone off on its own before he had a chance to think and aim. Later, he couldn't remember if he had pulled the trigger or not. It scared Marty, but Ed laughed, pretending that he knew what he was doing. He went back to the sandpit without his friend nearly every evening and in time learned to control the gun. All that remained to be done was to win the trust of Jim Coe, let him know that there was a box of money in Barron's house. He was sure there was more where that came from, enough for both of them.

There had to be a way to approach Coe and talk to him, and he fretted over it for several days. It was Marty, dumb, old Marty, who got the ball rolling. They were carrying a new toilet into one of the bathrooms when Marty nearly dropped the damn thing on Ed's foot. Ed yelled at him at the top of his voice and shoved him into the corner of the bathroom, where Marty stood like a wet dog. Marty never fought back; Ed knew that. Big and stupid, he just hung his head and sulked. Ed should have ignored him, but he was furious about the toilet and everything else. He continued to berate Marty until he was hoarse from yelling. Normally he didn't harangue his friend that badly, but his temper was easily stirred up these days.

Slowly Marty lifted his head and started talking about Grace. He had seen her with Coe, not once, but twice, he said.

"Shut up, you big klutz. Ya got no sense in that dumb head of yours." Marty was probably lying to get him to stop yelling.

That same day at noon, Ed went to the beauty parlor, but Grace wasn't there. They told him she had gone home. But when he got to her place, only Tif was there. Of late, he hadn't seen much of her, what with the job during the day and the rifle in the evenings.

"Where's Grace, Tif? I wanna talk to her. It's important."

But Tif was staring into space, deep in thought about something that was surely less important than his concerns. It was like talking to a wall. He repeated his question impatiently.

"She left a while ago, but she said she'd be back shortly," Tiffany answered finally. "What do you want from her?"

"It's private. I'm gonna wait."

And then they sat there. Tif retreated back into whatever dream she was dreaming while he got more restless by the minute. For want of anything better to say, he asked her if she wanted to come out to the sandpit with him and Marty sometime. She shook her head, and he wondered if she had even heard what he had said. And then he got mad, real mad. He couldn't help himself. The whole time he had been on edge, and now he let loose. Ed grabbed her arm and shook her. Later on, he couldn't quite remember what he had said to her. Something about working for old Al, how he hated it, and that it was all going to change. He wasn't really mad at her. It was just her bad luck that she was there and not Marty.

As usual, his outburst didn't last long. He was well satisfied, when he looked into Tif's startled eyes. At least he had managed to wake her up out of her indifference. She didn't seem to be afraid of him, not like Marty, just curious and maybe a bit worried. In any case, his tantrum had made an impression on her, as it should.

He moved his head close to hers and said in a low voice: "I gotta rifle from Casey. It fires thirty rounds, boom, boom, boom. Thirty rounds." He laughed.

"Why do you need a rifle like that?" There was a hint of fear in her eyes now.

"There are things goin' on here that ya know nothin' about."

"What do you mean?"

"I ain't tellin'." Her anxious face reminded him that he used to be her protector. "If I were you, I wouldn't hang around that guy Barron too much. He's no good. You still workin' for 'im?" She shrugged her shoulders. "Ya better make up your mind and quit. I gotta go now. Tell Grace I'll be back tonight."

Both sisters were at home when he returned after work. He felt that they had been waiting for him. Grace wasn't in a good mood. She kept looking at the watch over the kitchen sink. Tif was pale and seemed upset. He had scared her good.

"What do you want, Ed?" Grace asked. Before he could answer, she continued in an angry voice. "What's getting into you scaring Tif like that? She told me about your rifle and that you're up to something. Don't be stupid, Ed."

Smiling smugly, Ed sat down and asked for a cup of coffee. Grace walked to the coffeemaker, got a filter out of the cabinet, measured the coffee and poured water into the container. He followed every movement with hungry eyes. Surely, she would fall into his lap like a ripe apple rather sooner than later. When the coffee was done, he sipped it slowly, savoring the watery brew as if he hadn't tasted anything good like that in ages. He enjoyed letting the sisters wait a bit.

"Well, you're not thinkin' I'm workin' for Wiederspan forever, do ya?" he finally said. "I got some ideas, but it needs some plannin'." He put his cup down and pushed back a strand of hair that had fallen over his eyes. "Ya remember Jim Coe?"

Grace broke out into laughter. "Yeah, what's with him? Do you want to shoot him with that gun of yours?"

"Hell, no." He grinned. "I know some things and I'm gonna talk to 'im 'bout it."

Grace's lips puckered into a contemptuous smile, but he wasn't worried. She'd change her tune pretty soon.

"What do you know?" Tif asked.

"All I can tell ya is that there's somethin' wrong with this guy Barron, and me and Coe are takin' care of 'im."

"What do you mean? What does Coe want from Michael?" Tif's

voice was unnaturally loud, and Ed wanted to tell her to tone it down, when out of the blue, Grace put her hand on his sleeve, and he felt her foot under the table touching his lower leg. Slowly her foot traveled up his calf to his knee. When his leg started to twitch, the foot halted as if wondering if it was safe to go any further. In his pants his dick began a stormy little dance and blood rushed wildly into his groin.

"Well," he stammered. Grace smiled at him, and her toes softly dug into the hollow of his knee. "Barron's name ain't really Barron, and he is hiding. He's from Los Angeles." Ed took his hand off the table and, brushing against his agitated penis, put it on Grace's thigh. Her foot hadn't moved, but he didn't mind. With his hand, he was much closer to where he wanted to be. Her leg felt good, so soft. Underneath her tight, short skirt he moved his hand upward, but she grabbed it and yanked it away from where he was aiming. She had a smile on her face, and he knew that she wanted some more action. But of course, with Tif around it wasn't possible. Not now.

"So what about it? And what do you need the gun for?" Grace asked.

He recovered his senses somewhat slowly. "He got a gun, Barron does. I figure I need one too. With people like him ya never know."

That was all he was telling them. He didn't tell them about the strongbox with all that money, money that would buy Grace everything she wanted. He'd show her that he was clever, more clever than all the other men she'd gone out with. And she understood; she agreed right away to have dinner with him at Dub's. And this time, he'd be the one alone with her in the car. He'd make sure about that. When Ed drove home to change clothes, the warmth of Grace's flesh was still burning on his hand.

Ed didn't know how it had happened that Tif came along. He wanted to be alone with Grace, but when he had returned to the house to pick her up, Audrey told him that the sisters had already left for the bar. "You know how quickly the place fills up. They want to be sure that you all get a table," she said.

It was Thursday, prime rib night, Dub's family special, and it was always crowded on that day. When Ed arrived, most of the booths in the dining room were taken. The sisters were sitting at a square, wooden table in the corner. The low hanging lamp threw a dim light over them. Of course, Grace looked ravishing. He had read this word in one of his mother's romance novels which he occasionally skimmed through when he had nothing better to do. Grace and Tif were talking, but when Ed took a seat, the women became silent. He tried to revive the conversation, but his efforts went nowhere. Both women were sullen, absent-minded. Tif was staring at her Coke; Grace had her eyes glued to the door, barely paying attention to him. Every time somebody walked in, she came alive, only to slump down on her chair with a displeased look on her face. Who was she waiting for?

It was about seven when Coe walked in. Ed was struck again by the man's bearing. He wasn't tall or bulky, but he had presence. Maybe it had to do with the expensive aviator leather jacket he wore, but Ed was sure that there was more to it. It was the way he walked, the way he held his head up. Maybe he had a pistol strapped to his body. Ed had left his rifle in the truck, hidden under the seat. To know that he had a weapon made him feel good. Grace had seen Coe too, and waved, but he didn't notice her.

"Maybe he doesn't remember ya, Grace. I'll get him over here, if you want me to," Ed ventured, even though tonight he didn't really want another person at his table, not even Coe. Even Tif was one too many. On the other hand, he needed to talk to the man and, what would be even better, maybe he could pair him off with Tif later. This might be a good opportunity after all.

Grace started laughing in an almost hysterical fashion, and Ed wondered if she had had too much wine. "That's so funny, Ed. I am quite sure he remembers me." With that, she got up and walked to the door, hips swinging, shapely legs floating over the wooden floor. Coe seemed pleased when he saw her. As Ed watched them walk toward their table, Grace all smiles and flutter, Coe attentive and polite, he was annoyed that she had taken the initiative.

"How lucky can a man be to meet these two beautiful sisters here?" Coe said with a nod toward Tif.

Grace pursed her lips, and Ed thought that her mouth looked like a big, juicy strawberry, ready to be plucked and eaten. With effort, he tore his eyes away and greeted Coe.

Coe pulled a chair from another table, and instantly, the conversation became lively. Ed didn't have to rack his brain any longer to find something to talk about. Grace laughed, ordered more wine, and seemed to enjoy herself immensely. Only Tif remained sullen, but then he didn't care too much how she felt. Their prime rib dinners came, and Coe ordered a meal for himself.

Cutting into his meat, Coe started talking about the deal he had going with Heitman and Wiederspan. "A great business opportunity for Junction City. Mr. Heitman has discovered the remnants of an Indian village on a piece of property owned by Wiederspan. Spearheads, pottery chards, stuff like that."

Now Ed understood why he took off every day with Heitman. An Indian village. It could be true, but it could also be a smokescreen that gave Coe a reason to stay until Barron came through. Ah, this guy was slick.

"We might be able to develop it into a profitable enterprise," Coe continued. "With the right management and sufficient investment, it'll be a goldmine. Al Wiederspan can't wait to get started. He's a savvy guy." He laughed as if he had just thought of something funny.

"I dunno about savvy. Better watch out, old Wiederspan is a cheapskate," Ed said.

Coe turned to him. "Keeping busy these days, Ed? How's work?"

"Kinda slow. I'm just helpin' Wiederspan out right now. He got this emergency with them old pipes. Gettin' it ready for the plumber. I've done lots of repair work like that 'cause there's so many old houses here in town. Some of 'em are in real bad shape. Just look at the old Nielsen house, been empty far too long." Oh, he wanted a sip of beer, but he quickly pushed on. "Ever been there?"

Coe glanced at him briefly before putting a piece of bloody beef in his mouth. "Never heard of it. I'm not interested in old houses," he said blandly.

Ed was about to tell him that it was the name of the house where Barron lived, when in walked Michael Barron with his daughter. Jim Coe had noticed them too. Ed saw that the two men briefly locked eyes. There was a peculiar expression on Barron's face. Hate, fear? It was interesting. The little girl was trying to pull her hand out of her father's firm grip, but he bent down and said something to her. Then they walked to a booth that was as far away from them as possible.

Coe continued to talk about the Indian village. He mentioned that he might be able to offer Ed a job, one that would fit his talents, once the project went into the development phase. Ed liked the part about his talents. He nodded his head and began to speak loudly about Indians, old Sitting Bull, Geronimo, stuff he remembered from those little primary school readers. Grace thought he already had a job with Coe, and he didn't want her to ask any questions. But the two women didn't pay any attention to what he or Coe were saying. Tif had slumped down in her chair. She wasn't eating, she wasn't drinking. What was wrong with her? Grace, too, suddenly looked out of sorts, and Ed didn't know why. As far as he was concerned, the evening went well, and this time Grace would end up in his car. Tif could walk home, or Coe could give her a ride. He decided to ignore them both. Maybe this was his chance with Coe. Gotta be on the ball, he told himself. Grace would understand. He didn't even notice when the little girl approached them. She suddenly stood next to their table and began talking to Tif.

"Tiffany, Daddy said I couldn't come over here and talk to you, but I did it anyway." Her voice was full of reproach. She looked at Ed and the others in a scornful way as if it was their fault that her father wouldn't let her come here.

She now took Tif's hand. "Come, Tiffany, sit with us."

Suddenly, Michael Barron's gaunt figure loomed next to their table. He put his hands on his daughter's shoulders and moved her away. His face was grim, and his voice was full of anger. "Come back and eat your food, Emma. Sorry she bothered you."

Coe smiled, waved his hand dismissively and said that it was no bother at all. He enjoyed meeting this charming child. "I'm sure she's the apple of your eye, Mister Barron, and she ought to be. Children are so precious." He winked at the little girl.

Barron took no notice of him and marched his daughter back to his booth.

"I need to go to the restroom. Come on, Tif, let's go together." Grace got up and nudged her sister.

"Women like to do that," Ed remarked to Coe as he watched them disappear.

"What?"

"Go to the bathroom together."

The other man laughed. His eyes were still on Barron, observing him in a lazy manner, like a cat eyeing its prey and deciding to catch it later. A pleasant shiver ran through Ed. Barron was talking to his daughter. He seemed to be scolding her. The girl was staring at her plate. Maybe she was crying. Abruptly they got up and left.

"Strange feller, ain't he?" Ed remarked. Coe raised his eyebrows and looked at him questioningly. "I mean what's he doin' here in a small town? He's from Los Angeles, right? But he's tellin' nobody why he's here. I mean what does Junction City have that he can't get in L.A.? Don't look right to me."

"What do you know about him?" Coe asked.

"Writer, ain't he? I've been to his house a few times. I saw you there too. Doin' business with him, I guess."

"I don't know what you're talking about."

Ed leaned forward eagerly. "Ya know, Jim. Can I call ya Jim? Ya know I could be quite helpful to you. I mean, I know a few things and, uh . . . it could work well for both of us."

Coe stared at him silently. Ed saw the restroom door open and the sisters walk in. Grace was whispering something in Tif's ear. He had to hurry. "I understand you're from here, Jim, in a way. Your mother was." Coe's eyes were like two lumps of ice. Ed swallowed hard. He wondered if he had started the wrong way. He didn't want to make the man mad. He wanted to convince him that he would be an asset.

When Tif and Grace took their seats, Coe got up to leave. "I don't want to break up this delightful gathering here, but I have an early meeting with Mr. Wiederspan." For some strange reason, Grace got up too. "I'll leave you here with the beautiful sisters, Ed. You are a lucky man. Take good care of them." Coe disappeared before anybody could say a word. Grace fell back on her chair with a frown.

Stupefied, Ed stared at the door through which Coe had disappeared. He wondered if he should run after him, but then he remembered his real intention for the night, and he ordered another glass of wine for Grace. He wouldn't mind her a bit tipsy. Soon he would have to get rid of Tif. Coe was wrong if he thought he would take care of both sisters. Ed was only interested in one.

When they left the bar, Grace was swaying a bit, not much, enough to put his arm around her waist. He decided to drop Tif off at her house. She jumped out of the pickup and disappeared without saying a word. Grace wasn't fast enough, and before she could slip out of the cab, he reached over and shut the door. His stomach was churning, and his hands were clammy as he reached for her. She gave him a little peck on the cheek, and tried to open the door, but he quickly grabbed her head with both hands and dug his tongue into her mouth. Ah, she tasted of alcohol and cigarettes, and he couldn't get enough of her soft, warm tongue that she thrust against his so readily. Then she squirmed and moved her head wildly, and he wasn't quite sure if she was fighting him or if she was as aroused as he was. When she tore her head away from him and tumbled out of the pickup, he was disappointed, but in a way, he didn't mind so much. He had had a good taste of her, and this wasn't the end of it.

Chapter 19

A deep, impotent anger burned in Michael, as he drove home. Emma sat silently next to him staring straight ahead through the windshield. She too was probably angry because he had scolded her, and she didn't understand why he wouldn't let her speak with Tiffany. It had been unbearable to see her so comfortable in the company of those who were most repulsive to him. He cursed himself for having gone to the bar with Emma for dinner. The problem was that there was no decent food at home since Tiffany had stopped coming, and Emma had finally rebelled when he wanted to serve her another ravioli dinner out of a can. He glanced at his daughter who punished him with her unhappy silence. Was this the carefree childhood he had in mind for her? Her mother had failed her, and so might he.

And he cursed himself for having given in to his weakness. He was attracted to Tiffany, more than he dared to admit, but his head told him to stay away from her. Why hadn't he met her earlier when he was free and thought that love was a simple affair? He tried to fight against the jealousy that made his heart ache, but he couldn't get the image out of his head: Tiffany sitting next to Ed, so casually, as if nothing else mattered to her. And Coe, what did he have to do with them? Fear, doubt and insecurity were feeding off each other, plunging his mind into misery.

"Daddy, why couldn't I talk to Tiffany? She's our friend." Emma's voice was sad. Did he hear the sound of tears? He wasn't sure.

"She was busy, honey. She was with her friends. I don't think she had time for us." It felt good to blame her, if only a little bit, but he knew it wasn't right.

"She didn't look very happy. I don't think they are her friends."

"Well, why would she go out with them otherwise? Her sister was there too."

"But Tiffany isn't like her."

"What do you mean?"

"Tiffany is nice. The others aren't."

"Why do you think the others aren't nice?"

"I don't like the way they look. Please, Daddy, make Tiffany come back to us."

"I don't know, honey. These are her friends and family. She grew up with them. After all, we are strangers here." He might have gone on like that, venting his hurt feelings selfishly if he hadn't heard a small sob next to him. A wave of shame flooded through him, and he put his hand out to touch Emma's face. Was this the way to be a good father? Couldn't he do better than dump his frustrations on his six-year old daughter, the very person he had set out to rescue from sadness?

He saw the letter as soon as they walked into the house. When Emma bent down to pick it up from the floor, he told her to leave it where it was. It was an advertisement, he said. He'd throw it away later. He locked the front door, made sure the windows were closed, and turned on every light downstairs. Then he went upstairs where Emma was waiting for him to tuck her in. She fell asleep while he read her a good night story.

As he looked at her round, sweet face, illuminated by the lamp on the nightstand, the old ache came back, and he asked himself if he should call it off. He had meant to do the right thing by her, but maybe it had all been a big mistake. Maybe he should bring her back to Marcia, file for custody, and hope that the court would be on his side. Would they charge him with kidnapping? Would they believe that Marcia was a drug addict, unfit to be a mother? Would he be locked away in jail and Emma put in a foster home?

Slowly he went downstairs. The letter was still on the floor by the door. Somebody must have pushed it underneath. He picked it up and scrutinized it. A sealed, business size envelope, nothing written on it, smudges where someone had licked the gummed paper. In the living room he turned off the lamps except for the small, old-fashioned glass lamp on the table next to the sofa. Emma was safe upstairs. There was no need for the bright lights now. The person who had been snooping around his house was long gone. But he couldn't help himself, he felt unpleasantly exposed as he looked at the black bay window. He regretted that he had never bothered to put up curtains. Resolutely, he turned his back to the darkness and walked to the sideboard. With trembling hands, he opened the bottom drawer. Underneath papers and books, his fingers touched the cold metal. For a few seconds he held his breath, listening to the silent night and his rapid heartbeat. Cautiously he pulled out the pistol.

When he walked to the sofa, the old floorboards creaked, a welcome sound in a night that held strange secrets. He sat down and put the small, black weapon on the table in front of him. Without haste, he took out his pocketknife and cut open the envelope. He felt calm now; even his heartbeat had slowed.

LEAVE TOWN IF YOU WANT TO STAY ALIVE. The words were printed in large, bold letters. Was this a childish prank or a real threat? Laughter welled up in him, hysterical and nervous, but he never uttered a sound.

That night, he put the pistol on his nightstand. He woke up often and searched for it in the darkness. Once he must have pushed it off in his restless sleep. It hit the floor with a thump so loud, he thought a shot had been fired. He was exhausted when morning dawned. Neither a long shower nor several cups of coffee could overcome his fatigue. When it was time to wake Emma, he had decided that only two men could have written the letter, Ed or his dimwitted friend. Why? What did they know? He was too weary to think clearly.

He fixed breakfast for Emma and drove her to school, absent-mindedly listening to her chatter, muttering a word or two, nodding his head. Before she jumped out of the car, he grabbed her by the arm.

"Emma, wait right here for me after school. Don't wander off, do you hear? Don't go back to the schoolyard to play. You must stay here by the curb and wait for me." His voice was husky, and the words tumbled out of his mouth rapidly. Emma looked at him, confused and a bit amused. He wanted to shake her to make her understand that this was serious, when the shrill sound of the bell startled him.

Emma put her small hand on his shoulder and kissed him on the cheek. "Don't worry, Daddy. I'll be all right." Then she jumped out of the car and ran towards the line of children who had assembled in front of their classroom. He waited until the teacher came out and ushered them in. How often had he watched this little routine! Now he was thankful that it was so ordinary, so uneventful.

On his way home, Michael stopped at the grocery store. It was early, and not many people were there. He thought he recognized the fat man who was pushing a shopping cart with several bags of dog food. He was the one he had seen with Ed in front of the bar. The man briefly looked up as Michael walked past him. Two older men in overalls, their grimy caps pushed back on their heads, stood by the meat counter talking. When he passed them, they stopped their conversation, then picked it up again when he was out of earshot. Were they talking about him, or were they just discussing the price of meat? Had he seen them before? And the fat man? Why had he looked at him? Get a grip on yourself, Michael told himself, there was nothing sinister about these farmers or the fat man who knew Ed. Lots of people in Junction City knew Ed. It meant nothing. Slowly he walked to the cashier, put bread, milk and coffee on the counter, feeling strangely detached from his surroundings. It must be the lack of sleep.

He turned on the heat in the car as he drove home. It was a cold fall day. The cottonwood trees at the turn to his house had lost nearly all their leaves. Their gnarled branches sighed mournfully in the ever-present wind. It was an appropriate melody for his misery. He wondered how he would get through the day. Write? Impossible. Call Vincent and ask him what he should do about the anonymous letter? Pressing the bag of groceries against his chest, he slowly walked toward the house.

When he saw a figure move by the front door his first thought was his pistol. Why had he left it in the house? Then he recognized Tiffany, and relief washed over him, only to be chased away by anger, a white, furious anger that was irrational and self-pitying. He continued toward the door. The boards of the porch creaked under his steps. It sounded like the chatter of invisible people who were speaking in a strange tongue. He fished the key out of his pocket and slowly turned it in the lock. Tiffany was watching him without saying a word. He held the door open for her, his eyes on the gray floorboards. In the kitchen, he unpacked the groceries, trying to think of something to say that wouldn't betray his emotions.

"Do you want some coffee?" he finally asked. Tiffany nodded her head. He tried to keep his hands from shaking and cursed under his breath when he spilled some of the ground coffee beans on the counter.

"Let me do it." Tiffany took the coffee can out of his hands. She put cups, spoons and milk on the table. Gracefully, she moved through the kitchen, and he followed her with his eyes. Her faded, oversized sweatshirt concealed her body, and she appeared thin and frail. Some strands of hair had come loose from her ponytail that was held together with a clasp studded with fake pearls. When the coffee was done, she poured it into the mugs and sat down. Warily she gazed at him over the rim of her steaming cup.

He stirred his coffee, unable to form a clear thought. All he wanted to do was touch some of her fragile beauty, but he couldn't do it. The more he ached for her, the more his jealousy grew, and he wished he wouldn't suffer in this absurd way. And underneath it all was the terrifying fear that somebody out there wanted to harm him and Emma.

Finally Tiffany broke the silence. "Michael, I can explain why I went out last night with my sister and Ed."

"You don't need to explain."

"But I want to. I know I told you I wouldn't see Ed again."

"Listen. You know that I don't like your friend Ed. I also don't like Jim Coe, and I don't particularly like your sister. But who am I to tell you who to go out with? I have no right to do that." He was trying to increase his pain by hurting her. Just like last night, when he told Emma that Tiffany was among friends, and he and Emma were the strangers who didn't belong.

"You don't understand, Michael." She looked at him with steady eyes. "I went out with Ed because I wanted to find out what he is up to. He said things about you and Jim Coe, and I was worried."

"What did he say?"

"He said that he and Coe are onto something, and it has to do with you. That's all I know. My sister is seeing Coe, but I don't think Ed is aware of it."

She lowered her head, and her ponytail fell over her shoulder exposing her slender neck. Michael reached over and followed its delicate line with his fingertip. His resolve to stay aloof, angry, had vanished. When she raised her head, her eyes, dark and unhappy, met his.

"I came here to start all over, Tiffany. I had a plan, and it all seemed to make sense. But now, I am not sure. Things haven't turned out the way I hoped, and I don't quite know what to do now. I have enough on my plate with Coe. Now you are telling me your friend is mixed up with him. I should have known."

"Ed has a rifle, Michael."

"Has he told you why he needs it?" It didn't surprise him that the little, scrawny fellow had a weapon. He might think that he needed more than his fists.

Tiffany shook her head. "That's what I wanted to find out, and my sister was going to help me."

She refilled their cups. Michael followed her and put his arm around her shoulders. With his chin he motioned toward the living room. There he dropped down on the sofa and leaned back. His body ached from tension and lack of sleep. Gently he pulled Tiffany close to him and began to murmur his carefully kept secrets into her soft hair. He told her about himself, about Marcia, and that he had abducted Emma. It was a relief to unburden himself, at least for the moment, but guilt and shame accompanied every word he uttered.

"I thought we would be safe here, out in the country, away from people. My lawyer had set it all up. He assured me that nobody would find out." Michael laughed bitterly. "But there is no security in life, is there?"

"Your wife, what did she do when she found out that Emma was gone?" Tiffany asked, her head resting on his chest, her body leaning against him.

He put his hand under her chin and lifted it. Maybe it would be easier if he didn't look into these trusting eyes, but he wanted her to see him for who he was, a desperate, helpless man.

"She notified the police the next day when the nanny arrived and didn't find Emma. But the police asked all kinds of questions which she couldn't or wouldn't answer, and she became afraid. She backed off, withdrew her complaint and hired private detectives."

It was Jim Coe who had found them. But Michael had no idea why Ed was getting involved in his sordid affair. He told Tiffany that he had found Ed snooping around the house. "I chased him off, and I thought he got the message when I held a pistol under his nose."

He got up and from the sideboard took the letter and handed it to Tiffany. Anxiously, he watched her as she unfolded it, waiting for her to say something, but she remained quiet, her head bent over the paper, a pink flush spreading from her throat to her face.

"What does it say?" She handed the paper back to him. Her hand was shaking.

He was perplexed. "Can't you read that?" He said it before he could think. Of course, he should have remembered her reading problem. But could it be so bad that she couldn't even read eight simple words?

"I told you I can't read. And if I am upset, it's even worse. If I had some time, I could figure it out. The words aren't long. But we don't have much time, do we?" Her face was deeply flushed now, but there was a shy determination in her eyes.

"I'm sorry, Tiffany." He sat down next to her. "It's enough if one of us can read this crap, isn't it?"

She shook her head. "No, it's not enough. What does it say?"

Michael told her. Then he tried to laugh it off. "It sounds like an overused phrase from an old-fashioned detective story, doesn't it? Do you think Ed could have written it or that simpleton he runs around with?"

"Marty?" Tiffany didn't think that Marty was capable of it. He never did anything on his own initiative, only when Ed told him. "Ed? Maybe, but why? Why would Ed want to chase you away or scare you? Ed says he's working with Coe, and Coe wants money from you. Coe wouldn't want you to disappear, right?"

They tried to find a central thread that would tie it all together, but they couldn't find one. Tiffany was adamant. "Ed is not a bad person, Michael. He's never done anything criminal. Maybe he cuts a corner here or there. It doesn't amount to much. He has always been a friend to me, ever since high school."

"Maybe the man is different from the boy." Michael felt anger mixed with jealousy rise in him again. He knew he had no right to feel this way. "I can't trust him, Tiffany. What was he doing at my house in the middle of the night?"

"I don't know what he's getting himself into. Maybe it has something to do with my sister. He's crazy about Grace. He'd do anything to get her."

When Tiffany left, Michael felt that his whole life was hanging by a thin thread, yet he felt strangely reassured. He wasn't quite so alone any longer.

Chapter 20

Tiffany drove back to town and straight away went to the motel to get her old job back. She found Mr. Wiederspan in one of the defunct bathrooms working with Marty and Ed. Her employer was glad that she wanted to work again. Several hunters were coming tomorrow. The duck season was in full swing. Liz had complained about doing overtime, and he couldn't stand her griping any longer.

Liz was indeed happy when Tiffany told her that she was back at work. "About time," she grumbled. "I know you needed some space after your dad passed away, but mourning should be over now. Life goes on. And these hunters are coming. The mess they make in their rooms! Muddy boots and beer bottles everywhere. Well, you know what it's like. It's too much for me alone, and I told Al so. He didn't want to hire another gal because you'd be back, he said."

"How about if I take the early morning shift again and then come back at night, the way we used to do it?" Tiffany asked. Liz hated getting up early, and Tif actually liked being in the office when everybody was still asleep.

"Are you sure, honey? Then you'll have to scrub the toilets. Not that I'd mind giving up that job."

"That's okay."

"Sweet Jesus, I've been saved."

Liz disliked any kind of work, especially cleaning toilets and showers. She barely did any housework in her own home and hated doing it for strangers in the motel. Instead, she preferred sitting in the office, smoking, watching TV.

"How's Mr. Coe? Is he staying?" Tiffany tried to sound casual. She didn't want to arouse Liz's suspicion

"Oh, you'll like him, even though he's quite fussy. Needs new towels and sheets all the time, wants the floor vacuumed, and he likes his bottled water. Why can't he drink water out of the tap like everybody else? I asked him once, and he pointed to his head and said that the water is polluted here. It makes you crazy. Shallow wells, agricultural run-off. Well, I don't know anybody in Junction City who got crazy because of the water. Anyway, he gives me good tips."

Just after nine o'clock the next day, the hunters showed up, and Tiffany had her hands full. They were loud, boisterous men with padded jackets, heavy boots and coolers full of beer. They laughed and shouted and slapped each other on the back for no reason at all. They came every year, and Tiffany was familiar with their habits. Today they would sit in their rooms, sort through their gear and drink beer. She knew it would be a lot of work to clean up after them every morning. Empty beer bottles, dirty paper plates, wet towels on the floor, tobacco spit in the sink.

She was going through the registration forms when Mr. Heitman appeared in the office. His small face lit up when he saw her, and he lifted his slender hands as if in prayer. "Ah, you are back, Miss Tiffany. That's delightful." She had told Mr. Heitman earlier that he could call her Tiffany or Tif, like everybody else, but he had insisted on this formal address. "Maybe you can help me. I have mentioned it to Miss Liz, but she doesn't even try to do something about it. These hunters, the noise. One cannot concentrate, and I have to draw up detailed plans. I'll be gone for two days, but when I come back . . . please, please make sure that they stop shouting and stomping around, or maybe you can move them to rooms farther away from mine?"

"Do you want me to keep the same room for you?" Tiffany asked.

"By all means. I am leaving certain personal items and important

151

papers there." With jittery hands, he put his key on the counter. "I don't want to take the key with me. One can misplace it. It happened to me several years ago. I have never forgotten all the problems I had because of that mishap. Please, Miss Tiffany, make sure the room is locked at all times. The papers are of utmost importance. I have given Mr. Wiederspan a copy of the excavation plans for the site, but he is most careless, and I worry he could lose them." He spoke in a whiny, high-pitched tone, and his hands were fluttering up and down following the cadence of his voice.

"Do you mean the Indian site? Mr. Coe has something to do with it, hasn't he?" Tiffany was barely able to hide the eagerness in her voice. Mr. Heitman didn't seem to notice.

"Yes, Mr. Coe has been a most valuable partner. We are very fortunate that he is interested in this project and has offered his help. The site that I have discovered has immense educational potential. Unfortunately, nothing happens without the business community. We who are concerned with educating the young have to accept that. I am contributing the educational, historical aspect to this enterprise if I may say so, and Mr. Coe, a respected businessman, is in charge of financing our project. But let me be clear—the ultimate goal is expansion of knowledge."

"An educational enterprise and Mr. Coe is putting money in it?" Tiffany was astounded. In Junction City money and education had nothing to do with each other.

Mr. Heitman's eyes sparkled with excitement. "Let me explain, Miss Tiffany. I found the site on a stretch of land owned by Mr. Wiederspan. It was once inhabited by several groups of Indians, the earliest of which might have been the Folsom Culture. A considerable number of arrowheads point to that period. A rare find, a very rare find." He leaned forward and whispered, "Nine to seven thousand B.C." Tiffany didn't know what to say, and after a moment of silence, Mr. Heitman continued, "A site worthy of an archeological excavation. I know of several universities that would be interested and broached this idea to Mr. Wiederspan. Unfortunately, Mr. Wiederspan is not a philanthropist and therefore not interested in a scientific excavation and the eventual display of the artifacts in a museum. It was our good luck that Mr. Coe solved the dilemma. He suggested the development of a unique enterprise, a combination of commercial establishment and museum, similar to a theme park, based on sound educational principles. Tourists will visit the site and enjoy the attractions, among them educational films and authentic reenactments for which I will be the historical consultant. In a gift shop, modeled on those established by famous museums like the Smithsonian, visitors will be able to purchase enlightening souvenirs. Mr. Coe has already interested several big investors."

The longer he spoke, the more melodious his voice became. He stressed certain vowels and words, and he continued to move his hands like a conductor in front of a choir. An expression of self-satisfied importance spread over his usually reserved features. But the long speech seemed to have left the small man breathless, and he started to cough. When Tiffany offered him some coffee, he declined. He was anxious to leave and show his finds to some specialists who would establish beyond doubt the exact time period when the site was first inhabited. He'd be back in two or three days.

He was already by the door, when he turned around. "There will be many jobs for people here, Miss Tiffany. I am sure you could find a more appropriate and rewarding occupation in our Indian park." He smiled, cocked his head and shuffled out.

When Ed and Marty appeared a little later, Tiffany asked them if they knew anything about this theme park. "It sounds strange, Ed. A theme park like Disneyland?"

Marty began to ramble about Indians and bows and arrows, and before Ed could answer Tiffany, Al Wiederspan stormed into the office and told the two men to get on with their work in the bathrooms.

"How many rooms rented, Tif? Are we going to make some money? Come, girl, let's have a look at the reservations."

He leafed through the forms, counted the nights his rooms were occupied, and multiplied them by the daily price. "Not much. Three rooms for the hunters and then Mr. Heitman. Don't know if I can charge him," he murmured. Then he smiled at Tiffany. "Things are going to change, Tif. I'll be rich, girl, and you'll be better off too. No lay-offs in the slow time. No, you'll have steady employment because we'll be booked solid. An Indian theme park, what do you say? It's Coe's idea, and he'll get the money rolling. But it's my land, and that's what's going to make me rich." He slammed his hand on the desk and scattered the registration forms across the counter.

She was ready to go home after her morning shift when Ed and Marty walked into the office again. They were done with the bathrooms. Ed swore that it was the last time he was working for old Al, and Marty nodded in agreement.

"Yeah, we ain't gonna work for 'im no more. He ain't payin' enough for all that dirty work."

Ed turned to him with a frown on his face. "I'm talkin' about me, Marty, not you. For you it's different. Ya should work for Al 'cause it's all ya can do."

Marty looked at him surprised. "What d'ya mean? I wanna work with you. We always been workin' together, Ed."

"Well, things change, don't they? You gotta look out for yourself, Marty. Ya can't always wait for me to tell ya what to do. Ya know, ya gotta look around and kinda find your own way."

Marty was upset. He opened his mouth, but no words came out. Tiffany felt sorry for him.

"We always stuck together, Ed. You and me and Tif," he finally managed to say.

"I just told ya, things change. Listen, I might go other places, do other things."

Marty stared at him, silent, crestfallen.

"What ya lookin' at me like that for?" Ed scolded his friend. "I'm still here. I haven't gone yet, but I'm not takin' care of you no more."

"Don't be mean to him," Tiffany said. "Marty has always trusted you, and you've always watched out for him. What are you talking about anyway?"

Ed shrugged his shoulders. He grinned. "Come on, ya two, let's go for a ride. I wanna show ya somethin'."

When they squeezed into the pickup, Tiffany managed to sit by the door rather than in the middle. Both men smelled of sweat and work, and she wanted to make sure that the window stayed open. Every time Ed made a right turn, Marty's soft body fell against her. His flabby flesh and its sour, unwashed smell repulsed her. She didn't want to be in the cab with these two men, but if she could find out what Ed and Coe were up to she would gladly endure it.

The sky was overcast and a cold wind blew from the north. Tiffany hadn't been at the sandpit in many years. A thin turf of grass covered the crest of the sand-hills whose slopes had been crudely dug up a long time ago. No blade of grass would ever grow there again. It was a desolate place. She was shivering and turned up the collar of her jacket. Ed told them to hurry because it might rain soon. With care, nearly tenderly, he pulled a longish parcel out from under the driver's seat and unwrapped it. Tiffany was startled when she saw the rifle in his hand. It was of medium size, black, with a magazine attached. Guns were nothing new to her. Nearly every man in Junction City was a hunter. Her father had hunted, and so did all of her uncles. As a young girl, she had occasionally accompanied her father, and sometimes he had let her carry his rifle for him, but he had never taught her to shoot it. The weapon that Ed was holding up in his fist looked different from anything she had ever seen before.

Ed ordered Marty to set up some beer cans on a barrel that stood against the sandbank. Marty did so eagerly, and then rushed back to join Tiffany, who stood a few steps behind Ed. She closed her eyes and covered her ears with her hands as the shots came rapidly in a staccato scream that didn't seem to end. When she opened her eyes again, she was surprised that the sand-hill was still there.

"Let's check my shots," Ed chuckled, holding the gun high in the air like a victorious fighter.

Beer cans were scattered everywhere on the ground, and the barrel was full of holes. Ed pointed his gun at several of the cans and insisted that he had blown them off the barrel.

"This gun gives power, I tell ya, real power. I'm not takin' shit from nobody again, not from old Al or nobody. Wanna try?" He fumbled with the magazine, and then held the rifle out to them. Tiffany and Marty shook their heads.

"Why do you need a gun like that, Ed? What has Mr. Wiederspan done to you?" Tiffany asked. She was shaking.

Ed broke into a high-pitched cackle. "I don't mean Al. He's not important no more. I got my eyes on another person. He's threatened me, and nobody's gonna get away with that."

"What are you talking about? Who has threatened you?"

Ed shook his head and grinned. He wrapped the rifle in the piece of burlap and carried it back to his pickup where he stuffed it under the front seat again.

Marty and Tiffany were trailing after him. "Marty, what is he talking about?"

Marty briefly glanced at her and then quickly looked away. She knew it was useless. Marty would never tell on Ed. In a way, she had hoped that Ed was just bragging when he had told her that he had a rifle. It wasn't unlike him to mix fact and fiction, and his schemes almost never came true. But this time it was different. Tiffany was horrified.

She was barely paying attention when Ed suggested going to Casey's. She only awoke from her reverie when she heard the dogs. Behind the fence, they were growling and snarling, their fangs exposed and saliva dripping to the ground. One was running back and forth on the hard-packed dirt. The other dog was straining against the fence, every muscle quivering, ready to sink his sharp teeth into her throat. A faint smell of dog feces and urine hung in the air. When Casey called the animals back, they whimpered, flattened their bodies against the ground, and then slunk off behind the trailer.

It was close to noon and Casey was alone. Tiffany wondered if he ever really worked. He claimed that he drove a cement truck, but she had never seen him in one. He invited them into his kitchen where he was eating lunch. As he squeezed behind the wobbly kitchen table, he apologized for finishing his meal. "Can't let it go cold, right?"

Marty eagerly contemplated the remnants of a steak and a half-eaten baked potato.

"What's up? Wanna beer or maybe some ice tea for the young lady?" Casey daintily cut a piece of fat from the meat.

"That rifle you got me works fine, real good," Ed said.

Casey frowned. "I don't know that I should've given it to you, Ed. I'm not sure you'll be using it right. But then, if people ask me for a gun, I like to get it for them because I believe it's every man's right to carry one. No questions asked. Me and my friends, we think the world will be a safer place when everyone is armed." He paused, and Tiffany felt his gaze on her. "But we want to keep things quiet here, don't we? You gotta be smart."

"Don't worry, Casey," Ed said. "I know what I'm doin'. It's just a precaution, that's all. Ya know, I should've gotten a rifle a long time ago. We need to be armed. That's right. Otherwise they trample all over ya."

Casey nodded his head. "The damn anti-gun lobby, they're going to make babies out of us, defenseless babies. We can't allow that."

Marty had been moving his beer can from one hand to the other, placing it on the table, grabbing it again with his pudgy hand, barely taking a sip. He was now shifting restlessly on his chair. When he started speaking, he wasn't addressing anybody in particular. "It fires a lot of rounds. Ya can't stop it. It just fires."

Ed turned to him impatiently. "That's the point, ain't it? It's supposed to fire, you dumb klutz."

"Marty has a point," Casey said. "It's a dangerous thing, a weapon like that. You gotta know what you're doing, Ed. They can't trace that rifle to me. I always make sure about that. But you better not cause any trouble. First and foremost, a weapon is for self-defense, Ed. Don't forget it." With a piece of white bread, he wiped up the mixture of meat juice and blood on his plate.

Tiffany wasn't ready when he turned to her. "How are you today, Tiffany? Haven't seen you in a long time. Still working for that man in the Nielsen house?" He appeared friendly enough, but Tiffany was apprehensive.

"Off and on. I'm back at the motel."

"It's hard for a man raising a little girl on his own. Her name is Emma, isn't it? I've seen her at the schoolyard. Nice little girl. Where's the mother? Divorced probably."

"I don't know. I just do housework for them."

"Come on, you must know somethin'," interjected Ed, but Casey silenced him with a stern look.

"He picks her up after school, doesn't he?" Casey continued.

Tiffany tried to laugh. "Why are you so interested in them?" Emma! He shouldn't be asking about Emma.

"I'm really not. But this is a small place. Can't help noticing newcomers. Same with this guy Jim Coe. Now I hear he's going to make Al Wiederspan rich." Casey laughed and his belly shook. "Al thinks he's a great businessman, going to throw money at him. This Coe makes everybody think he's their sugar-daddy."

"Jim Coe knows when somethin' good comes up, and I can help 'im. He's all right," Ed quipped.

"I heard he's Grace's new man."

Tiffany saw Ed stiffen. "What d'ya mean? She's not with him. She's with me."

"Is that so? What do you think, Tiffany?" Casey smiled at her.

She didn't answer. She looked at Ed, who hastily gulped down his beer. Did he really not know or did he not want to know?

Casey shrugged his shoulders and told them that he had to get ready for the hunters. They were on vacation and often arrived already in the afternoon for a good game of poker. If they wanted to stay, fine, but he had to set up the tables now.

"Can't stay, not today. Gotta meet somebody." Ed got up.

"Don't tell me I didn't warn you, Ed," Casey called after them as they walked to the door.

The pickup rattled loudly, and Ed steered it like a maniac. Right, left, he seemed to aim for every pothole. Nobody spoke during the trip back to town. Marty was glum.

Tiffany tried to master the anxiety in her voice when she turned to Ed. "You're going to meet somebody tonight? Grace?"

"Maybe. I ain't tellin'."

How she hated them all, Casey, Ed, Marty. They played their little games, made innuendos and didn't tell her the truth.

When Tiffany got home, her mother was sitting in front of the TV. Cigarette smoke drifted through the recently decorated living room and mixed with the vapors of new carpet and fresh paint. Quietly, Tiffany sat down across from her on an overstuffed armchair. Audrey paid no attention. She reached for her drink, eyes glued to the TV.

"I've gone back to work at the motel, Mom."

"Have you seen Grace?" She mumbled the words and her speech was slurred. "She's gone all night and barely shows up at work. Is she still with that new guy? I hope so, but you can't trust men. They never turn out the way you think. Remember that." Briefly, she glanced at Tiffany, her glassy eyes half hidden under heavy lids. Then she turned to the TV again. "Your father, a handsome guy, but he never got anywhere. Didn't even give me a house. After all these years, I haven't got a house. The bank owns the house." Her voice was taking on a shrill, whining tone.

Tiffany left the room, but her mother never noticed. She rambled on in the pitiful manner of a drunk. Hadn't she been the most beautiful girl in Junction City? She could have had Carlton, a dentist. Why hadn't she played her cards right? Randy just didn't know how to get ahead. Every time now, when her mother drank, she talked about her father that way. Tiffany tried to seek refuge in the remembrance of the good moments they had shared as a family, but these memories were few and fading fast. The face of her handsome father, when he was young and strong, was always overshadowed by the face of the dying man. Her ache for him was like the gnawing hunger pains of a person who was slowly starving. Was it love she was longing for? Sometimes she saw the face of Michael in her mind.

Chapter 21

Ed had trouble getting rid of Marty after their visit to Casey. Marty complained that it was still too early and he didn't want to go home yet. In a way, Ed didn't blame him. Marty lived with his older brother Marvin, who, even for Ed's standards, was a singularly bad-mouthed, short-tempered man. He didn't mistreat Marty. Marty would have told him if that were the case. But Marvin kept his younger brother in a perpetual state of fear and unease. Sometimes Marty quietly stole into the living room to watch TV with his brother. If Marvin remained silent, it meant Marty could stay. However, more often than not, Marvin was in a bad mood. Then he scolded Marty for being dumb and useless, a burden on the brother, and Marty quickly retreated to his room or the old garage that stood empty. Ed sometimes felt sorry for his friend.

By comparison, Ed had an easy time at home. He had his room at his mother's house. It cost him nothing and was convenient. His mother did his laundry and cooked for him, the way she had done throughout his life. He was the youngest, and all his siblings had moved out of the tiny wood-frame house a long time ago. Sometimes one or another came back for a short while when hard times befell them, but they never stayed long. His older sister had once admonished him to be nicer to their mother, but he had shrugged her off. What was wrong with yelling at the old woman when she had forgotten to iron his shirt? She never complained. After all, the old man had been worse.

When he dropped Marty off at his house, his friend lumbered away sullenly, dragging his feet as if he were pulling a heavy weight. Ed drove away in a hurry. In his rear view he saw Marty standing forlornly in front of his ramshackle house watching him leave. Ed cursed him and the foul-mouthed Marvin and pressed his foot down on the gas pedal.

When he knocked at Coe's door at the motel, no sound came from the other side. However, the window was lit, and Ed was sure that Coe was inside. Then he heard footsteps, and the door opened a crack.

"What a surprise, Ed. Can I help you with anything?" Coe sounded friendly enough, but he didn't look too pleased.

"If I could come in, Jim. I need to talk to ya."

Reluctantly, it seemed to Ed, Coe stepped back and let him enter. Ed noticed the new pink and green bedspread on the king size bed. It was rumpled. On the nightstand next to it stood two empty glasses. Why two? A cigarette was smoldering in the ashtray that was full of stubs, some smeared with lipstick.

"I can't quite imagine that we need to talk about anything. But now that you're here, what's on your mind?" Coe sat down on the shabby armchair and pointed to the other one, equally worn and shabby. "Do you want to finish our conversation from last night?"

Suddenly Ed's mind went blank, and he stared at the other man, frantically trying to say something, but the words didn't come. Coe watched him expectantly. Finally Ed stammered, "Well, yeah, Mr. Coe, Jim, I mean . . . there wasn't time last night." Why couldn't he think clearly? Was it Coe's manner, so cold and self-possessed? Ed started to sweat.

"Go ahead, Ed. Or maybe I should tell you something? Set you straight about a few things?" He paused, and Ed felt as if Coe's eyes were burning holes into him. There was an unmistakable threat in his voice. "You think I'm from here. I'm not, and anyway—what's it to you? But you're right about Michael Barron. He's from Los Angeles. Now, I'm curious. How did you find out about him? He's very discreet, you know."

Ed cleared his throat. "Well, let's say I overheard ya. I was there one night when you was visitin', just by accident. My truck was overheatin' and I thought I could ask Barron for some water." He relaxed a bit when his fib spilled forth so easily. He was always good at covering up. He had learned that however flimsy his lies were, they got him through more often than not. "Ya know how it is with them old cars."

"I don't drive old cars." Coe raised his hand and smoothed back his hair. "As I told you, I'm not from here, and I am thankful about that. This place is a dump. But you obviously know that my mother grew up here. The house Michael Barron lives in belonged to her. I sold it to him. My mother died some months ago. A blessing, her mind was totally gone, couldn't remember anything. Sometimes she called me Dan, sometimes Jack and other names. The last time she came back here was when Uncle Jack died, but I don't think anybody recognized her then. She was with her latest husband. After that, her mind started to go. I used to think it was that husband of hers that did it to her, but I'm not so sure anymore. Maybe it was seeing the old house again. Anyway, she is gone now." Jim Coe gazed at Ed with a far-away look in his eyes. "Well, I'm sure you're not interested in my mother."

"I remember your uncles." If Coe wanted to talk family, Ed could tell him a few stories.

"They were quite crazy, weren't they? At least, that's what my mother told me." Coe said.

"It was only Jack. Dan was normal."

"Are you sure? They lived like paupers, and my mother told me that they were rich. You call that normal?" Anger flickered in Coe's eyes.

"Maybe they was rich. We never seen it. They had a lot of land, I guess."

"Yes, and there was a lot of money, too. Dan had stashed it away in the attic together with some securities. A considerable amount, but the mice and rats chewed it all up." Coe burst out in a bitter laugh. "And my mother's last husband, Ed, his name was Ed like yours, he made sure that the money from the sale of the land that belonged to the Nielsens disappeared quickly. Oh well. It's an old story."

Coe was silent now, lost in thought. Ed stared at the floor, wondering how to proceed. As far as he was concerned, everybody had a sob story, but mice eating dollar bills, that was tough, he had to admit. Finally, he cleared his voice. "It's about this guy Michael Barron. I can help ya, Jim."

Coe focused his eyes on him again. "Help me? I don't think I need help. I am a busy man, and I prefer to work alone. Anyway, I'm done here pretty soon. Just a few more meetings with Wiederspan, and it's all settled."

"I don't mean the project with Wiederspan. I hadn't thought about that. I was talkin' 'bout your business with Barron. Ya wanna get money out of 'im. I can help ya. I can do the dirty work, put the screws on Barron real tight." Now it was out.

"I'm in the investment business, Ed. What would you know about it? I'm asking Barron for money that I'll invest for him. You must have misunderstood the nature of my business. It's all perfectly legal. There is no dirty work, as you call it." He rose. "And now, Ed, I must ask you to leave. I'm expecting a visitor, not for business." He smiled at him knowingly.

Confused, Ed got up from the armchair. Did Coe dismiss him just like that? Maybe he hadn't expressed himself clearly. The two men stood facing each other. When Jim Coe, who was only an inch or two taller, took a step toward him, Ed shrank back. And then the anger, his old companion, reared its head. It began in his stomach and burst into his esophagus like a hot burning flame.

"You're blackmailing 'im, Jim. Ya can't tell me any different. You ain't no investor or consultant or whatever. You're from Chicago, and you got a police record there. I know all about it." The words spurted out of his mouth before he could think.

"I think you better go."

164

Ed didn't move. He knew he had to soften his tone. "Look, Jim, I don't mean to offend ya. All I wanna say is that I wanna do business with you. Ya call the shots, and I do whatever ya like."

Coe stared at him coldly. "It's all about investments, Ed. It's a tough business. Not everybody can learn it and come out ahead."

Ed lowered his head and continued stubbornly. "You're the boss, and I wanna learn. Your mother didn't like it here, and I don't like it here either. When it's all worked out, maybe ya can give me a leg up in Chicago. It's a dead hole, Junction City is. I wanna move on with Grace."

"With Grace? Is she your girlfriend?"

Ed lifted his head and saw the hint of a smile on Coe's face.

"Yeah, me and Grace, we're real tight. She ain't happy here. I wanna give her a better life, ya know, with nice clothes, a good car, stuff like that."

The smile was gone from Coe's face as quickly as it had appeared.

"You're all wrong, Ed. I don't want a partner. I'm a very independent person. I set up my own business; I make my own decisions. No interference from anybody, that's how I operate. You talk about blackmail. I don't take kindly to that. I don't engage in it, and if I were you, I wouldn't engage in it either. It's a dangerous business. People get hurt." He paused. "People get killed. Just read the newspaper."

His voice was cold and sharp. Ed wanted to tell him that he wasn't afraid, that he could be trusted, that he was smart in all kinds of useful ways, but Coe held up his hand and continued. "I don't need any help, Ed, especially not in my business with Barron. When it comes to Al Wiederspan and the theme park, maybe we can talk. I'll think about it." Coe grabbed his arm with more strength than Ed expected from a man of his slender build, and forcefully steered him toward the door.

When he walked to his pickup, his body was twisted into one big, tense knot, his stomach was feeding a low flame of anger. The conversation had taken a wrong turn someplace, and Ed couldn't put his finger on it. Maybe it had something to do with all this talk about Coe's mother. The guy had a chip on his shoulder. Ed couldn't quite understand it because his own mother never figured in his thoughts at all. But maybe it could still work. If Coe wanted to get him into the theme park business, he'd go along with it for now and wait for Coe to teach him about "investments," if that's what he wanted to call it. Right now, he needed a cigarette and a beer. Maybe Grace was at Dub's.

But Grace wasn't there. When he asked about her, nobody had seen her. He drank a few beers, deeply inhaled his Marlboros and slowly started to unwind. When he left, he felt mellow. As he drove along Main Street, he passed the motel. The blue neon sign shone brightly. "Sunshine Motel," a name that struck him as ridiculous today because the wind was blowing and it would start to rain pretty soon. Below it, it said in smaller, red letters "Vacancies." Several parking spaces in front of the rooms were occupied by the hunters' trucks, Coe's Lincoln Continental, and a white car that looked like Grace's. Ed squinted his eyes, but he was already past the motel before he had a good look. He shook his head. Too many white cars in Junction City, too many beers.

Chapter 22

Five cars in front of him, four cars behind him. One car pulled away, a dirt-splattered jeep. An odd car among all the sedans that lined the curb. Probably a father who spent more time hunting than waiting for his child in front of the elementary school. Michael put his car in drive and moved forward. There was Emma. She had seen him and waved at him. In her hand she held a white piece of paper.

When she threw herself into the seat next to him, she clutched an envelope tightly in her fist. Michael looked at her fondly. Her flushed cheeks, her lively eyes always reminded him that he had done the right thing.

"I found this on the ground." She held up the envelope.

"On the ground? Somebody must have dropped it."

"No, it's for me. My name is on it."

Michael took the letter from her. Emma's name was written in smooth and precise letters. Adults print this way, not children. Adults use business-size envelopes. He tossed it on the dashboard and maneuvered the car away from the curb.

"It was suddenly under my foot when I looked down." Emma continued. "Do you think it could be from Mommy?"

Michael looked at her sharply. "Why do you think it could be from Mommy? Mommy doesn't know where we are."

"Maybe she has found us, and she doesn't want us to see her because she's afraid that we'll go away again. That's why she wrote a letter." There was no joy in his daughter's voice.

"No, Emma, it's not from Mommy. She's still in the hospital trying to get better. You mustn't worry about her." They never talked about Marcia because Emma never asked about her. She didn't ask because asking meant finding out the truth about her mother and the truth might hurt. Even his small daughter knew this. He gladly acquiesced in their shared secrecy because he had no good answers. Michael tried to keep his eyes on the road, ignoring the envelope, whose reflection gleamed in the windshield.

Emma was silent now. She opened her school bag and pulled out a book. It was one that Tiffany had given her, about a rabbit and a squirrel. She began leafing through the pages, stopping here and there to look at pictures or read a few sentences.

"Is it a good book?" Michael asked.

She nodded without looking at him.

"How was school?" He wanted to make her talk and reassure himself that she was all right, troubled by neither the letter nor her mother's absence. He wanted to hear her happy, cheerful chatter.

"All right." Her voice revealed nothing, but the brief reply was uncommon for his talkative daughter. Usually, she was eager to tell him about her school day, about her teacher, the other kids, or one of the many events that interrupted the daily routine: the local firemen who gave them a ride in the fire truck, somebody who had brought a pet, a party. Reports like these normally filled the time until they reached home. But now she remained stubbornly silent. He felt miserable and helpless.

He slowed down the car as he turned off the road. There was a certain comfort in approaching the house that had sheltered them for the past months. He thought of the rugs that Tiffany had chosen for the living room, the flowers she had put on the dining table. All these touches had made their home into a cozy refuge. But with the envelope on the dashboard came Coe's image, the malicious smile, the mocking eyes, and Michael's short glimmer of happiness was replaced by sad resignation. He wanted to protect Emma, but his carefully laid plans had started to fray weeks ago, and now they were unraveling fast.

As they walked toward the house, he took Emma's hand into his and felt comforted by the touch of her warm palm and small fingers. This was real, he thought, and squeezed her hand.

"Look." She pointed to the sky. High above them, a flock of geese flew south. They stood still for a while and watched the fluid V-shape that formed and reformed accompanied by the hoarse whooping of the birds. Emma asked him where they were flying and if they would come back. When he told her that they would do so in the spring, she clapped her hands and smiled.

While Emma was in the kitchen getting a snack, he quickly went upstairs into his study. With his penknife he opened the letter. GET OUT WHILE YOU CAN. He compared it to the one he had received earlier. Same paper, same envelope. Whoever was behind it didn't ask for money but wanted them to leave. Why? They posed no threat to anybody. All they wanted was to be left alone. Was Coe behind it, trying to ratchet up the tension? Michael felt as if an invisible web ensnared him. The more he moved and thrashed to free himself, the tighter the web got. They would have to move on, but he needed time; time to plan the next step, to cover his tracks, to keep Emma safe.

He had mentioned the possibility of leaving to Vincent, but his lawyer had been evasive and edgy. Often when Michael called, he wasn't in, and when he managed to get him on the phone, the lawyer sounded gruff and unfriendly. Michael suspected that he was trying to extricate himself from the whole affair, whether from lack of interest, lack of sufficient remuneration, or because he was suddenly concerned about the legality of it all. Michael couldn't tell. So far Vincent hadn't sold the house in France and didn't seem interested in doing so.

Michael sat down at his desk and switched on the computer. Then he began typing, and to his surprise his fingers flew across the keyboard without hesitance.

Dear Vincent,

My affairs have taken a turn for the better. I do not require your services anymore. Please, stop all proceedings concerning the sale of my house in France. I will take care of it myself. Thank you for all you have done. I hope the enclosed check covers your expenses.

Sincerely Yours,

Michael Barron

He wrote a check for a generous amount, addressed an envelope and enclosed the letter and check. When he sealed it, he felt relieved. For the first time since he had left Los Angeles with Emma, he was pro-active. It felt good.

The next morning, on their way to school, Emma chattered happily and didn't seem to have a care in the world. Michael was glad. She had forgotten the letter.

"Emma, after school, you'll wait for me by the front door back there. Don't stand by the curb. When you see me, come to the car." He tried to sound cheerful, matter of fact, but he knew that Emma would find his request strange. A few days ago he had told her the exact opposite: stay by the curb and wait for me.

"Why, Daddy? I always wait at the curb. The other children wait there too."

"There's too much commotion. I sometimes can't see you among all the children. And what if somebody pushes you?" He slowed down as they were approaching the school.

Emma frowned at him, but then she glanced out of the window and a smile spread over her face. Two squirrels were chasing each other up a maple tree. She quickly threw her arm around him, kissed him on the cheek and grabbed her school bag. Had she listened to his instructions? He watched her skip along the sidewalk and disappear among a cluster of children.

It was too early, and he decided to stop at the donut shop for a cup of coffee. There was a buzz of animated voices in the room when he

170

walked in, quite different from the dull atmosphere in the afternoon. At this time of the day, the place was filled with locals, mainly small businessmen, farmers and the retired. They briefly glanced at him, then turned to their neighbor again. A tall, fleshy man in a dark suit nodded to him. He nodded back. The man looked familiar, but Michael couldn't recall where he had seen him before. Then he remembered. He was the owner of the funeral parlor. He had seen him at the church hovering over the open coffin, putting the finishing touches on the flower arrangements. An odd man, morbid in an amiable way. Michael was glad when he could retreat to a table in the corner, sip his coffee and escape into his thoughts.

Nobody paid attention to him when he left the coffee shop. He drove to the post office and dropped the letter to Vincent in the mailbox. Then he continued on to the motel. A few mud-splashed pickups were parked along the row of rooms and among them, nearly hidden, was Coe's sleek town car.

He parked his Buick out of sight, at the end of the building. When he walked around the corner, he nearly bumped against Al Wiederspan.

"Well, now, Mr. Barron. So early in the morning? How are things? Your house is done? Not a bad house, but lots of repairs, right?" The old man's eyes sparkled.

"Yes, it's nearly finished. There are just a few minor things left."

"Can I help you with anything? Is it Tiffany you want to see? She isn't in yet."

"No, it's not Tiffany. I've come to see Jim Coe." So much for hiding his car and his visit, Michael thought bitterly.

"Number eight it is," the old man smiled knowingly. "And I can guess why you're here to see him. Business, isn't it? I've just talked to Jim myself. We've signed the papers, and I've given him a check. Not a small sum, I tell you. But of course, we need more money, local money and from the outside. Good for you, Mr. Barron. You know a good deal when you see it. This will be a big boost for Junction City, and we'll all come out ahead."

171

"Yes, that's the idea."

"You won't regret it. An Indian theme park. It's going to be an educational enterprise. Heitman will see to that. And it's going to be big. Coe will see to that. I've had this land down by the river forever. Fifty acres, just brush and weeds. But that's going to change now. We'll get more investors. Coe will bring some in from the outside. I'll work on the locals here. Glad you're on board with us. You're a member of our community, Mr. Barron. You might want to join us at the Rotary Club."

Mumbling that he'd be delighted but was in a hurry right now, Michael took his leave. He walked quickly to room number eight and knocked. Light steps moved across the floor and the door swung open widely. Coe's welcoming smile turned to surprise when he saw Michael.

"It's you. I thought old Wiederspan was back with another check." He laughed.

"We need to talk."

"Come in. I didn't expect you, but it can only be good news, right? Today must be my lucky day, which means I'll be able to wrap things up and move on." He motioned for Michael to take a seat on one of the armchairs.

The chair was low and uncomfortable. Michael leaned forward resting his elbows on his knees. Coe sat across from him leaning back, thoroughly at ease.

"I don't know if it's good news," Michael said.

"Things are going splendidly, Michael. I could even tolerate a bit of tardiness from you. Al Wiederspan just gave me a check for $30,000 to invest in my company that will develop his worthless river land. The theme park, you know. Looks great on paper. Every bank will be happy to do business with me. I was involved in a thing like that in Flint, Michigan, years ago. We were building a factory that was going to make valves. It was to be built in a blighted area, get people jobs, get them off welfare. You know how they always look for people to get off welfare. Well, we gave the mayor a great outline, and he and his people swallowed it all, hook, line and sinker. We got good money for a nonexistent factory. The funny thing is, later they built a real factory there, tires, not valves. I could swear they used our bogus plans." Coe took a cigarette and lit it with a silver lighter. "So, what's up?"

Michael pulled the two letters out of his pocket and threw them on the small table that stood between them. "I have been getting these lately. Do you know anything about it?"

"What are they?"

"That's what I want to know from you."

Coe picked up the letters and turned them over in his hand. A mask dropped over his face, freezing his smile into a watchful, menacing guise as he read the messages.

Was he the hunter? Who was the hunted? Once before, Michael had seen this look on his face. Coe would do whatever was necessary to survive the chase and be the winner.

"When did you get these?" Coe asked.

"The first one last week. My daughter brought the second one home yesterday."

"Why didn't you tell me right away?"

"Why should I? I didn't think you had anything to do with it. Now I am not so sure."

"Don't be ridiculous. Only an idiot or a simpleton would think up something like this." He put the letters back on the little table. "But I think I know how to take care of the problem. Don't worry, you won't be getting any more of these. I can promise you that." His eyes had the hungry look of the street kid who knew how to survive in the dog-eat-dog world.

Chapter 23

Just before Tiffany got off work at noon, Mr. Heitman returned from his fact-finding trip. His narrow face was glowing with pleasure. He wore a new pair of khaki pants, a blue cotton shirt, and a brown vest with many zippered pockets, the type worn by hunters and fishermen. But the most remarkable part of his outfit was the brand-new cowboy hat that he had fastened with a string below his chin. Tiffany couldn't help but smile at the man, who usually wore poorly fitting suits and white shirts with striped ties.

Carefully he put down his suitcase. "Miss Tiffany, we can now begin with the excavation of the Indian village," he said in his slow, exacting way as if he were addressing a school class. "I consulted a friend of mine, a professor of anthropology at Anchorside College in Sioux City, and he gave me the most valuable information." He pulled a small package from one of the pockets in his vest and unwrapped it carefully. In it were two spear points made from stone.

"Indians were living here thousands of years ago. My friend is convinced that we are dealing with the Folsom Culture." He held up one of the spear points. "We won't know for sure until we have done the carbon dating. I have made arrangements with my friend, but it'll cost some money. I will have to talk to Mr. Coe about it." With trembling hands, he wrapped the precious items again and stowed them away in his vest. "You see, Miss Tiffany, we have to proceed in a very scientific manner, if we want to do this right."

The poor man was a bundle of nerves, nearly too jittery to talk, but he droned on, even though Tiffany was barely paying attention to him any longer. Indian cultures, carbon dating, excavations. Her mind was on other things. She looked at the clock on the wall. Liz was supposed to take over from her, and she was late. Just then the door opened and her coworker walked in.

The large woman mumbled an unintelligible greeting. Indifferently she glanced at Mr. Heitman, who made every effort to ignore her and continued to talk to Tiffany about different methods employed in archeological excavations. Liz lit a cigarette, turned on the TV and plopped down on the swivel chair.

"Maybe you want to come out to the site sometime, Miss Tiffany," Mr. Heitman was saying.

"Yes, maybe." Absentmindedly, Tiffany nodded her head.

Liz raised her eyebrows in mock surprise. She stubbed out her half-smoked cigarette and turned to the small man. "Well, Mr. Heitman, is there anything else you want? It's my shift now. Tif is off." She pushed Tiffany to the side and grabbed a key from one of the hooks. "You need the key to your room, Mr. Heitman? Here it is. Have a good day."

He looked at her, alarmed. With a shaking hand he took the key, picked up his suitcase, and muttering a faint, "Yes, thank you," rushed out of the office.

Tiffany frowned. "You didn't need to be so curt with him, Liz. "

"Come on, honey. The man is a long-winded bore, and I don't get why you're so patient with him. You know what? This guy Michael Barron likes you. It's with him you should spend time, not with fools like Heitman. An Indian village? Who cares? Good riddance, I say! Don't waste your time with weird people."

"I didn't understand all that stuff about carbon dating, but it's quite interesting that Indians used to live here a long time ago."

"Forget about the Indians. It's Michael Barron I'm talking about." Liz lit another cigarette and inhaled deeply. "If you don't mind having a kid thrown into the whole thing, I don't think you could do better. I never liked you running around with Ed. You two don't suit each other."

"You're imagining things. I work for Mr. Barron. That's all." Tiffany put on her denim jacket.

"Oh yeah? I've seen him look at you. Man, he looks needy, real hungry. I feel sorry for him. When he's talking to you, you think he's drowning. Men like that aren't cut out to be alone. He has a kid, but that's not enough for that type. I once knew a guy, a truck driver. He stopped here once in a while, years ago. The quiet type, didn't say much. But he had this look in his eyes, kind of desperate, same as Barron. I sometimes wondered if I should've gone to bed with him, like giving food to a starving man. He was lonely; he needed love. Not just sex, love. Well, I never did go to bed with him; he never asked me. Can't say I wouldn't have if he had. God, my hubby would've killed me if he'd found out." Liz chuckled, and her ample bosom shook.

When Tiffany left the office, she didn't know what to do. So far, she hadn't learned anything that might help Michael. Without thinking, she started her car, backed out of the parking space and drove down Main Street, then right onto 3rd Street where the pavement petered out into a dirt road. Marty lived in this part of town. The homes looked as fragile as those houses of cards that she and Grace used to build as children. Her own house was modest, but at least it stood in the section of town that had paved streets and sidewalks, and her father had always taken great care of their home and the yard.

Slowly she came to a halt in front of a small house. Paint was peeling from its green siding and white trim. An old sofa with broken springs stood on the porch. The front yard was littered with trash, discarded lumber and old tires. The house didn't just look dirty and neglected. Many houses in Junction City did because they were old or built badly and people were too poor to keep them up. Marty's home struck Tiffany as utterly wretched. There was a desolation about it that neither paint nor a thorough cleaning could cure. Maybe it was a blessing that Marty's dull mind didn't comprehend how miserable this place was.

A path overgrown with weeds led up to the house. When she knocked at the door, the dirty piece of cloth that covered the window next to it moved. Then the door opened a crack. Marty's brother squeezed his squat, muscular body through the opening and looked at her warily.

"What d'ya want?"

"Is Marty here?"

"You're Ed's girl, right? I need to have a word with 'im. Marty says he owes 'im money, from work at the motel. Ya tell Ed if he ain't comin' clear about the money, I'll put the screws on 'im. Marty ain't smart, but nobody's cheatin 'im. Ya tell Ed that." Marty's brother turned around, but before he slammed the door shut he motioned toward a rickety shack that stood next to the house. "He's in there."

The rusted shell of a car partially blocked the access to the structure, which at some point had served as a garage. Battered by wind in the summer and snowstorms in the winter, it leaned precariously to one side. Nobody had ever bothered to strengthen the flimsy building. The big garage door in the front had shifted with the shed and was now wedged unevenly in its warped frame. Several old tires and a broken bicycle were stacked against it. It was obvious that nobody was using the garage to park cars. Tiffany walked around the side looking for another entrance. When she passed a small window, she glanced through a film of dust into the dimly lit room. Marty was sitting on a barrel among a disorderly clutter of debris. In his hand he held a short piece of metal. He weighed it, scrutinized it and then threw it on the floor. From what looked like the remains of an old motor, he picked up another piece of metal. This too, he examined, weighed it in his hand and then listlessly dropped it on the ground where it landed with a loud clang. Now he got up and walked around the barrel, his head bent, his foot kicking against piles of rubbish as if he was searching for something particular.

When Tiffany knocked against the window, he lifted his head and stared at her, startled. "Can I come in?" she called.

Pointing to a door in the corner, he nodded his head. As she entered, a smell of dust, rotting wood and animal waste assaulted her. Marty had taken his seat on the barrel again. His hands were dangling between his legs; he looked at her resentfully.

"What d'ya want? My brother, he don't like visitors."

Stepping carefully, Tiffany made her way across the trash-littered floor. "I just talked to him. He said Ed owes you money."

"I dunno. Ed, he give me some, but Marv says it ain't enough." Marty stared at the floor and bumped the heel of his foot against the barrel.

The foul smell was overpowering, and Tiffany only dared to breathe in shallow, small gasps. "What's going on with Ed, Marty? I've been worried about him lately. You know, the gun and the way he talks."

"I dunno. He don't tell me nothin'." His voice was low; his eyes were guarded.

Tiffany knew she had to proceed cautiously. Marty would clam up if she appeared too pushy. "I don't want Ed to get into trouble, Marty. This guy, Jim Coe, I don't quite trust him. Do you know why Ed is working with him?"

"I don't like 'im either. And Casey don't like 'im. He told Ed to stay away. I think he's right."

"Why did Casey get him that rifle? Ed never had one like that."

"It's a big one, ain't it?" Marty murmured, and Tiffany had to move closer to understand him. "Ed don't like the man in the Nielsen house. He made 'im mad. That's why he got the gun." He paused, then lifted his head and added in a loud voice, "Can't tell ya anymore. It's a secret."

Tiffany started to feel hot, and the stale air of the garage made her nauseous. From the outside, footsteps were approaching the garage. She put her hand on Marty's arm. "Marty, you tell Ed to leave Michael Barron alone. He mustn't make trouble. Michael is none of his business. It's all a misunderstanding."

Marty's eyes fluttered nervously, and he cocked his head. The footsteps were coming closer.

"Marty," she pleaded, "did you ever write a message to Michael Barron? Or Ed? Did he write something?" She knew she sounded desperate, nearly hysterical. Marty smiled at her maliciously. She regretted that she had ever tried to be nice to him. Then the door was flung open, and light filtered into the dust-filled haze of the garage.

"We gotta get to work now." Marty jumped up and rushed past his brother. She wanted to run after him and make him tell her what he knew. But she just stood there, paralyzed.

"Lady, I gotta lock up. I don't have all day." Marvin's broad figure was a black shadow in the doorway. Hastily, she stumbled across the cluttered floor. Outside, she took a deep breath, thankful to fill her lungs with fresh air.

Marvin closed the door behind her and fastidiously turned the key in the padlock. Was he afraid somebody might steal some of the rubbish? Marty was already sitting in the passenger seat of his brother's truck. His big, round head with the greasy hair was bent low, touching his chest. Now Marvin climbed into the cab, and the pickup coughed to life. Tiffany felt the sadness and misery in the hunched, mute shapes of the brothers, who were sitting close together, yet seemed miles apart. In a way, she was relieved to see them drive away.

Chapter 24

Ed had a lot of free time, some cash in his pocket and the prospect of plenty more. Life wasn't bad. Coe would get back to him sooner or later, he was sure of that. The man couldn't afford to ignore him. All Ed had to do now was sit tight.

Hoping to find Grace, he drove to the beauty parlor. When he parked his truck by the storefront window, he recognized Audrey, who was sitting in a barber chair reading the newspaper. Just then she lifted her head, her bleary eyes staring into space. It was obvious that she'd let herself go ever since Randy had died. She drank too much and smoked too much. She was going downhill. Not so Grace, who was cutting somebody's hair. She had her back to the window, and Ed admired her shapely hips in tight jeans, the full, soft arms, the heavy, blond curls that fell over her shoulders. Of late, she looked more beautiful than ever. He touched his hair and wondered if he should get it cut.

Just then Al Wiederspan, Grace's customer, swiveled around on the chair. Of late, Al had been rather mean to him because he claimed that he, Ed, had done a shoddy job in the bathroom. A leak had sprung up, and Al insisted that it was his fault and hadn't paid him his full wage. Ed was furious, and they had some words about it. It had been a nasty exchange, but old Wiederspan didn't relent. In return, Ed had kept money back from Marty. Right now he didn't care to meet Al, and he started his truck again.

It was nearly twelve, when he pulled up to his house. The old woman probably had a stew boiling on the stove, and he was hungry. As he slipped out of his cab, he heard the soft motor noise of an expensive car. Then he saw it out of the corner of his eye: a sleek, white automobile that slowly rolled toward him and came to a stop behind his pickup. There was only one car in town like that, and the man who owned it was Jim Coe. Ed's heart beat faster. Coe was getting down to business and he, Ed, was ready. He slammed the door to his pickup shut and waited, his thumbs tucked behind his leather belt, his chest pushed out, his shoulders squared.

"Ed, I've been looking for you." Coe was slowly walking toward him. There was not a wrinkle in his clothes, and Ed wondered how he managed to look so impeccable all the time. Coe smiled, but there was a strange flicker in his eyes. "Let's go for a ride. We've got to talk things over."

Ed's first impulse was joy at riding in the fancy town car, but his instincts told him to be careful. There was something odd about Coe today. He had to watch out.

He heard the front door of the house open, and the timid voice of his mother called. "Ed." What did the old woman want from him now? He was a grown man. She should leave him alone. Besides, he wasn't hungry any longer.

Coe was already getting into his car again, and Ed quickly followed him. It was a marvelous vehicle. He had never driven anything but used pickups, the ones you get for seven or eight hundred dollars. Their engines were always noisy, their tires bald, and their seats torn. Ed leaned back against the cool, tan leather seat and listened to the nearly inaudible purring of the motor. Smoothly the car rolled over the dusty street away from his house, onto the paved highway. On and on it rolled, until they were back on some narrow dirt road where gravel crunched under the tires. It all sounded like music to Ed. He too would get such a car and glide through the countryside, up and down Main Street, past the beauty parlor and Al Wiederspan's motel.

181

Jim Coe wasn't saying anything. When Ed asked him where they were going, he received no answer. Finally, the car came to a halt by an old alfalfa mill that was rusting away at the side of the dirt road. Jim Coe opened the window and lit a cigarette. Cool air streamed in. Ed was getting restless. The smell of cigarette smoke made him yearn for a smoke too. Why didn't the man offer him one? He felt in his pockets, but there was none. He had left his cigarettes in the pickup. A peculiar, eerie sigh came from the mill. Birds? Old boards creaking? Metal pieces swaying in the wind? Ed began to feel a little sick and a strange sense of desolation overcame him. It must be the fresh air, he told himself as he coughed to get rid of a tickle in his throat. Or he might be catching a cold.

Coe was staring out of the windshield, one hand on the steering wheel, fingers tapping softly, the other hand holding the cigarette. When he turned to Ed, his face was rigid, his eyes cold. Uneasy, Ed squirmed. Suddenly Coe leaned toward him.

"Excuse me, Ed," he mumbled and reached into the glove compartment from which he extracted some papers. When he leaned back again, he held up two envelopes. "Look familiar?"

"What ya mean?" Ed was confused.

"Now tell me, Ed. You wrote these letters, didn't you?" Coe's voice was like frozen metal, so cold it would tear the skin off your fingers when you touched it. A mournful shriek pierced the fog in Ed's brain. A wild animal in distress, maybe caught in a trap?

"I dunno what ya talkin' about." What was this about? Didn't Coe want to make a deal with him? All of a sudden, Ed knew what that black, shiny thing in the glove compartment was that he had just seen but barely registered. He wondered if Coe had locked the car doors. He thought he had heard a clicking sound earlier. Ed felt really sick now. He wanted to throw up.

"Well, Ed, have a look at these. Maybe that'll refresh your memory."

He glanced at the words printed in bold letters.

"Somebody write that to you? I didn't do it." His voice was loud, the words tumbling out hastily.

"Don't play dumb, Ed. These have been written to Barron."

"I swear, Jim, I've no idea. I ain't talkin' to nobody about Barron except you. All I wanna do is help ya. Ya gotta to believe me." Ed's thoughts were racing. Was somebody setting him up? Coe, Barron? He didn't understand what was going on.

"Why should I believe you? Where I'm from, you have to earn people's trust, and I don't trust you, Ed. Neither do I trust that idiot friend of yours. I'm sure you told him everything."

"Ya can trust me, Jim. I'm on your side. And it ain't Marty. He couldn't think up nothin' like that."

With a quick movement Coe leaned forward and grabbed Ed by the collar, shaking him like a rubber doll. "I warn you. You stay out of my business, and you stay quiet, or you'll be a body in the ditch. If you ever butt into my affairs again, if I only think you're interfering, you'll regret it. Get that? You better tell your friend." He loosened his grip and threw Ed against the door. "Nobody crosses me, nobody. Now get the hell out." Coe wiped his hand on his pants, as if trying to clean it after his contact with Ed's collar.

A soft click unlocked the doors. Quickly, Ed slipped out. He watched the car turn and drive away, leaving behind a gray cloud of dust that settled on his cowboy boots. He kicked the gravel and cursed. Shaken, weak, he didn't feel well, and now he had to face the long walk home. If he was lucky, he could hitch a ride.

By the time he got to his house, he was done in. He yelled at the old woman when she was hovering over him with her baked beans and hot dogs. He had no appetite, but he needed a smoke. In his pickup, he fumbled through the glove compartment and finally found a pack of cigarettes. With jittery hands, he lit one. God, that felt good. He leaned against the cracked upholstery, smoking, thinking, trying to unwind. But strangely, the first deep drags of the Marlboro brought images of Randy. It seemed a long time, since he had died, although it had been only a few weeks. There were many ways of dying, and death through smoking didn't seem so threatening any longer.

He opened the window a crack, and threw the cigarette butt out. He was calmer now. As he drove away, he saw his mother's face in the window staring after him. The old woman could keep her lousy food for now.

He didn't bother to check Marty's house but went to the garage right away. He knew it was Marty's favorite place when he was at home. Squinting his eyes, he peeked through the window and was glad when he saw his friend sitting on a barrel, staring into space. He knocked against the dirty glass pane, and Marty's face lit up when he recognized Ed. Eagerly, he motioned for him to come in.

"Hi Ed, where ya been?"

Ed looked around for a place to sit. There was an old camping chair with all but three strips of the plastic seating gone. He sat down cautiously. "Well, ya know, here and there. What ya been up to, Marty?"

"Workin' with Marv." Marty grimaced. Well, yeah, Ed knew Marty didn't like to work with his brother. "Marv ain't here now, but he's mad at ya. I dunno when he'll be back." Fearfully he glanced at the window.

"What's he mad about?"

"The money, ya know. He says I ain't got enough."

As a rule, Ed and Marvin avoided each other, which wasn't always possible because they did the same kind of jobs, and often met at the same work sites. Marvin went out of his way to antagonize and belittle Ed. He criticized the way he did his work and sometimes acted as if he, Ed, was a tad slow in the head, like Marty. What annoyed him was that he took most of Marty's money, and Marty rarely had any to spend. It wasn't the first time that Ed had held money back from Marty. He did it to buy his friend a beer or a meal. It was only fair. Why should he use his own money for Marty? Sometimes, the accounts got muddled, what was his and what was Marty's money, but it never amounted to much. He took care of Marty, and Marty trusted him. It was too bad that this time he had to hold back quite a large sum. It wasn't his fault. It was Al Wiederspan's fault.

"Fuck your brother. Tell 'im it's none of his business. I get the jobs for us. We work 'em together. It's between you and me. I'll get Social Services after 'im. The way he treats ya, an' the way the house looks. A pigsty." He was talking himself into a real fury.

"No, don't do that. We're pals, right, Ed? I don't need no money." Marty's voice was fearful. Ed knew Marty didn't like it when Ed talked like this. When he was younger, Social Services had put him into a home for neglected children. It had not been a happy time for him.

"The thing is this, I got enough on my hands with Coe. I don't need your damn brother bothering me."

Marty squirmed restlessly on the barrel. "What's with Jim Coe? I thought you an' him are workin' together now."

"I ain't got no clue what's eatin' that man. He showed me some letters, looked like anonymous letters, ya know, when ya don't know who wrote 'em. He thinks I wrote 'em. Hell, why would I do that?"

"So you ain't workin' with 'im no more?"

"Work with 'im? The guy threatened me. Told me he'd kill me if I cross 'im." Ed got up from the lawn chair and started pacing back and forth in front of Marty. "I wouldn't move a finger for that guy. Ya know that ain't a small thing when somebody threatens to kill ya."

Marty followed him with his eyes. "What d'ya mean? He's gonna kill ya?"

"I ain't done nothin'. But somebody is writin' them letters. I dunno who's doin' it or why. Coe is mad, real mad. He asked about you. He wanted to know if you wrote them letters. I told 'im ya didn't write 'em."

"He thinks I wrote them letters?" Marty was thoroughly bewildered.

Ed nodded his head. "Marty, I know ya can't write such letters, but he don't know that. That guy could bump us both off. I be dead and you be dead. Get it?"

"He wanna kill us?" There was more surprise than fear in Marty's voice. He chuckled. "We'll get 'im before he gets us. Ya'll fire all them bullets into 'im with your gun before he can blink an eye."

Ed shrugged his shoulders. "Don't be stupid." But of course, Marty was right. That rifle of his was powerful. However, he didn't intend to use it on anybody. The thought actually scared him. "Don't tell anybody about this business, especially not that brother of yours. We don't wanna have no more trouble." The cluttered, dusty garage with its musty, sour smell began to get to him. It was time to leave.

Marty got up from the barrel and walked with Ed to the door. "I'm not gonna say no word. We'll go back to work together, Ed, ain't we? The way we used to? I don't like workin' with Marv."

"Yeah, sure, just sit tight."

Ed was on edge. He needed to talk with somebody, badly. One couldn't really talk with Marty who didn't have enough brains to understand things. Maybe Tif would help him sort it all out. She might still be at the motel. When he got there, Liz was sitting on the swivel stool behind the counter watching TV.

"She isn't here, just left." As usual, Liz spoke to him in that disapproving tone that he detested. Then, out of the blue, she told him to leave Tif alone.

"The girl has better things to do than hang out with you." She glared at him snootily.

How dare she talk like that? He and Tif had been friends forever. Obviously, Liz didn't know that he was doing Tif a favor by taking her under his wings, and when he told her so, the big woman laughed.

"Listen, if you haven't noticed, this guy Michael Barron is quite fond of her. Why don't you stay away? Tif is a nice girl, doesn't have much of a life at home. Give her a chance."

And then she told him a story about some truck driver who had stopped here in the past. She wished she had taken care of him somehow, done something for him, but she hadn't. He didn't know what the hell she was talking about. As far as he could tell, it had nothing to do with Tif. Liz was distantly related to Marty. He had considered her normal, but now he wondered if she too had lost her marbles. Maybe there was something in the family. He felt his temper rise at the woman, who was lecturing him from behind the counter.

He was already through the door, when he turned around and yelled, "You're crazy. Ya'll belong in a nut house, you and your family." Then he slammed the door and left Liz standing there, speechless, the cigarette dangling in the corner of her mouth.

Aimlessly Ed drove through Junction City, past the tavern, past the beauty parlor, out into the country. The truck rattled over uneven dirt roads. He didn't pay attention to where he was going. He was mad at Coe, at Liz and at Marty for being so useless. When he saw the old alfalfa mill, a surge of shame gripped him. He slowed down and stopped. The wind was picking up, rattling the corrugated metal sheets of the mill's roof. With shaking hands he lit a cigarette. Was it the dust or the smoke? A coughing fit made him double over the steering wheel. Ed threw the cigarette out of the window. He was nobody's fool. One last thing, he would do one last thing, and that would show them all.

At home, he threw several checkered shirts, a pair of pants, socks, underwear into an old canvas bag. He looked around the room that he had occupied since he was a little boy. Dirty clothes littered the floor, blankets and sheets were crumpled on the bed, an ashtray overflowed on the nightstand. A dusty, half-finished model airplane stood on the otherwise empty bookshelf. He couldn't exactly remember when he had made it. Maybe he was twelve or thirteen. His mother had given it to him for Christmas, and he had been excited about it, because usually he just got a shirt, socks or underwear, stuff he needed anyway. This was a toy, and that was special. He had started putting the pieces together right away, and the model was nearly done when the old man bumped against it. It fell to the floor and broke apart. His father didn't say anything. He just went into the kitchen and got another beer from the fridge. Christmas as usual: father drunk, mother trying to act as if this was a happy holiday for them. Ed showed her the ruined airplane. She put it on the shelf in his room, broken and unfinished, and that's where it had stayed ever since. A reminder of Christmas past and Christmas to come. Ed took the plane and crushed it in his fist. The thin, plastic parts snapped easily and fell to the floor.

With his foot he pushed the canvas bag under the bed. He'd come back later and get it. There were things he had to do first. He drove to the beauty parlor where they told him that Grace had gone home earlier. It was just as well. They'd be less disturbed there. When he got to her place, he had to knock against the door several times before she finally answered. She wore a pink bathrobe, and her hair was disheveled. Had she been sleeping in the middle of the afternoon?

"What do you want? Tif isn't home," she said. Her drowsy voice brought forth images of a warm bed, a soft body, the smell of sweaty embraces. Shivers went down his spine.

Ed pushed past her. "I need to talk to ya."

Grace protested, but he continued toward the kitchen where he threw himself on a chair. Pulling her bathrobe tightly around her, Grace looked at him curiously, a frown on her face, the beautiful mouth curved down in a mocking smile. Ed wondered how much he should tell her.

"Grace, I gotta leave town for a bit and I wanna ask ya to come with me."

"What happened? Why do you want to leave town? Have you robbed a bank?" She giggled as if she found that idea amusing. Anger stirred in him, but he managed to keep it down.

"I'm set up to get some money, and then I'm gonna get outa this hole. I want ya to come with me. What d'ya think, Grace? A nice apartment, a big town with bars and shows. We can do it all, the two of us." He leaned forward eagerly. Surely, she would understand that he was doing it for the both of them.

With swaying hips Grace walked past him toward the sink. There was only a flimsy bathrobe between him and her naked body! The desire to feel her suddenly overwhelmed him. In one swift movement

Ed pulled her on his lap. She tried to wriggle free of his embrace, but he held her tight in his arms. Her movements excited him and his heart was beating like a hammer, when he buried his nose in her neck and pulled the bathrobe from her shoulders.

"Let go of me," she shrieked.

But Ed had her firmly squeezed between his legs, with one arm clamped around her waist. With his free hand he explored the warm, voluptuous softness of her breasts. This felt good, so good. It was as far as he had ever gone, and he wasn't going to stop now. He would show Grace how good he would be for her. He would prove it. Let her wriggle in his arms; it was thrilling. He knew she was as excited as he was. They were both breathing heavily, when all of a sudden he felt a sharp pain on his scalp. Somebody was brutally pulling his hair and yanking back his head. Surprised, he let go of Grace.

"Stop! Stop! Are you crazy? What are you doing, Ed?" Tif was staring him in the face, aghast.

Grace had run to the farthest corner of the kitchen, clasping her bathrobe. She looked afraid and furious at the same time.

"Get out of this house!" She yelled at him. "Out and don't you ever dare . . . . " Her voice rose to a hysterical pitch. "Don't you ever come here again! He'll kill you! I swear, he's gonna kill you!" She sobbed and raced out of the room, her curls shaking wildly. Ed didn't understand why she was mad. He had meant her no harm.

Tif was saying something, but her words made no sense. Slowly he got up and walked to the door. He'd sort this out later. Now he had to get ready for the important thing. Grace would come around, she'd have to. A sense of failure stirred in him, and he felt very tired, too tired to listen to Tiffany, who was still talking to him. His brain was fuzzy, and his body ached.

In the front yard he stopped and turned around. Gently, Tif put her hand on his arm, and he wondered if he should tell her what his intentions were toward Grace. Then she could tell her sister, and Grace would understand that he wanted to do the right thing by her. If she wanted, and he didn't see why she wouldn't, he was going to be her steady man, not like the others who used her and then left.

"Ya know, me and Grace, there's somethin' between us. I know we can make it together. Maybe this ain't the right time. I got a bit carried away, but I didn't want to upset 'er. Tell 'er that. I'll make it up to 'er."

"She's not interested in you, Ed."

He grabbed her arm and shook her. "What d'ya know? You tell 'er what I said. You tell 'er." He was yelling the last words, and she flinched. It wasn't the way he meant to say it.

Like a horse that has lost his rider and returns to its stable by instinct, Ed was unaware that he was driving home. He was confused, very confused. The small, smelly room with its familiar disorder looked pleasant and welcomed him back. He wanted to drop on his unmade bed and stretch out his legs, but first he had to make a phone call. When that was done, he got a bottle of beer out of the fridge and opened it with shaking hands. Then he lay down on his bed, lit a cigarette and sipped the beer. He began to relax as smoke streamed into his lungs and out of his nostrils. He'd just lie here for a bit and calm down. Before he fell asleep, he saw a parade of familiar people pass before his closed eyes: old Wiederspan, Marty, Liz, Tif, Grace, Jim Coe. Their mouths were moving. They were speaking at the same time, but it was all gibberish. Then they faded away, one after the other, and dark, soothing emptiness enveloped him. Did he dream that Marty was in his room and that he told him about Barron's strongbox and the alfalfa mill?

Chapter 25

The telephone call came when they were eating dinner. Another telemarketer, he thought as he rushed into the living room, annoyed that his mealtime with Tiffany and Emma was disrupted. But it was no telemarketer. He recognized the voice right away, and the caller didn't try to hide his identity.

"I know about ya, Mr. Barron, or whatever your name is. I know about that strongbox with the money. Bring it to the alfalfa mill tonight, 11 pm. That's all I want. Don't do nothin' stupid. I'll notify the police if ya do. And don't ya worry. Soon as I get the money, I be gone. You can stay here with your daughter as long as ya like."

Before Michael could say anything, Ed had hung up. He went back into the kitchen, finished his dinner, silent, unable to respond to Emma's happy chatter or Tiffany's worried glances. Later, he carried Emma upstairs. He felt her light body as she squirmed in his arms. He heard her laughter as she called to Tiffany to come up and say goodnight to her. Like a robot, he went through their routine, all the while trying to put his thoughts in order, suppress his fury at another crook, this one a spiteful villager who shouldn't have any hold over him but who had dealt him the final blow.

When he came downstairs, Tiffany was standing at the bottom of the stairs.

"Michael, who was that on the phone?"

"Your friend Ed. He blackmailed me. He wants money, otherwise he'll go to the police. He wants to meet me tonight." Maybe now Tiffany would understand, once and for all, that her friend was no good.

"Michael, he doesn't know what he's doing. He has a gun. Don't go." Tiffany grabbed his arm. The blood had drained out of her face.

He pulled her toward him and held her in his arms. "Maybe we should pack up and leave. You and I and Emma. We could go away, far away from here and nobody would find us." Did he mean it? He didn't know, but it sounded so simple. Just pack and go.

"Michael . . . ." He saw confusion and doubt in her eyes.

"Come with me, Tiffany." If she loved him . . . but did she love him enough to walk away from her friends, her family, her life in this miserable town?

"I want to, Michael, but there are things I have to take care of here. My mother, she is losing the house, and my sister. They might be out on the street. They have always relied on my father and . . . ."

He loosened his arms around her and took a step back. How could he expect her to join him and become what? A runaway? Never safe, never happy. "Of course. And I don't want you to spend your life as a fugitive. It was a stupid thing to suggest."

"You don't understand, Michael. I want to go with you, but I have to take care of them, too." She murmured the last words so softly that he could barely understand them.

"Where is the alfalfa mill?"

"It's not far from here. Don't go, please. Ed is not himself. It's Coe who is leading him on."

"This has nothing to do with Coe. This is between Ed and me, and I don't think it'll be difficult to convince him to back off. Can you stay here for a few hours until I get back?" How he yearned to tell her that he loved her, that he wanted to do right by her. Instead, he made them both feel miserable.

"Of course." She raised her head, and he saw a quiet resolve in her eyes.

Was it his frustration that made him call Coe? He didn't know, but he was right about one thing: this latest development had nothing to do with the slick criminal. Coe was surprised, then furious. Ed, he shouted into the phone, had been warned by him. "I'll take care of that louse and his retarded friend. When I'm done with them they'll be silent, they won't dare whisper a word. You stay away from the mill, Michael. I'll handle it. Ed is playing on my turf. This is my business."

The moon and the stars were hidden behind a thick layer of clouds that muted every tone and extinguished every light except the forlorn beams of his headlights. The endless prairie had disappeared into impenetrable darkness. Michael gripped the steering wheel so tightly, his arms ached. When he relaxed his hands, a sigh of relief escaped him. It was only a soft groan, but to his ears it sounded not unlike a wail of distress.

Michael thought about Emma, Tiffany and the house somewhere behind him in the night. Before he had driven away, he had looked back and seen Tiffany on the porch, a dark silhouette against the bright light that spilled forth from the door. The house held all he wanted, and he would do anything to protect those he loved.

Slowly, as the car rolled through the night, he began to feel more confident. The small, yet heavy weapon in his pocket pressed against his thigh, and he glanced at the extra package of cartridges on the seat next to him.

About half a mile from the alfalfa mill, he parked behind a cluster of bushes. In the darkness his car was barely visible as a black mound, a boulder maybe, or a discarded piece of farm machinery. Cautiously he walked to the mill, not daring to use his flashlight. The gravel grated under his shoes, and he stepped off the road and walked on the withered vegetation of the shoulder. Thorny plants, wet with dew, grabbed his ankles and pierced his thin socks. The silence was complete, even the grass had stopped rustling.

It was just past ten when he saw the mill looming ahead of him. In its defunct, desolate state it reminded him of the ruined shell of a house after a bombing raid. He approached it cautiously, stopping every once in a while, listening for unusual sounds. There was no guarantee that Ed hadn't come earlier and was waiting for him. But all was quiet. Michael switched on his flashlight and crept along the outside wall following the narrow beam of light, until he saw a grassy tussock below a gaping hole that had once been a window. A cluster of bushes grew around it. It was a good hiding place, and the window gave him a clear view of the interior of the mill and the road on which Ed would be approaching.

He switched off the flashlight and sat down, his back against the wall. Better to trust his ears than stare through the hole at the empty darkness. It was still early, and Ed might not show up before the agreed upon time. The stillness weighed on Michael. He would have welcomed the wind, the constant background noise on the prairie, but this was one of those rare nights when there was not the slightest hint of a breeze. The alfalfa mill stood quiet, grass, trees and bushes were at rest, a thin veil of dewdrops was floating down from the sky.

The wait seemed eternal. He tried to make himself comfortable, but the earth was cold and hard. When he stretched out his legs, his pants got stuck in thorns and weeds, and he wanted to curse. Resigned, he settled against the wall again, listening, the pistol in his hand. Once some metal pieces grated against each other. He wondered what made them move in this calm night. Was there any chance that they could fall down? He turned up his collar and dug his heels into the grass.

When a precise, sharp sound whipped through the night, it rang as loud as a shot, but most likely was nothing more than a twig snapping. Gripping the pistol with a shaking hand Michael cautiously peered through the opening in the wall. He scanned the outlines of the collapsed wall across from him and the pile of rubbish in the middle of the building searching for a movement. Minutes passed; no sound disturbed the night. Maybe he had been wrong, and his imagination had played tricks on him. But he knew it was not so. A branch had snapped under somebody's foot. Was the other person listening to the darkness as intently as he was, waiting to hear if somebody else was hiding in this desolate place? He was glad to have the thicket at his back whose branches were jabbing into his canvas jacket. Nobody could approach him unseen or unheard from behind.

He heard the soft clink of a stone dislodged by a footstep. Then he saw him. For a fleeting moment, a figure moved past a wide opening in the broken wall, a jet-black silhouette against the dark sky, and then the wall swallowed him up again. Michael listened, but no sound gave the other man away. He had stopped and was listening also. Close to the spot where he suspected the man to be, a sliver of sky was visible through a crack in the wall. Should the man move past that spot, Michael would be able to see him. But neither shadow nor stealthy sounds revealed the invisible man.

Who was waiting in the darkness? Ed? He was early. There was still half an hour to go. Gradually, Michael became aware of a new sound. First, it was only audible as a faint hum, then the noise of a coughing, rattling motor came closer. A farmer on his way home after some beers at Dub's? He hoped the car would pass, even though with every second it became more unlikely. The man in the mill must have heard it also.

White, quivering headlights pierced the night. They swayed from right to left as the vehicle drove through potholes and erratically followed the old track to the mill. Then Ed's pickup came into view. Slowly, haltingly, it lurched forward. When it stopped abruptly by the building, the motor died in a screeching howl. The driver turned off the headlights, and for a short moment everything was quiet and dark again. Then the night burst into a sharp glare, and the old mill was bathed in the merciless brilliance of the high beams. It streamed through every crack and fissure in the wall. Michael, who was cautiously peering through the broken window, saw Jim Coe crouching behind a pile of bricks a few yards away from him. In one hand Coe held a pistol; with the other hand he tried to shield his eyes against the light that blinded him.

From some place close to the pickup came a booming voice. "Got ya, Mr. Coe." There was a childlike triumph in these words, and Michael knew only one person whose voice sounded like a man's, but had the immature quality of a child's. What the hell was Marty doing here? Where was Ed?

"Ya think you're so smart, but you ain't. Ya ain't scarin' us, Mr. Coe. I know ya're here, but Ed ain't here. We knows ya come to do bad things, and me and Ed, we ain't gonna stand for it. This is our place. Ya go back where ya came from."

Marty was stepping into the full glare of the light holding a rifle with a long barrel in front of him, his face a mixture of fear and pride.

Michael scanned the area by the bricks where he had last seen Coe, but it was empty. Then Coe's voice came out of the darkness, hoarse with suppressed fury.

"Drop the gun. Put your hands behind your head and walk forward until I stay stop."

Marty squinted his eyes, trying to penetrate the night.

"Did you hear what I said, you fool?" Coe's disembodied voice was a low snarl. "Drop the gun. Hands up, behind your head, and move forward."

"I only wanna tell ya to leave us alone. Me an' Ed, we got nothin' to do with them letters."

Michael saw Marty turn his head from right to left in an effort to locate his invisible adversary. His eyes fluttered nervously, and he lifted one hand to wipe the sweat from his forehead. Was he losing his nerve? But Marty held onto the rifle. Suddenly, a shot shattered the silence and hit the ground in front of him.

"Do what I told you!" Coe's voice shrieked through the night.

With an agility that Michael had not expected, Marty raised the weapon and started firing. An explosion of gunshots detonated against the concrete walls, the metal girders, the ground in front of him. Pandemonium tore the night apart. Quickly, Michael retreated behind the wall as bits and pieces of cement and rock flew past him. When the shooting stopped, he edged toward the opening again.

Marty's body lay on the ground in front of the truck, bathed in the bright glare of the headlights. It was very still, a crumpled heap, arms and legs at strange angles.

"My God." Michael had only whispered the words, but suddenly the beam of a very powerful flashlight was blinding him, and Coe's voice cut through the stillness.

"Come down, Michael."

Hardly aware of what he was doing, Michael swung his legs through the hole and slid over rubble and debris toward the motionless body. He staggered back, when he came to a stop, and fought against the nausea that was about to overwhelm him. What had once been a face was now a mass of brain, blood and splintered bones. One or more bullets must have entered at the top of the head and torn away part of the cranium.

"Not much experience with such an ugly sight, eh?" Coe aimed his pistol at Michael as he touched the body in front of him with the tip of his shoe. "Why did this stupid fellow have to meddle?" He sounded strained. "And what are you doing here, Michael? I told you to stay away, didn't I? Now you're an accessory to this unfortunate shooting. How do you like that?"

"Why did you kill him?" Michael gasped.

"He tried to kill me. You saw that, didn't you? Self-defense, that's what they call it."

Michael was silent. He was sick. Coe told him to hand over his pistol, and he did so readily. He didn't care anymore.

"We have to hide him," Coe said. When Michael didn't move, he motioned with his gun. "The guy is heavy. You take one of his legs." With his free hand Coe grabbed the other, keeping the pistol pointed at Michael. They left a trail of blood and brain as they pulled the dead man toward the wall. Marty's body was warm, and the flesh of his leg was soft like a child's. Michael felt faint and let go of the leg. With his back to the dead man, he crouched down, overcome by nausea.

"I admit it's not a pleasant sight." Coe snorted contemptuously. "I

197

should have aimed better. After all, that guy provided a lot of target. Get up, we don't have time for your sensibilities."

They proceeded to haul the body into the shadow of the wall. Once they were out of the light, Michael regained control over his stomach. With effort, they pushed the dead man into a thicket of low growing bushes whose branches closed mercifully over him. Even during daylight, he would be invisible to the casual eye.

"We have to get a plastic sheet, a blanket, something to hold the body. And then we'll have to get rid of it." Coe lifted his pistol and playfully aimed it at Michael again. "You don't have many choices any longer, Michael. Neither do I. I tried my best to warn this idiot off. Unfortunately, things didn't go quite as I had planned."

"Marty had nothing to do with it."

"How should I know? He's Ed's friend. After your alarming phone call, I saw him hanging around the motel, and we had a little chat. I let him know that I was aware of Ed's latest threat against you. He played dumb, if that makes any sense. I told him that I would take care of Ed, once and for all. I didn't expect that idiot to show up at the mill."

"What about Ed?"

"That's his pickup over there. He won't be coming here. We'll have to take care of the truck later. Let's go to your place now, Michael, and see if you have anything useful to wrap this thing up."

Michael stumbled ahead of Coe, unable to form a clear thought, unable to grasp the enormity of what had happened. In vain, he tried to block out the images that raced through his head: Marty in the bright light of the headlamps, Marty dead on the ground, his face gone. It surprised him that the night was still quiet and serene. Somehow, he expected police cars to appear with flashing lights and howling sirens.

As Michael drove through the silent darkness, Coe's headlights glowed steadily in his mirror, a reminder of the horrible event he had witnessed. It was like a bad movie script that needed to be rewritten. He was a writer, he would invent a new story, a happy ending. But he knew it could not be done. When he turned onto the dirt road, his house rose on the grassy plain before him, forlorn and unprotected. He didn't want to bring home the misery that had taken place out there in the night. How would he explain it to Tiffany? But Coe's headlights were right behind him, threatening, relentless. A door slammed, and then Coe's face peered through Michael's window. Michael glanced at the dashboard's clock. Just past 11.

Coe was impatient. "Don't just sit there. Hurry up. We have work to do. It's going to be a long night before we're rid of the body. They'll find him eventually, but not until I am safely away. And you better think about your departure also."

Michael got out of the car. He felt Coe's warm breath and smelled his aftershave as the pistol dug into his back pushing him toward the house. Just then, the porch light flared up and Tiffany stepped through the door. She smiled when she saw him. Had she noticed the smaller man behind him?

"You should be in bed, Miss, and in your own, not his." Coe stepped forward, the pistol directed at both of them, motioning them into the house.

Chapter 26

When Tiffany looked at Michael, she gasped. His eyes were dark and his face was deathly pale. She had never before seen anybody whose suffering was so unmistakable in his ravaged features.

Coe ordered them into the kitchen. He walked over to the sink and let water run over one hand, then over the other, switching the pistol from one to the other. Michael also washed his hands. Tiffany found it strange that the two men were doing this. They didn't speak, they didn't look at each other, yet some understanding seemed to tie them together. What had happened out there by the mill? Michael appeared very much alone, and she yearned to help him. There was a cut on his wrist and it was bleeding. When Tiffany offered to get a Band-Aid, Coe glanced at Michael, who was absent-mindedly staring at the gash.

"I guess he needs some tender loving care, but don't do anything stupid, Tiffany, and be quick about it."

The two men were silent when she returned. Carefully she took Michael's hand and turned it so she could apply the dressing. Maybe her touch softened something in him. When she raised her head, he was looking at her, and his distraught eyes drew her into his anguish.

"Is she taking good care of you, Michael?" Coe's mocking voice interrupted the stillness. "Those sisters know how to make a man feel good, don't they?"

Tiffany glanced at him. She knew about the mocking voices of mean-spirited people because she had many years of practice dealing with them. As a child she would conjure up the image of her father, the person she loved best and who loved her best. It enabled her to rise above the insult. Sometimes it had been hard because she was young and vulnerable. But now it was effortless. Michael sat right next to her. She didn't have to imagine the face of the man who loved her. She could stretch out her hand and touch him.

"Grace is the older of you two, isn't she? You must be quite a few years younger, or maybe you just look very young." Coe stared at her with shameless eyes. "Young isn't bad, Michael, right? I myself prefer an experienced woman, and Grace certainly has been around." He broke out into laughter. "But some prefer to come in at the beginning. Is that what you like?"

Michael's face had turned a deep red. He was sitting upright now, as taut as an arrow, ready to punch the man. Tiffany put her hand on his trembling arm, but he didn't seem to notice.

"Easy, Michael," Coe said. The mocking tone was gone. "Don't be so touchy. Believe me, I have no interest in this girl here. I have not much of an interest in her sister either."

"Then you should leave her alone. She is not a bad person." Tiffany didn't want to talk about her sister, but she wanted to give Michael time to regain his control. She kept her hand on his arm, pressing it softly. If she could only take the edge off his fury, then he'd realize that he must not let Coe provoke him.

"Of course not. A woman who has that much fun in bed can't be a bad person. No, a bad person is different. That's somebody who's trying to cheat you. It's somebody who crosses you the wrong way. You might want to tell your friend Ed about this little philosophy of mine. But I think he already knows it."

"Well, what do you want now? We can't sit here all night," Michael interrupted him. He spoke calmly now.

"Let's get a blanket or a large plastic sheet. You must have something like that. And you, young lady," Coe said to Tiffany as he tucked his pistol away under his blazer, "you stay right here, don't move. You don't want anything to happen to him, do you?"

She shook her head and watched the two men leave the kitchen. It didn't take long, and they came back. Michael, tall and stooped, was carrying several large plastic sheets under his arm. His mouth was compressed into a thin line, his eyes were tired, yet alert. Anguish simmered under cold determination. Tiffany saw the man again who had checked into the motel many months ago.

"It'll be an hour or two, Tiffany. Lie down and try to get some sleep. Don't worry about me."

He stood in front of her, rigid, the plastic sheets between them. Quickly she embraced him. All at once, the stillness in the small kitchen was shattered by a ferocious, deep barking somewhere in the dark night outside. Then the wild racket stopped abruptly and Tiffany heard voices, but they were drowned out when the terrifying howling started again, closer than before. Dogs. She looked at Michael who was listening as intently as she.

"What's that, Michael?"

"I have no idea," he murmured. He dropped the plastic sheets and pulled her toward him.

The gun in his hand, Coe rushed to the window, his eyes narrow slits, his mouth half open, exposing his irregular teeth. His air of glib vigilance gave way to the scared look of a hunted animal. There was no doubt in Tiffany's mind that he would fight mercilessly to save his skin. He was a ruthless man.

"What's that?" Coe repeated her words. His eyes were searching the shadows outside.

Nobody replied. Tiffany and Michael stood still, holding each other. The barking was very close now, and the sound of heavy boots could be heard on the porch. Coe took a step toward them.

"Police? Did you call the police, Tiffany? You wouldn't be so stupid, would you?" he said through clenched teeth.

"Dogs," Michael answered. "The police here don't use dogs."

All of a sudden Tiffany felt herself yanked away from him. She

202

was too surprised to resist Coe's brutal force. Michael tried to pull her back, but Coe kicked his leg violently. Michael stumbled and let her go.

"Stay back." Coe held her in an iron grip, his pistol against her temple.

Suddenly the door was filled with the straining, quivering bodies of two enormous dogs. Saliva dripped in white, foamy flecks from their teeth, and their fiery eyes were glowing with the bloodthirsty madness of the chase. Tiffany shrank back against Coe, who held her in front of him like a shield. The barrel of the pistol dug into her temple painfully. She saw Michael regain his balance and rush toward them, but any movement in the kitchen was a provocation for the dogs, and they howled fiercely and strained forward. What were they waiting for, what was holding them back?

Her mind was racing to find an answer to this insanity. This was Junction City, and such things didn't happen here. It was unreal, absurd. Emma! The noise! Where was she? A new wave of panic gripped her. Nobody seemed to remember that there was a little girl upstairs in her bedroom. Would she suddenly appear before these beasts, scared, looking for her father in this chaos? When Tiffany strained against Coe, his elbow dug into her stomach and took her breath away.

A loud voice yelled at the dogs, and instantly their savage bark changed to a suppressed snarl. Out of the corner of her eye, Tiffany could see two shadows in the hallway, one tall and bulky, the other scrawny and small. Why was Casey here with his dogs? What did he have to do with Michael or Coe?

Stepping into the doorway, Casey calmly surveyed the situation. His hands were resting on the massive heads of the dogs, stroking them gently. Slowly, as if against their will, they lowered their bodies and lay down, alert, trembling, ready to pounce on anybody who could be a threat to their master.

Ed stood next to him, his frantic eyes flitting back and forth between Coe and Michael. There was a strange wildness in his wasted face. Something had pushed him over the edge. He was holding a short, compact rifle with a long barrel, similar to the one that Casey had slung over his shoulder. They wore hunters' camouflage vests, and their pockets were bulging with ammunition. They were ready for war, but oddly enough, Casey looked as good-natured and friendly as always. Tiffany found it hard to believe that he was here to do them harm.

"Who did it? Which bastard killed Marty?" Ed's voice was shaking with rage. He raised his gun and aimed it at Michael, then at Coe.

The sudden movement brought the dogs back to their feet. In a sharp voice Casey ordered them to sit, which they did reluctantly. Coe pressed Tiffany against him, forcing her to stand straight and cover him as much as possible. She could feel his heart beating against her back.

"I'll kill ya'll. I don't care. I'll kill both of you. That's what ya deserve an' you'll get it. You'll pay for it."

Tiffany heard a sob in Ed's voice. He was at a breaking point. He didn't know what he was doing. In a way, he was as crazy as the dogs. If she could only talk to him, maybe he'd snap out of it. She knew him, the way his temper could flare up and drown out all common sense. But her captor held her tight, gun cocked, ready to shoot.

"You do that, Ed, and she's dead before you can pull the trigger. I told you to stay out of it. Go home and take your friend and his dogs with you. Everything will be all right then. There's nothing for you to do here." Coe tried to sound calm and reassuring, but the hand that held the pistol against her head, was shaking.

"Nothin' will be all right. Did ya kill Marty? Why did ya do it? He was just a dumb fella." The sob in Ed's voice was growing louder. "Them dogs found 'im. They tore 'im up. His face, ya can't see his face no more." He was staring at them wildly.

"Ed," she called to him. "Ed."

His eyes shifted to her, and she thought she saw a glimmer of sanity.

"Ya wanna kill 'er too? She ain't done nothin'. Let 'er go."

"You let me pass with her. I won't harm her if you let us through.

I take her with me, just for a short while."

"Let 'er go, ya bastard!"

"You don't understand, Ed. I didn't kill anybody. Barron did. He thought Marty wrote those letters and went out there to kill him."

Ed laughed spitefully. "Is that so? Barron ain't got a gun in his hand, but you do, Coe. Maybe Marty was after you because ya threatened me. He was my friend, and he wanted to protect me. Maybe ya both killed 'im." He sobbed. "You'll all pay for this. Ya ain't gonna get outa this alive."

"Tell him the truth, Coe," Michael said in a hoarse voice. "Tell him that his friend shot at you. Maybe by accident, I don't know. You lost your nerve, Coe. You killed him."

Casey had taken the rifle from his shoulder and planted it in front of him like a walking stick. The dogs were much calmer now. When Ed lifted the gun in a sudden, quick movement, they didn't even stir. Only when Casey cleared his throat did they lift their heads and perk their ears. A nervous tremor went through their bodies. They were waiting for the signal to start the assault.

"Ed, the situation is under control. We don't need any more of this confusion." Casey's voice was pleasant, yet determined, not unlike that of a father who speaks to his wayward child. Then he addressed the group in the kitchen. "I want you both to go. Leave Junction City, leave no traces, and don't ever return. We give you our word; neither Ed nor I will report you. If you, Mr. Coe, want to take this young woman with you because you don't trust us, do so by all means. But I would advise you not to harm her. Take her as a security, and then let her go. And you, Mr. Barron, I think your time is over in Junction City. I don't know why you came here, but I don't think you want to stay after what has happened."

The dogs whimpered softly and put their heads on their front paws.

"I'm not going without Tiffany. If you want to let Coe go, that's your business, but he can't take her with him," Michael said.

"Be quiet, Barron. You got nothing to say here. I'm taking her and you stay back. And you, Mister, keep away from me." Slowly Coe inched forward with Tiffany pressed against him. The dogs sat up, their bodies quivering, a deep growl rising from their throats, but they calmed down when Casey touched their heads.

"Everybody back!" Coe yelled.

Ed was watching him intently. His gun was still cocked against his shoulder, but it was as if he had forgotten about it. The kitchen was very quiet now. Only the raspy, quick breathing of the dogs could be heard.

"Make room. Get the damn dogs out of the way." Coe briefly took the pistol from Tiffany's temple and aimed it at the dogs.

Casey gave a sharp command and took a step back into the hallway. The animals followed him slowly, crawling backwards, their eyes focused on the people in the kitchen, ready to charge should their master give the command. Ed wasn't stirring. Tiffany tried to meet his eyes, but they were fastened on her captor. Casey was standing behind Ed now. He lifted his hand. Maybe he wanted to pull Ed back, when a deafening shot exploded in the kitchen. Tiffany felt Coe's grip loosen, and she fell to the ground with him. Somebody lifted her up instantly and carried her away as two dark, massive shadows flashed by her and with a loud, terrible sound, pounced on the crumpled body on the floor. She heard the ripping of fabric. All she could do was scream in terror and bury her face in Michael's shoulder.

Casey's voice rose above the pandemonium and, miraculously, the dogs stopped. Their bodies trembled as they lifted their foaming mouths and stared at their victim who lay on the floor in front of them, motionless. Casey called out again, and the dogs retreated. But they had tasted blood. They hesitated and cautiously advanced forward again. This time Casey's voice lashed out at them. He grabbed their collars and fastened a metal chain on them.

Tiffany was sure that Coe was dead. Either the dogs or Ed had killed him. Clinging to Michael, her eyes searched the lifeless body on the floor. She heard a groan, then Coe lifted his head and slowly got up. His trousers were torn, and blood oozed from a deep gash in his calf.

Otherwise he seemed to be unhurt. His hands were empty, his face contorted with pain. He must have lost his pistol in the unexpected assault. Coe looked at the dogs, then at Casey and shook his head in disbelief. Ed, his hair standing up wildly, his face as white as a sheet, threw his rifle away and was advancing slowly. In a flash his fist shot out and hit Coe in the face. With as much force as his skinny body could muster, he threw himself at the wounded man and grabbed him by the throat. Both men staggered and would have fallen, but they tumbled against Michael. With one swift movement Michael pushed Tiffany behind him. She shrank into the corner of the kitchen, as he aimed a pistol at Coe and Ed.

"Enough! Get out of here, all of you." The men didn't move. "Out!" he shouted. Tiffany saw the pistol shake in his hand.

The dogs. Where was Casey with his dogs? When she looked toward the hallway, they were gone. Only a few dark spots on the wooden floor, left by their saliva, hinted at their terrifying intrusion.

Slowly, the two men staggered out of the kitchen with Michael following them. Coe was limping. Tiffany heard them walk down the steps of the porch, and then, after what seemed to be a long time, she heard the sound of a car's engine, then another motor started with a slow rumbling sound. Ed's truck. She recognized it well, the stuttering exhaust, the roaring howl when Ed revved up the motor. The noises faded into the night and stillness surrounded her. She strained her ears, uncertain if the nightmare was over.

When she looked around her, she gasped. Ed's shots had blown a cabinet and its contents to pieces. Splintered wood and broken china covered the floor. And there were stains of blood and scraps of blood-soaked cloth where Coe had been attacked by the dogs.

Emma! A new wave of alarm swept over her. Frantically, she rushed upstairs, but the little girl wasn't in her room. Her bed had been slept in; now it was empty. Her clothes were neatly folded on a chair. Tiffany ran downstairs and called her name, at first hesitantly, afraid that her loud voice might stir hidden ghosts, bring back those who had brought terror into this house. But Coe and Casey and Ed couldn't hear her now. They were gone. Her voice rang through the house louder. Nobody answered. Then she ran out onto the porch and stopped and listened into the night. Somewhere she heard soft murmuring voices.

Out of the shadows, Michael stepped into the light, carrying Emma in his arms, walking toward the house in long strides. Emma was clutching her stuffed monkey, which was nearly as big as she. They halted for a moment when they saw Tiffany, and waved. It looked like they had just gone out for a stroll. Or maybe they wanted to get a good look at the stars? There was nothing unusual about them except that Emma wore her nightgown.

Tiffany lifted her head. A wind had come up and broken the cloud cover. The sky no longer shrouded the earth in complete darkness. A multitude of stars sparkled in untroubled serenity. Indeed, she sighed, it was a lovely night, a night to turn one's eyes away from the earth and gaze at the heavens above.

Chapter 27

Casey told Ed to follow him in his pickup. Ed's head was in turmoil, his stomach a painful knot. The letters, Coe's threats, then the dogs tearing Marty apart. It had all happened so fast, one terrifying event following another, and he didn't understand how it all fit together. But Marty, my God? A sob came from deep down in his throat. He tried to keep it inside, but it wasn't possible. Then a cry of distress, muted, yet loud and tormented, escaped from his open mouth into the close confinement of the cab. He listened, shocked.

The tail-lights of Casey's jeep swayed in front of him. He kept his eyes on them, but in his mind he saw Marty's body, a pile of flesh, and the two dogs above him, keeping him down with their paws while tearing at him with their terrible fangs. Their heads were swinging back and forth, and strangely shaped pieces were hanging from their foaming mouths. And the noise, that horrible noise, when they crushed his bones. With trembling hands Ed had shone his flashlight on them and cried for Casey to come. When the fat man finally arrived, sweating and breathing heavily, he called the dogs back, but it wasn't easy. With his rifle butt he had to hit them until they let go. My God, it was a terrible sight. Blood everywhere, Marty's skull blown apart, his face crushed. Ed ran into the bushes and threw up.

Now his truck rumbled through the night past the familiar signposts, but he saw nothing. With his fist he pounded the steering wheel. More sobs began to pour from his mouth like a death chant. His wails filled the cab with an anguish that had no place to go. Ed had never before in his life felt like this. He yearned to have Marty next to him, laughing his stupid laugh, trying to find a cigarette for him. At last, Ed stopped crying out and let his tears flow silently down his cheeks. He had never cried for anybody like this, not for his old man, not for anybody. But Marty was his friend, his only friend. Marty had trusted him, and he had died because Ed had screwed up.

Ed wiped his nose on his sleeve. He should have killed the dogs right away. He could have easily done it out there by the mill. He had one of Casey's guns. When he had staggered back to the bloody scene, he had raised the gun and taken aim. The dogs were tied up by a tree at that point, an easy target. Casey was crouched over what was left of Marty.

"The dogs didn't kill him, Ed," he'd said.

"Them dogs killed Marty!" Ed's finger was on the trigger, jittery, ready to pull.

"Hold on, Ed, I'm telling you the truth. If you don't believe me, come closer. I'll show you something." Casey sounded so sure of himself, as if he was some crime scene investigator. "I can prove to you that my dogs didn't do it. They only kill on command, my command, and I didn't give it. Marty was dead when they found him." Casey got up and stared at the lifeless, mutilated body. In his hand he held a shell casing.

"I'm gonna kill your dogs if you're lyin' to me." Ed had moved closer to the body, even though he was afraid to look at it again. And then he saw with his own eyes that Casey was right. It was infuriating in a way because it would have been so easy to shoot the dogs and have revenged poor old Marty. But somebody, not two dumb dogs, had killed him, shot him in the head. Ed could see a bullet lodged in the skull, or whatever was left of it. It wasn't the dogs that had spilled Marty's brains. It must have been that bastard Barron. He had made a mistake. He had waited for him and had killed poor Marty instead.

Casey pulled an old glove out of the pocket of his jacket and extracted the bullet from the soft, gray mass.

"We don't have any proof that Barron did this, Ed. He doesn't strike me like a man who shoots another man. It could have been anybody. It could have been Coe." Casey cleaned the bullet by rubbing it in dirt and then put it in his pocket.

"Coe? Why should he be at the mill? I never told 'im."

"Maybe he found out. Maybe Barron told him."

"Then let's go to Barron's place. Let's see what he says. I'll make 'im pay, or whoever did this. I'll make both of 'em pay." Ed's voice was shaking with fury. Dumb, old Marty, why did you come here? Why did somebody blow your brains out?

It seemed ages ago that he had woken up in his room, and the old woman told him that Marty had borrowed his truck. Going to help Ed, he had said to her. Ed knew right away that something bad was going to happen. If only he hadn't dozed off, after he had made that phone call to Barron. If only the old woman had woken him up, before Marty took off with his truck. But she was afraid, didn't even dare knock at his door. He had cursed himself for having left the keys in the truck. But that wasn't the worst of it. The rifle was under the front seat.

Casey had offered to drive and help him look for the fool. Ed didn't like his idea of bringing the dogs along, but Casey had insisted that they could be handy in tracking Marty down. They were good bloodhounds, he said. Bloodhounds, indeed! Ed already knew that Marty would be at the alfalfa mill.

Casey's jeep ahead of him was making a sharp turn. Ed followed and came to a stop in front of the fat man's trailer. When he turned off the truck, it was suddenly very quiet except for the wind that had started earlier. A sense of emptiness filled him. As he listened to the night, pictures, like in a film, appeared before him: Barron's house, the kitchen, Tif. She had looked so calm when Coe had held her against himself with the pistol at her head, even when the dogs were barking wildly. And Barron, he had seen a pain in his eyes that was not unlike his own pain. It wasn't the look of a killer. Ed touched his face and felt

211

that it was wet. What was happening to him?

He sat in the car and waited for Casey to safely lock his dogs away. He was gone for a long time. It was a relief not to see those brutes and not to hear them. As long as they were out of his sight, Ed didn't have to think about what they had done to Marty. He still felt that they ought to be destroyed, even if they hadn't killed Marty. He had always considered them dangerous. Bloodthirsty monsters. But he knew that Casey would never let that happen.

Ed slumped back against the seat listening to a clanking noise that was accompanied by the deep voice of Casey. He was feeding those beasts. Hadn't they eaten enough? The thought brought another wave of despair, but the fury was gone. More out of habit than to calm himself, he lit a cigarette. Marty was dead. Good, old Marty. He'd never find another buddy like him. He'd see what Casey had to say, but as far as he was concerned, he'd like to hand Coe over to the sheriff and then see him fry, yes, fry. He'd ask if he could attend the execution. Because that's what they owed him. That's right. They didn't kill too many people in this state, but surely, a man who killed a borderline retarded fellow, they'd see to it that he'd get the death penalty.

There was a knock against his window. Casey's broad, bearded face gazed at him through the dirty glass. Ed got out of the car and stumbled after him trying to avoid the holes that the dogs had scratched in the hard ground. Casey switched on the light in the living room. Everything looked very ordinary. It smelled of beer and stale air. Nobody would have guessed that this was a meeting place for high-stakes card players.

"How you keep your customers away, Casey?" Ed asked. He didn't want to meet any of them tonight.

"When the front light is off, nobody comes. And it's late anyway." Casey dropped down on the old, green couch where not too long ago Grace had made out with one of the boys from the lumberyard. "Ed, we got to be smart now."

"What d'ya mean? Smart? I'm smart. We gonna go to the sheriff and tell 'im what we seen. Coe killed Marty, Barron said so. He was there at the mill. That bastard Coe threatened me and I told Marty who got it in his stupid head to help me. Coe will fry for it."

"We didn't see him kill Marty. You have no evidence."

"Well, we got the bullet."

"A bullet without the gun won't help."

"Who got the gun? Coe ain't got it no more. Somebody got it, with fingerprints on 'em."

"I believe Barron picked it up in the shuffle. But it's all beside the point. The point is, we want this affair to fade away."

"Listen. My buddy was killed tonight. I ain't got nothin' to do with it. You ain't got nothin' to do with it. So what are ya talkin' about?" He jumped up and started pacing back and forth in front of Casey.

"Sit down, Ed, and listen to me. I sent some letters to Barron to get him out of town because I knew that Coe was after him. Coe is a guy wanted by the police. How long, do you think, before they'll be here? Then they'll check us out, you and me. I don't know about you, but I can't afford to have the police after me. It's not the gambling. There are these other things. I've got to keep a low profile." Casey glared at him sternly, and Ed sat down again, but he found it hard to keep still. His legs were twitching and twisting. What was Casey saying? Didn't he see that now was the time to get rid of Coe once and for all?

"I'll keep ya out of it, Casey. I promise. But I gotta do this. I can't let Marty lie there and let Coe get away with it." He knew his voice was getting shrill. He couldn't control it.

"That's exactly what we have to do. The dogs mangled him pretty bad. They'll never figure out that a bullet killed him. We have it, and I picked up the shell casings and bullets that Marty fired. Should the police find any that I overlooked, they'll think kids did some target-practice. All you're going to do is report him missing. Or better, leave it to his brother. They'll find him eventually."

"They think the dogs killed 'im? They gonna shoot your damned dogs." Ed looked at Casey suspiciously.

"Don't talk like that. They won't know my dogs were there. There are enough stray dogs, wild dogs, coyotes here. If they want to shoot dogs, they can shoot those. My babies were here all night with me, and you were here too. You swear to that and I will too."

"I dunno, Casey. I wanna see that guy Coe get it." Babies, what the fuck! Wild beasts, that's what they were.

"If he goes, you go. He'll drag you and Barron into it and nail you for murder or blackmail or accessory to murder. And Tiffany, she's somehow mixed up in it. You don't want to hurt her, do you?"

"She ain't done nothin'. I ain't done nothin'." He tried to think, but everything was a jumble in his head. "What 'bout Barron? He'll keep quiet?"

"Sure, he will. He's got something to hide. He won't talk to the police."

All of a sudden, Ed was tired, dead-tired. Marty gone! He buried his head in his hands. After a while he got up. His legs were wobbly.

"I gotta go. I dunno what to do. I'm so damned tired. I gotta go."

Casey rose in that jovial innkeeper's way that he had and put his fleshy hand on Ed's shoulder. "It's over, Ed. You listen to me, and everything will be all right."

"Yeah, I guess so," he mumbled and made for the door. All he wanted was to get home to his bed. That little wooden house, which he shared with the old woman, had never seemed more inviting to him. Tomorrow, he'd think about it all.

Chapter 28

There wasn't much left of the night, and Michael was too shaken to sleep. But Emma was tired and Tiffany looked exhausted. She was very pale under her bronze skin, and as he watched her with his daughter, huddled together on the couch in the living room, their arms around each other, he saw her long lashes close over her eyes more than once. But he had not been able to calm his taut nerves. All he could think about was what had happened during that night, and over and over again, a new surge of panic gripped him. Only children, he thought, could live through this turmoil and still be capable of sleep. He felt like a father to both of them. He felt very old.

Emma had escaped most of the upheaval. She told him that the dogs had awakened her, and she had peeked over the banister and seen Ed and the fat man with the animals. Then his wise daughter had grabbed her favorite stuffed animal and gone down to the lake to the little shelter that they had built together. It was a small wooden platform nailed into the lower branches of a gigantic cottonwood tree. They had spent many afternoons there in the summer fastening a tarpaulin over it, planning their next improvements and inventing stories about dangers, rescue and escape. The shelter was to be their safe haven in case of some disaster. The threats they imagined were quite humorous, such as stepping on the green patch of grass in front of the school and arousing the principal's fury. Once Emma suggested that it could also serve as a shelter in case her mother's thugs, she called them friends, were coming.

But they didn't elaborate on this idea. They had become tongue-tied, and their carefree mood had disappeared that afternoon. Never again had they spoken of Marcia in the shelter. It was Emma's place, filled with laughter and fun, and they both tried to keep it that way. In the summer, it was hidden behind a curtain of rustling green leaves. In the fall, when the leaves turned yellow, Emma said that they were sitting in a room with walls made of gold.

He had found her there, wrapped in a blanket, clinging to her stuffed animal. She had looked at him with wide, wary eyes but had not asked any questions. When he said that the men were gone and had taken their dogs with them, she got up, and he helped her down the wooden ladder. He took off his jacket and wrapped it around her. She lay her head against his heart, the way she always did when he held her close. She was shivering. He kissed her on the forehead and told her everything would be all right.

When he suggested that they all go to bed, Emma took Tiffany's hand, and they went upstairs together. Emma went straight into his bedroom and jumped into the middle of the queen-size bed. She pulled the blanket up, settled the stuffed monkey next to her, and closed her eyes. This was not a night to sleep alone, his wise daughter seemed to say. Tiffany had remained by the door. She would sleep downstairs on the sofa, she whispered, but he shook his head.

"You want to sleep down there all by yourself? No curtains in the windows. The sink in the kitchen is dripping. No, you wouldn't sleep well." He pulled her toward him and lifted her face. His eyes examined her closely, then he kissed her on the temple where not too long ago Coe's pistol had grated against it. "This was a terrible night. We need some comfort. Emma does, I do, and you do. You are exhausted. Stay here." With that, he let go of her. He gently moved Emma to the far end of the bed. Then he took off his shirt and jeans and cautiously slid into the middle of the bed. With his right arm, he cradled Emma's small body, and with his free hand he pointed to the empty space next to him. Blushing and avoiding his eyes, Tiffany stared at the wooden floor. He loved her for her innocence and would have liked to tell her how much he needed to have her close to him now. But there would be another time, a better time, for this.

Hesitantly, Tiffany slipped out of her jeans. He followed her movements, seeking comfort in her smooth, long limbs, in the dark hair that flowed over her shoulders, in the arcs of her slender body. She nestled against him, her leg touching his, her head resting on his arm, and he buried his face in her hair that smelled of sweetness and youth. It wasn't long before he heard her breathing in the calm rhythm of the sleeper. Slowly he pulled his arm away and leaned on his elbow, his face bent over the young woman next to him. There was a fine line around her mouth, and two thin lines between her brows. Otherwise her skin was flawless, tanned, with a touch of copper on her cheeks. She'd love France, he thought. She won't mind the sun and the shimmering heat in summer. Then he turned to Emma whose blond curls were matted to her forehead. The old ache was back in his chest, as he looked at her round face and smelled the sweaty scent that children give off in the warmth of a bed. He put his arms around both of them, and his heart was full when he finally fell into a fitful sleep. Once he awoke feeling Tiffany's face against his shoulder and Emma's small, delicate body on his other side. He lingered for some time in the shadowland between sleep and wakefulness before slumber overcame him once more.

Emma only asked one question, when she woke up in the morning. Did Mommy send the men?

He shook his head. "No, Emma, Mommy didn't send them. Don't worry. They won't come back." She looked at him in a curious way. There seemed to be some doubt in her eyes, and he felt he had let her down. He gently touched her cheek.

For two days a storm whipped rain and wind across the prairie. The cottonwood trees lost their last leaves, and the color of the gray, murky lake beyond the house blended with the turbulent sky. The old house sighed and shook, when the fury of the wind unleashed itself. More than once Michael thought that the thin, wooden walls would crumble under the onslaught, but to his surprise, the house withstood the assault. At night the temperature dropped, and in the morning a thin layer of ice covered the grass.

While Michael and Tiffany spent the days in silent dread, their nights were filled with desperate lovemaking. Shy at first, Tiffany lost her reticence and responded to him passionately. Whenever he woke up at night, an unknown happiness washed over him, and he pulled her into his arms. When he bent over her in the early light of morning and kissed her, she opened her eyes, smiled and buried her head against his shoulder. He felt as if he had searched for her all his life.

They didn't leave the house for those two days. When Emma asked if she could go to school, he told her that school had been cancelled because of the storm. It wasn't true, but he didn't want to let her out of his sight. She wasn't safe here anymore.

They sat by the radiators and listened to the hot water gurgling and hissing in the old-fashioned heaters. Tiffany tried to call Ed but only got his mother on the phone, who told her that Ed was in his room and didn't want to see anybody or talk to anybody. The old woman sounded distraught. When Michael asked Tiffany if she wanted to go home, she shook her head. So they waited and listened to the radio and wondered when they would hear a report about a missing person or a dead man. They didn't talk about it, but he knew that they were both steeling themselves for the same news.

Michael was torturing himself with thoughts about where things had gone wrong, how he could have avoided the disaster that had taken place at the alfalfa mill. When he had removed Emma from Marcia's house it had been an impulsive decision. At first, there was no plan. All he wanted to do was get Emma away. It was a rescue mission, not an abduction, not a kidnapping. And later, when there was a plan, he thought he could make it work in Junction City. School, friends, a parent who loved her, Emma would be all right. But it hadn't worked out that way. Should he have taken Emma to France? Would they have been any safer there, an ocean away from Marcia? He hadn't even considered it at the time.

How much did Ed and the fat man know? What would they tell the police? They could be coming for him any day. He had only one option now: get away, far away. In France, maybe, he could start over. He would write his plays again, and he'd clear things with Marcia. She'd realize that he only wanted the best for her and for Emma. In France, there was time to work all this out.

In a fit of fury, he had burst out in a rant against Junction City and the men who had turned his life upside down. Tiffany had listened to him silently. He had yet to explain to her what had really happened and what had gone so wrong. But he himself hardly understood it all. Ed, Coe, Marty, the fat man. Strangers with ideas and plans, unknown and incomprehensible to him, had wreaked havoc on his life.

Michael stared down at the papers in his hand. There was a small suitcase in front of him, half filled with notes and books. The wastebasket next to it was nearly full with crumpled sheets of paper. Tiffany stood by the window and gazed through the wet glass panes at the land that was drenched with rain. She didn't move when the floorboards creaked under his steps. Gently he put his hands on her shoulders and turned her around. But before he could say anything, she shook her head silencing him. There was a sad smile on her lips that stabbed him like a knife.

He took her hand in his. "Tiffany, I want to talk about—"

"Not now." She turned toward the window again. "It's Marty. You know, I never liked him. I thought he was stupid and dirty. And I was always a little angry when Ed brought him along. He made all of us look stupid. But Ed didn't mind. I never understood that. I minded."

Michael stroked her hair. "It's okay. It's over."

"He didn't deserve to die. He never really understood anything."

They had heard it on the morning news on the radio. A body had been found. Nobody had been reported missing, and it had not yet been identified because it was badly mutilated. It could possibly be a transient who had camped out in the old alfalfa mill. They kept listening

219

to the radio, and at eleven o'clock, the young, cold voice of the announcer came on again and reported that the body had now been identified. It was Marty Sorensen, whose brother, Marvin Sorensen, had notified the sheriff's office two hours earlier that he had been missing for a few days. He had stated that his brother sometimes stayed away and that he hadn't thought much about it until he heard the police report this morning. It was a well-known fact that Marty Sorensen had mental deficiencies, and his brother said that of late he appeared to be getting worse. The sheriff's department was making a thorough investigation, but it was widely believed that Marty Sorensen was attacked by wild dogs and succumbed to his wounds.

The air was fresh and cool when Michael stepped out on the porch. Sun bathed the land in a bright, golden light. Not a cloud was visible in the pale blue sky. The storm was over; calmness had descended upon the earth and sky. For the past two days, he had thought of nothing but that terrible night. In his mind he had seen ugly images, and the storm had only reinforced his despair. Was it possible that the world was now starting anew, fresh and clean? He looked toward the west from where the clouds usually advanced. Not a single disturbance threatened this brilliant day.

Slowly he walked to the car drawing in deep breaths of sharp, cold air, trying for a brief moment to forget his errand. Tiffany was standing by the bay window with Emma. He knew they were both watching him. The thought of Emma's face dampened his short-lived happiness. She hadn't asked him where he was going. Only her pensive eyes raised unspoken questions.

He drove along Main Street, avoiding several large tumbleweeds that the storm had driven into town. He passed the motel. Coe's car wasn't there. Then he drove down the next block past the sheriff's office. Two police officers, young men whose shirts stretched tightly over their muscular chests, were coming out of the old brick building. There was something very upright about them, and Michael envied them. As he glanced in his rearview mirror, he saw a woman talking to them. It was Grace. She was gesticulating with her arms, and the policemen were laughing. Michael had slowed down to a crawl, but a large gas truck appeared behind him blocking his view. The beefy face of the driver stared into Michael's mirror, and he increased his speed. He couldn't help but wonder if Grace, too, had something to do with what had happened at the mill.

Tiffany had described to him how to get to Ed's house. It wasn't difficult to find it among the ramshackle dwellings that lined the unpaved street. A dismal place, strangely at odds with the beautiful day. In the barren, fenced-in backyard, empty except for a clothesline and an old doghouse, he caught a glimpse of a thin, old woman hanging up laundry. When he pulled over and turned off his engine, she briefly lifted her head. The loneliness of a life spent washing and cooking with rarely a measure of happiness stared out of her haggard face. She bent down again and took a piece of gray clothing from the basket. As he walked toward the fence that separated them, she paused and watched him with timid eyes. He could tell that she expected nothing but bad news from him, and he wondered if anybody had ever come to her with good news.

Trying not scare her away, Michael spoke softly. "Hello. I'm looking for Ed. Is he at home? Tiffany sent me."

"Tif? I ain't seen her in a long time." Her face brightened only to be replaced by a look of anguish, so visible, so deep-seated, that it took him aback. Life had kept her down, people had shoved her around, used her, abused her. Her suffering was permanent, timeless. He could sympathize with the old woman because he too was suffering, but it was only a brief flash of shared pity that he felt. His misery was not to be of the lasting kind. He would not let himself succumb to it. He felt ashamed that he had stayed in the house for two whole days, inactive, prostrate, wretched.

"I need to talk to Ed. It's important." He tried to sound friendly and smiled but realized right away that he had made a mistake. Nobody ever smiled at the woman, and she became mistrustful.

"Ed ain't here. I dunno where he is." She bent down, picked up her basket and shuffled away.

"I know he's here. His truck is over there. Will you please tell him that I need to talk to him?" he shouted after her.

She slowed down and stopped. Then she turned around and walked back to the clothesline where the laundry was fluttering in the breeze. Irresolutely she shook out a wet shirt sleeve and stuck one more pin on a sheet. Without looking at Michael, she mumbled, "He ain't well. He's in bed."

"Leave us alone." A husky voice came from the house. Michael didn't know if this command was meant for him or the old woman.

Ed was walking unsteadily toward him. He was pale and unshaven. His wispy, unkempt hair hung over his forehead, and his clothes looked as if he had slept in them for several days. He stopped in front of Michael and glared at him with red-rimmed eyes.

"I need to talk to you. Tiffany tried to call you several times, but your mother always said you were sick."

Ed threw a threatening glance at the old woman, who quickly scurried away. Then he took a step toward the fence, and Michael caught a whiff of his unwashed body. "What d'ya want?" His breath smelled of cigarettes and alcohol.

"Coe is gone, Ed. It's over."

"Yeah, it's over for Marty."

"We all have a share of the guilt."

"Coe killed 'im. Bastard! I dunno why Marty went there. Well, I guess I know. But you're right, it's all over. Coe left and ya better hit the road too." Ed's eyelids quivered. His voice was hoarse and he coughed.

"Who is the guy with the dogs? What does he have to do with it?"

"Casey. Talk to him. He got it all worked out. Him and his damned dogs." Ed grabbed the fence with his bony hands and thrust his face close to Michael's. The stench from his mouth was overpowering. "Marty's dead. Who cares if a bullet did it or them dogs? Go away!

Maybe Casey is right. You brought it on!" He staggered and steadied himself against the fence. Then he turned around and stumbled back to the house.

Michael threw one more glance at the dilapidated house that hid the joyless lives of its two inhabitants before he drove away. He was thankful he didn't have to look into the desolate face of Ed's mother again.

Casey turned out to be a very congenial man. He didn't hesitate to invite Michael in.

"A cup of coffee, Mr. Barron? I was just getting ready to brew a fresh pot." His voice was calm, his demeanor undisturbed. Whatever had happened that fateful night did not seem to bother him greatly.

Michael nodded his head and watched the fat man moved in the sparsely equipped kitchen with the grace of a dancer. His body bounced from the cabinets to the stove, to the refrigerator, and with a flourish he placed a coffee mug, milk and sugar in front of Michael, who had taken a seat on a flimsy metal kitchen chair, not unlike the ones that he had in his own kitchen. Casey beamed at him cheerfully, lifted his cup and with great relish took a long sip of the hot liquid. Without haste he put the cup down. "Now, Mr. Barron, what can I do for you?"

"I don't think that's so difficult to figure out. You and I know that Marty wasn't killed by wild dogs, as the police seem to think."

Casey studied him indulgently, as if he were a young child, who had asked an inappropriate question and needed a patient adult to set him straight. "Let me tell you one thing, Mr. Barron. It is in your interest to forget about this whole affair. My babies, if I may say so, saved the situation. They got a little out of hand, I admit that. But they are big, strong and healthy. Sometimes their instincts take over, and even I have a hard time restraining them. That night they were a bit too keen. But you have to admit, it turned out for the best for all concerned. The police are satisfied. Coe, I assume, is gone. Poor Marty. I know, Ed is taking it hard, but he'll get over it. And you, Mr. Barron, are free to go without worrying about Coe. He already had a long criminal record. Now he has added murder to it. I don't think he'll pester you again."

"What's your role in all of this?" Michael wasn't satisfied. What did the fat man know about him and Emma? What part, besides being the owner of two murderous dogs, did he have in the nightly events that led to Marty's murder?

"Be satisfied, Mr. Barron. I only came along to help Ed. What else do you need to know about me? Take Tiffany, she's a nice girl, and leave." He smiled and showed a row of strong, yellow teeth. "I never thought she and Ed made a good pair. Ed is clumsy. He doesn't know a thing about women."

"I am not here to talk about Tiffany," Michael interrupted him.

"There's nothing else to talk about." Tilting his head back, Casey took another gulp of coffee. Michael hadn't even touched his. "You should leave. Put the house up for sale. That's the most sensible thing you can do. You are a sensible man, aren't you, Mr. Barron? We spread the word that you got a job in one of those big cities where you came from. Everybody will understand. You never quite fit in here anyway. The police have closed the case. That's what we want, right? You don't want them to change their mind." He broke into a soft chuckle. Like his elegant movements, it didn't seem to suit his massive body and the broad, bearded face.

Michael leaned forward and stared into the eyes of the other man. Casey might be soft-spoken, but his eyes were hard and cunning. "I can't just walk away from this. I don't want to be a fugitive on the run with a child and a woman who have no part in this. I need to understand what happened. I had some part in it and I am fully willing to accept my share of responsibility. I saw Coe kill Marty. I didn't kill him; your dogs didn't do it. But what I don't understand is why Marty came to the mill, and why you were there with your dogs."

"Marty was the town's fool. Doesn't every town have one? Like a town's drunkard? He had no future. You know what happens to people like him eventually? They end up in a government institution."

Casey pulled his face in a grimace. "Why don't we ask why you went to the mill? I think you wanted to scare Ed, confront him, maybe threaten him a bit. Not very nice, Mr. Barron, and not very clever. You should have taken heed when I wrote those two letters. Lots of things could have been avoided then." Casey paused, a stern look in his eyes. Michael remained silent. "You could have been killed in that little rendezvous instead of poor Marty."

"Why did you write those letters?"

"That's my little secret. Let me just say that I was less concerned with you than with Coe, a criminal from Chicago. You were a handy tool to get rid of him. I figured if you went, he'd go." Casey finished his coffee, got up and took the cup to the sink.

With his back to Michael, humming a little melody, he turned on the tap and held his hand in the water. When he started rinsing his cup, Michael realized it was time to go. The fat man wouldn't tell him anything else.

Chapter 29

Mr. Beasley was sweeping the front porch of the funeral parlor when Tiffany walked by. She tried to ignore him, when he called her name, but he called again, louder, and waved to her.

"A sad, sad ending, isn't it?"

She stared at him blankly pretending not to know what he was talking about.

"Marty, I mean. He was your friend, wasn't he?" Mr. Beasley's watery eyes blinked, and he shook his head.

Tiffany had always suspected that Mr. Beasley secretly gloated over every death in town because it meant business. The watery eyes were part of his professional appearance. They gave him the look of a man who was always grieving.

"The police are done with the body. Not much of a body. We won't have an open casket. The face, the head, you know, most of it is gone. I can do a lot with a face, the makeup we have is marvelous, but I can't perform miracles." He smiled at her ingratiatingly.

Marty's face flashed through Tiffany's mind, the round, good-natured smile, the innocent eyes. She didn't want to hear about dead faces, beautified by Mr. Beasley and Grace.

"I have to go, Mr. Beasley."

"Well, yes. But wait a second. You see, I have a small problem. Well, it's not really a problem, but maybe you can help me."

"Help you?" She couldn't imagine what he wanted from her.

"It's about the funeral." He took a step toward her. "It's going to be the day after tomorrow. Marvin wants it done fast. I don't blame him. It'll be simple. Marvin picked a plain casket, one of our less expensive models, but still elegant. All my caskets are elegant. This one is metal with a decorative border, lined in dark-red satin, very tasteful even at that price."

"Mr. Beasley, I don't have much time."

"Wait, wait. I see you are in a hurry, but this is important. The problem is this." He lowered his voice and moved his face close to hers. Tiffany took a step backwards, but he followed her. "Marvin refuses to buy any flowers for the funeral, No flowers at all," Mr. Beasley whispered.

He withdrew his face a few inches and looked at her expectantly, obviously wondering how she would take this amazing piece of news. When she didn't say anything, he frowned and then continued in the same soft voice. "I have never arranged a funeral without flowers, and I'm not sure it can be done. I have suggested to Marvin to go with the cheapest flowers, carnations. He asked me what they cost, and when I told him it would be around a hundred dollars for a simple, but beautiful, floral arrangement, one on the casket, another in a vase between the candles, he refused. Just refused."

Mr. Beasley shook his head in consternation. "So, when I saw you, it occurred to me that maybe you could talk to Marvin. Not a pleasant man, but you were Marty's friend, and you must know the family a bit. Somebody has to explain to Marvin that a funeral without flowers is hardly a funeral at all."

Mr. Beasley grabbed her arm and pressed it gently. "I think you're the right person to explain this to Marty's brother, Tiffany. Remember that beautiful funeral I arranged for your father? Your mother didn't spare any expenses. She knew how we, the living, should take our leave from our dear departed. Please, go to Marvin and tell him that you know about such matters. He shouldn't deny his brother this last beautiful moment on earth." Mr. Beasley's misty eyes watered more heavily, and

Tiffany feared that he was getting ready to deliver one of those sermons that he usually reserved for the family of the deceased.

"Mr. Beasley, you know yourself that Marvin is not the type to care for flowers. All he wants is to get Marty buried as soon as possible with as little expense as possible." She shook his hand off. The startled funeral director dropped his broom and stared at her, perplexed.

"I'll see what I can do about it," she murmured and quickly walked away.

When she opened the front door of her home, the new odors, left behind after the redecoration, hit her like a foreign object. They blended with a faint trace of liquor, perfume and the smell of cigarette smoke. Even though her father had been dead for some time, she still expected the acrid odor of a very sick person. She had never minded it. It had been a sign that her father was still alive.

To her surprise, Grace was at home. She sat on the overstuffed couch in the living room surrounded by empty cups and full ashtrays, watching TV. The curtains were closed, and the room appeared gloomy despite the new furniture. On her way to town, Tiffany had tried to think about how to say good-bye. She had a few phrases prepared, something like *He has asked me to come with him. He needs somebody to take care of his daughter. I'll be in touch. I'll write.*

No, she couldn't say that. Normal people said such things when they took leave, but in her family nobody wrote letters or cards, and it wouldn't be exactly easy for her to do so. *I'll call.* That was better. Grace and her mother were always on the telephone. They called the beauty parlor, the hospital, the undertaker, and when her father had died they had called their friends and their relatives. But of course, Tiffany couldn't call them from Europe. France, Michael had said. She didn't know anything about France. She had never been out of her home state.

Grace stared at her in a hostile manner. "What do you want? You haven't been home in a while."

"I'm leaving, Grace." She didn't want to say it this way, not so abrupt and final. She wanted to be nice about it. Maybe Grace would

228

miss her a little. But the angry look in her sister's eyes flustered her, and she yearned to be done with it all, to be gone from this place where she didn't belong anymore.

"You're leaving? Where're you going? Everybody seems to be leaving. Mom and I, we might be leaving too. When the bank takes the house away." Grace laughed without joy and lit another cigarette.

Would they ever be able to take care of themselves? When Tiffany searched her heart, she couldn't find that old, familiar sense of responsibility for them. Somehow they would be all right. They would limp along, muddle through. The bank would defer payment, Grace would buckle down and work harder, and her mother would learn to save.

"I'm going with Michael."

"Is that where you've been these past few days? My little sister has finally discovered men. How is it with him? Is he good in bed?"

Why does it always have to be like this? Can't we be like sisters? She had so often longed to love Grace, but her sister had made it difficult. There were times when Grace had shown concern about her. When they were young and other children had been too rough with her, Grace had occasionally stepped in. And she had tried to help her recently when Tiffany was worried about Ed. But she could never take her sister's kindness for granted. Anytime she did, Grace rebuffed her cruelly.

"It's not like that," Tiffany murmured.

"Men only want one thing, Tif, and that's sex. I know what I'm talking about. Don't let them fool you." Blue smoke circled around her sister's head, and she squinted her eyes. A fine, spidery net of wrinkles appeared on her smooth skin. Tiffany suddenly caught a glimpse of how Grace would look in ten years. Her beauty was already fragile.

"You know about Jim? He's gone, just gone. And this time I was so sure." Grace threw her half-burnt cigarette into a cup where it drowned with a faint hiss in the remainder of cold coffee.

"Did he say anything?" Tiffany could not feel sorry for her sister.

"They never tell you anything." Grace broke into a bitter laugh. "You don't know that yet, but you'll learn. He told Al Wiederspan that he had to meet with his investors. Before he left he got a few more checks. He said he'd be back soon and left an address and telephone number. I called the number. It's an answering service and they said they'd forward the message. But I know he's gone and won't come back. And I also know that he's screwed Al and the others."

"How do you know that?"

"The way he talked about them. He cleaned them out, and I don't care. Actually, I helped him. I gave him the names of people who might be interested in his scheme. I was glad I could do that for Jim. All I wanted was to go with him." The anger was gone from Grace's voice. Tiffany could not remember when she had seen her sister so defeated. Instinctively, she took a step toward her.

"Stay there. I don't need your pity." Grace stared at her with hostile eyes.

"Grace, he was no good. I'm glad you didn't go with him."

"I knew he was no good. I just thought he liked me enough."

Grace would have gone with him, even if she had known that he was a criminal, a killer. Tiffany sat down on the armchair across from her sister who hung her head until it touched her chest. Sadly she gazed at that wonderful thick, blond hair. Grace would grow old in Junction City. Her hair would turn gray, and she would dye it like their mother, too blond. It would lose its luster and its curls. Maybe one of these men who had been so hot for her when she was young and pretty would remember her beauty and marry her, if she hadn't smoked herself to death by then.

Grace lifted her head. "I even went to the police. I reported him missing." She stared at a spot on the wall, someplace to the right of the framed picture that showed her father in his football uniform. "They just laughed. They didn't take me seriously."

She paused and her eyes wandered back to Tiffany. "Do you remember Ted? He was a year ahead of me in school. Black, wavy

230

hair, tall, not bad looking. He's a policeman now. He was after me back then, and we went out a couple of times. When he started with the police, it was over. He thought I wasn't good enough anymore." She laughed, shrill, joyless. "Well, anyway, I told him that Jim was missing. He's an adult, he said, and I'm not next of kin." Grace buried her head in her hands, her red fingernails shining like pieces of candy among her curls. "But he didn't have to say that Jim left because he was tired of me. That's what he said. It's not true. That much I know. I was good for Jim, and he was good for me. I don't understand what went wrong this time."

Tiffany got up and walked toward her sister. Hesitantly she put her hand on her shoulder, and to her surprise, Grace didn't shake it off. It had been a long time since she had let her come so close. Tiffany's face touched her hair, which was soft and silky. When Grace lifted her head, tears glistened in her eyes. She smiled and pushed Tiffany away gently as she got up from the sofa.

"Let's not be sentimental, Tif. That never gets you anywhere." She went to the window. "Did you tell Ed to come here?"

"No, why?"

"He's walking up the driveway. Looks quite wasted. I guess Marty's death got to him." She turned around. There was a perplexed look in her eyes. "We don't really know how we feel about people until we lose them, do we? Tell him I'm not here. I can't stand the guy. Get rid of him, Tif."

Before she rushed out of the room, she quickly lifted her hand and touched Tiffany's cheek. It was barely noticeable, and later Tiffany didn't know if her imagination had played a trick on her. Even in her best moments, Grace had never shown any physical affection for her.

She met Ed at the door.

"Why'd ya leave your car at the gas station?" Ed didn't look well even though he was freshly shaven. His hand, which held a cigarette, was shaking.

"I felt like walking." She didn't tell him that she wanted to have

231

one last look at the place that had been her world for all of her life. Seven blocks from the gas station to her house. She had walked slowly, looking right and left. There was the library, the tavern, the donut shop, Mr. Beasley's funeral parlor, the school, the gift shop. She had taken comfort in the familiar sights and wondered if it was possible to step out of one's life and enter a new one. Without Michael by her side, she had felt unsure of the plan he had laid out for her. Was it fear of the unknown or fear of leaving certainty behind? Yet when she had reached her family's house, a premonition of endless years in the dreary household of three defeated women had overcome her, and she knew what she had to do.

"Why'd ya wanna walk if ya got a car?" Ed looked at her with bloodshot eyes.

"I'm leaving, Ed." This was the second time within an hour that she said these words. Grace had laughed her off, and she couldn't blame her. Saying it was one thing, doing it was another.

"Where ya goin'?" He didn't seem surprised.

"I'm going with Michael and Emma." That's all she could tell him.

Ed inhaled deeply, exhaled, and watched the smoke rise into the clear, brisk air. When he looked at her, his face was a distorted grimace. His lips were drawn back exposing stained, crooked teeth, one corner of his mouth was tilting upward, the other downward, and deep, vertical lines appeared on his thin cheeks. Tiffany couldn't tell if he was laughing or scowling. She assumed it was a scowl because she had never seen Ed laugh in such a strange way.

"We might go far away, to another country. I don't know when I'll be back."

The familiar cackle broke forth, loud and shrill, but without the spite that usually accompanied it. After a while he caught himself. "South America. They all go to South America. Maybe ya'll never come back. Might be just as well." He wiped his watery eyes.

Tiffany swallowed. She knew she had to say it because she might never have another chance. "Ed, I'm sorry about Marty."

"I don't wanna talk about it." He threw his cigarette to the ground.

She looked at his bent head, the thin, wispy hair uncombed as usual. He'd be lonely after she left. Marty was gone; she was going. The funeral was in two days.

"There won't be flowers at Marty's funeral," she said in a low voice.

"What d'ya mean?" He looked up, puzzled.

"Marvin won't buy any. I guess he doesn't want to spend the money. I thought, maybe, if I tell Michael, he'll take care of it."

Ed shook his head. There was a flicker of anger in his eyes, and she regretted that she had even mentioned the flowers. "I'll take care of it. He was my friend. Got nothin' to do with Barron." His voice was flat and without emotion. He fumbled for another cigarette, but instead of lighting it, he broke it in two and threw it on the ground where he crushed it under his dusty boot. When he looked at her again, the anger had disappeared from his face. It gave her the courage to ask him for help.

Michael had tried very hard to convince her that he had a good plan. He had told her that he would go through his lawyer in Los Angeles. "He'll do it just to get rid of me," he said. But she could tell that he was unsure. And then there was the matter of how fast the lawyer would be able to procure passports for all of them. Tiffany needed to talk to Casey. He might be able to help.

Ed didn't want to go with her. "I'm through with 'im," he said. "It's because of them dogs. I can't look at 'em again, ever." His voice broke off abruptly.

"Ed, we need passports, quickly. Casey wants Michael to leave. Maybe he can get the documents. Please, let's talk to him."

"I dunno. I don't wanna have anything to do with false papers. I got no stomach for this anymore. I got into somethin' I didn't quite understand, and in this business, ya gotta know all angles." He paused and thought. "Ya know, I feel sometimes as if it's me that shot Marty. If I hadn't told 'im that Coe was threatening me, he wouldn't've gone after 'im. I let 'im down." They were both silent. Then Ed motioned with his head toward the pickup. "Let's go."

Tiffany was surprised how easy it was to make Casey understand that he had to help them. There was no hesitation on his part. All he wanted were passport pictures and a sum of money. The money wasn't for him, he explained. He didn't care to make money that way. No, it was for the experts. That's what he called the people who fabricated such documents. Tiffany wondered where the experts were. Maybe Casey did it himself? She told him she'd be back with the money and the pictures as soon as possible. They could expect the passports in one week, he said. It was all so easy; it scared her.

Chapter 30

Marty's funeral was over quickly. There weren't many people, but Ed didn't care. Marvin was there, of course, his face sullen, poorly shaven, his gray suit crumpled and ill fitting. Liz shuffled into the church sniffling into a bunch of Kleenex. Ernie, her husband, sat in the pew looking bored. Some other people he didn't know mulled around the casket. Probably relatives who had never shown up while Marty was alive. The casket looked okay as it stood in the church surrounded by thick white candles and the red and white flowers that Ed had chosen, daisies and carnations. He didn't care too much for the little red carnations. They didn't seem fitting for a grown man like Marty, but it was all he could afford. Mr. Beasley had assured him that nowadays dainty flowers were quite right for men. He was the expert; he should know.

Ed wore the same old suit that he had worn for Randy's funeral. It didn't feel right going to two funerals within a few months. He hadn't thought about it until he put on that suit. It reminded him of how worried he had been about his own health when Randy had died from lung cancer. Well, he was still trying to cut down. But with all these things going on, he hadn't been able to concentrate on quitting.

It was strange that he was already used to the fact that Marty was dead. At first, it had seemed unbelievable, monstrous. He still missed him, but it was no good dwelling on it because every time he thought about Marty, he remembered the grisly corpse, the way it had been chewed up by the dogs. Then he felt like falling into a deep, black hole that was hard to get out of.

It had been like that for days after Marty's death. Ed had lain on his bed dozing, dreaming, drinking beer. He didn't think he ate anything during that time. When the old woman popped her head in occasionally, he was too weak to tell her off. And then that guy Barron showed up. The man looked pretty shaken, probably felt as lousy as he did. Somehow that made him feel better.

Ed stood by the entrance to the church shaking hands with people, the way relatives of the deceased do. Well, he had every right to do it. After all, he had bought the flowers. And they weren't cheap, whatever Beasley said. Time to look for a job again. His money was gone.

Al Wiederspan was slowly walking toward the church. He looked old in that black suit that was too big for him. He must have lost weight lately. With satisfaction, Ed observed that he didn't even stop to talk to Marvin. He shuffled toward Ed.

"Sad business, isn't it?" Al shook his head mournfully.

"Yeah."

"Marty was a bit slow, but a good worker, if you kept your eyes on him. Never had anything against him. Decent fellow." He paused and looked at Ed with misty eyes. "Life goes on. That's what they say. I got a job for you, Ed. Roofing. It needs two men. You know somebody else?"

"Well, not right off hand. Lemme think about it." He didn't know how Marvin suddenly appeared next to them.

"I'm lookin' for a job," Marty's brother mumbled gruffly. Ed was so surprised he just stood there gaping at him. "I know about roofin'. Have done a lot of it. Way back, Marty and me, we used to do it together."

What was he saying? Did he want to claim his brother in death after he had never given a damn for him in life? Ed felt anger well up, but he fought it down. He didn't want to be mad at Marty's funeral.

Old Al looked from one to the other. "Maybe it's fitting. I mean you two working together, now that Marty is gone." Ed didn't say anything. Marvin nodded his head. Before he strolled away, he said something to Ed about getting together after the funeral. Well, he wasn't quite sure if he wanted to work with that mean, foul-mouthed guy, but Marvin was gone before he could collect his wits.

"You know anything about Coe?" Al whispered, glancing around furtively.

Ed shook his head.

"You hung around him sometimes. Did he talk to you about his business?"

People were moving into the church and somebody started to play the organ. It was time to leave his place by the door. When Ed turned to go inside, Al grabbed his arm. "I think he took me in, me and several others. I asked Grace. She was at the motel every night. It wasn't decent, the way she carried on. But she won't tell me anything. I think he took her in too."

Ed tried to move away, but Al clutched his arm tightly and followed him into the church hanging onto the sleeve of his jacket.

"Heitman has talked to the police, but we got no papers, nothing in writing. It was in the mail, the bastard said. We never got anything. Thirty thousand. I lost thirty thousand dollars."

With a quick jerk Ed shook off the old man's hand. Wiederspan didn't seem to notice. He followed Ed and took a seat next to him in the pew. He must be in shock, Ed mused. People like him usually avoided Ed's company in public.

He didn't pay much attention to what the minister said. It wasn't necessary. He had already taken leave of Marty. His eyes fell on Tiffany, who was sitting at the end of the pew in front of him. She must have entered the church while old Al was pestering him. She had never really liked Marty, but he knew that she felt bad about this business. There was this peculiar expression on her face, quite different from the shy, quiet girl he knew. A few times, when she took care of her sick father, he had seen it. Confidence, determination? He wasn't sure. She looked straight ahead now, composed and serious, just as she had on that awful night in Barron's house when Coe was ready to blow her head off. One thing was clear; she didn't need him, her old pal, anymore. Somehow with Marty's death, everything had changed.

When Casey asked him several days later to take the passports to Barron's house, Ed didn't mind. It was strange that Casey referred to it as the Barron house, after it had been the Nielsen house forever. Ed thought it didn't make much sense to rename the old house when Barron was getting ready to leave. The passports looked great, like the real things. Nice, little blue books with gold letters and a fancy eagle on the cover. True, he had never seen real passports, but he was sure that they couldn't look any better than the ones Casey handed him. When he wanted to open one of them to see what they looked like inside, Casey snatched them from him and stuffed them in a Manila envelope.

Ed had asked Tif why she needed a fake one. After all, she hadn't committed a crime or needed to hide for any reason. She had told him that they wanted to leave as soon as possible, and Barron couldn't take a chance that their whereabouts might be traced to Junction City. Something to do with the little girl's mother. Tif didn't explain, and he didn't really care to know. At some future time, she had said, they'd come back and make it legal. Well, he didn't think so. He had heard that it was quite nice to live in South America. Even if you weren't rich, you could have a big house and maids. Why would anyone want to come back?

When he drove up to the house, he saw the little girl right away. She was sitting on the steps of the porch surrounded by all kinds of toys, watching him get out of his truck. Her gaze was very intent, and he tried to smooth down his uncombed hair with his fingers. He didn't like to be inspected.

"I know who you are. You're Ed," she said when he stopped in front of the porch.

He hadn't been back here since the night Marty died, and then he hadn't paid attention to anything. The house, he now noticed with surprise, had changed a lot. It did not much resemble the old Nielsen place anymore. The railing of the porch had been repaired and painted a soft yellow. Two white wicker chairs with brightly colored cushions and a small table between them made it look like in the magazines he sometimes leafed through at the barber's. A shame to leave it now. He turned his eyes to the girl, who was still examining him curiously.

It occurred to him that he hadn't seen her the night of Marty's murder. The little girl couldn't have slept through all that noise, not with the dogs and that crazy Coe. A dull pain pressed upward from his stomach into his head and eyes. It never lasted long, but it appeared every time something reminded him of that night.

"Yeah, I'm Tif's friend." Her steady gaze made him uneasy.

"Tiffany, it's Tiffany." She paused and seemed to debate something in her little head. "Tiffany and my Daddy are getting married soon."

Now that was laughable. He broke into a high-cackle sneer but quickly stopped because the child glared at him with such cold dislike that he was taken aback. "Wait a minute," he said. "I know Tif's goin' with ya dad, but I don't think it's for marryin'. She never said nothin' 'bout it to me."

"You are not her friend anymore. We are her friends now, and my Daddy will take her to . . . ." She hesitated and looked at him warily. Then her face brightened. "He'll take her to a place that's full of roses and pink houses and smells good." She wrinkled her little nose as if to indicate that he didn't smell very good.

It was South America all right. Why not tell him? He was getting annoyed with her.

"Listen," he sneered," if I don't help ya, you're goin' nowhere." He held up the envelope and waved it back and forth in front of her face. "I got somethin' and they need it. Get out of the way, ya little . . . ." Before he could finish the sentence with a nice swear word, the front door opened and Michael Barron appeared.

"Emma, go inside," he said. The girl frowned at Ed, grabbed a doll and disappeared into the house.

"What do you want?" Barron was standing above him on the porch glaring down. His voice was gruff and his eyes were full of contempt. It was obvious: the man despised him. But if he wanted those passports, he better be grateful and treat him right.

Ed raised his hand holding the yellow envelope. "I got somethin' for ya from Casey."

"Hand it over." Barron walked down the stairs.

This man and his daughter, they weren't thankful, they didn't show him respect. Ed pressed the envelope against his stomach and took a step backward. "Well, Mister, not so hasty."

"Listen, this business has nothing to do with you. It's between Casey and me. Give me that envelope."

Ed took another step backwards and another, and the tall man was coming after him in big strides. Of late, Ed had felt weak. Too little food and too much beer. Barron might think he was retreating. But that wasn't so. He was just trying to gain time and figure out how to punch a man who looked quite a bit stronger than him. Behind the large window he caught a glimpse of the obnoxious girl. Surely, Barron wouldn't make a spectacle of himself in front of his daughter. He was bluffing.

He stumbled, and instantly Barron was on top of him. His clean-shaven face was very close, and he felt Barron's breath against his cheek. It smelled faintly of toothpaste, which struck Ed as extraordinary. Most people he knew smelled bad on close contact. This bastard didn't.

Ed rolled over on his stomach, still clutching the envelope. It was now buried underneath him in the dust. Out of the corner of his eyes he saw Barron looming large against the pale, blue sky with his fist raised high. In anticipation of the blow he tensed his body, but nothing happened.

"No, no, stop." It was Tif's voice, and then it was very still. Slowly he turned his head and looked up. She was standing next to them, her face anxious, her hands lifted in a pleading gesture. Barron got on his feet without taking his eyes off him, and Tif quickly stepped between them. Ed was still on the ground, the envelope concealed under his body. He was coughing because dust had gotten into his nose and mouth.

"Ed, don't be silly." Tiffany bent down and put her hand on his shoulder.

He got up slowly and dusted himself off with his free hand, painfully aware that Tif and Barron were observing his every movement. With as much defiance as he could muster, he raised his head and what he saw startled him. It was Tif all right, leaning against Barron who had put his arm around her, but at the same time it wasn't the person he had known all his life. The way she stood next to that tall man, the way they held each other, it looked fitting. There was a strange kind of beauty about her. In a brief flash, he understood what Barron saw in her.

After that, there wasn't much to say. He gave Barron the envelope. Barron opened it quickly and reached into it. Three passports. Ed turned around and walked away. No point in lingering. When he drove off with a howling motor and kicking up a cloud of dust, he looked into the rearview mirror. Barron was talking to Tif, who stared after his pickup. As she became smaller and smaller, a feeling of sadness spread through him. Well, maybe it wasn't sadness, more a sense of emptiness, a strange longing that was vaguely familiar. When he turned the corner onto the county road, it came to him. He was a little boy, and his mother used to leave early in the morning to clean houses for people who had money. She always told him when she'd be back, but he worried constantly that she wouldn't come home. Time after time he had this nagging feeling of being left alone.

Well, that was then and this was now. He made a fist and hit the steering wheel. In the rearview mirror he could still see the gable of Barron's house. He wished he had looked at Tif one more time. Nervously he fumbled for a cigarette in the breast pocket of his shirt.

241

He had given up his fight against smoking. It didn't matter. People died from one thing or another. Randy had kicked the bucket in his early fifties. With some luck he would have more than twenty years to go. That was enough.

Chapter 31

That very last evening in Junction City Michael got a phone call from Vincent. The lawyer's voice was very friendly. He even tried some small talk, which wasn't like him. But Michael was busy. There were boxes and suitcases everywhere, and it was already late. Michael's monosyllabic answers finally forced the lawyer to come to the point.

"I have some news, Michael."

"Hm."

"I called Marcia several times, but nobody answered the phone. I left some messages, never got a call back. Finally I got hold of her friend, Albert. You know, the one who gets her the stuff."

Albert. He had heard that name before. He remembered that Emma had mentioned him. She had told him that Albert was strange, and that she was sometimes scared of him. He was the man who had staggered into the house with Marcia the night he took Emma away.

"Albert is living in the house now. He told me that Marcia is going to check herself into a clinic."

"Well, has she done it?"

"Not yet, but I told Albert if she didn't, she'd lose her little girl forever."

Michael tried to stay calm. He didn't know why Vincent had decided to insert himself again into his affairs. He hadn't asked him. On the contrary, he had paid him off handsomely.

"What do you want, Vincent?"

"Well, you know, a while back you asked me about the guy who sold you the house out there?"

"What about him?"

"I got some news about him. It seems that he surfaced in Chicago a few days ago. Some of his old buddies had been looking for him, and they ratted on him. Now he's out on bail, waiting for his trial on some drug trafficking charges. I thought you'd be interested. He might get a few years, but you know how it is. He'll be out soon."

"Thanks for letting me know, but I have nothing to do with the man. It was all a big misunderstanding. I'm not even sure we're talking about the same guy."

"Well, Michael, let me know if I can do anything else for you. The situation here might clear up soon, and now is the time to legalize the custody business. You know, if Marcia comes out of the program clean, it'll be difficult for you. I mean it'll be difficult even now. After all, you took the little girl away from her mother."

Michael was silent. The knuckles of his hand that gripped the receiver were white.

"I might be able to straighten things out, Michael." The voice hesitated. Then it came through clear and strong. "Abduction is an ugly word."

"I hear you, Vincent. I have to think about it. I tell you what. It's late, and I had a busy day. I'll call you back tomorrow, and we can talk about it."

"Yes, do that. Don't wait. As I said, I think the time to act is now. As long as she's on the stuff, you have a case."

"Yes, you're right." Michael paused. "Before I forget it, I sold that house in France. A Belgian journalist bought it. These Europeans always have plenty of money. He paid well." It was almost a pleasure to lie to Vincent.

"Good, I'm glad. I told you that's the way to do it." Michael couldn't remember that the lawyer had advised him in any way, but he sounded genuinely pleased, the way lawyers sound when things turn out well for their clients. Obviously, Vincent wanted his business back, and now he was assured that Michael was flush again with money. What could be better? He would be able to pay generously for a custody battle. And it would be a battle if Marcia was clean or not. He knew how single-minded, how determined she could be. She wouldn't give up Emma easily. It was not a risk Michael wanted to take.

"I'll call you back, Vincent. Good night."

"Okay, Michael. Take it easy. Don't wait too long. It's all a matter of timing."

Michael put down the receiver softly and stared at it with a frown. Was Vincent trying his hand at blackmail? Had he told him the truth about Marcia? Suddenly an appalling thought crossed his mind. What if the lawyer was working for her? Would he work for the highest bidder? Probably. If Marcia paid Vincent well, the sly fox would hand Michael and Emma over to her on a silver platter and tell everybody that justice had been done. He shook his head, trying to rid himself of these thoughts. It didn't matter anymore. Tomorrow the telephone would be disconnected and Vincent would get the message fast. He was a smart man.

Tiffany was sitting by the window when he entered the living room. She turned around and smiled at him. A brief flash of happiness chased his dark thoughts away. He had experienced moments of joy with her, but they had been momentary, frantic, because his anxiety never quite left him. When he felt her beside him at night and took her slender body in his arms, he wondered if she would still be there in the morning. When he woke up during the night, drowsy with sleep, he would search for her with his hand and be surprised that she was lying next to him. But the time was close when he would not have to doubt and worry. He'd feel her at night and trust that she'd be there in the morning.

Tiffany seemed much more at ease in this madness that had turned his world upside down than he was. With calm self-assurance she packed, discarded things, took care of Emma, cooked their meals, cancelled their utilities. He sometimes wondered if that shy, insecure

245

girl, that he had met months ago in the office of the Sunshine Motel, had vanished altogether.

Once in a while, he still caught a glimpse of this other person. Earlier that day she had helped him clear out his desk. There were stacks of papers on the floor, some typed, some handwritten, and he was trying to organize them in folders and boxes. Tiffany was bending over one pile of papers, scrutinizing the top sheet intently. A dark shadow crossed her face. He put his arm around her, but she didn't seem to notice.

"What is it, Tiffany?"

"You remember what I told you, don't you?"

Of course, he did, but it mattered as little to him now as it did before.

She held up the paper and pointed to a three-letter word. "Look at this. Such a short word and I don't know what it says."

"It doesn't matter, my love. I'll teach you. Once we're away from here, we'll have time, and we'll work on it every day."

"It takes me a long time to figure out if this is a "b" or a "d." Is it . . . ?" Her hand shook slightly. "Is it 'bay' or 'day'?"

"It's 'day'." He took the sheet of paper and put it back on the pile. "I promise you, you'll be able to read. Everybody eventually learns it. Some take longer than others."

She looked at him doubtfully. "There was a time when I thought that too. I tried to sound the words out like the other kids did. I waited for the miracle, but it never came."

He stroked her hair. "I know, my love. But that is over now. You'll have a competent teacher; at least I'll try to be one. You know that I don't just read words, I also write them. That should eminently qualify me."

She lifted her hand and touched his cheek. "I wonder how this will work out. You are a writer, and I can't read. Sometimes strange things happen, even in Junction City." A smile stole into her face. "You know, everybody thinks this is such a normal, boring town, but it isn't. Casey writes anonymous letters, Al Wiederspan invests in a bogus scheme, Mr. Beasley creates heaven on earth, and you fall in love with me, the dumbest person in town."

"The most beautiful woman in town. The very first morning when I woke up in that lousy motel, I thought about you. I remembered your face very clearly, even though I wasn't in love with you then. Wait, I probably was in love but didn't know it yet. Your reading disability, it's like a vision problem. It can be fixed. Nobody has given you a chance."

"Except Ed."

"Has he taught you to read?"

Tiffany laughed and put her arms around his neck. "No, he didn't teach me to read, but in his own way he taught me that I was okay. It was the best he could do. You'll teach me to read, and then I'll read all your plays and scripts. And I'll be smart, and you won't be ashamed of me."

Chapter 32

It was later that night that Tiffany went home for the last time. The living room was dark except for the bluish glow of the TV and a small lamp that threw its light on the new furniture. She made out a figure on the sofa, hunched over, the hair tousled. Was it Grace or her mother? For a brief moment, mother and sister merged into one person, and there she was, the little girl, the skinny teenager, the young woman, facing them alone. A storm of emotions flooded through her. At the beginning, she had been desperate for their love, then worried about their love, and then overwhelmed by a sense of responsibility for them. If she couldn't rescue them, who would? Tiffany sighed. She should have kept an eye on her mother and sister during these last few days in Junction City. They should have talked about the bank and the mortgage. Instead she had pushed them out of her mind. As she now stood in the doorway, she was surprised that she did not feel any guilt. Yes, she could leave them.

Her mother was wearing her faded pink bathrobe. In one hand she clutched a glass filled with the amber liquid that had become her companion, in the other she held a cigarette. She was drunk, very drunk, and gave no sign of recognition when Tiffany entered the room. With a shaking hand, she now brought the glass to her mouth, took a sip and then glanced around the room with vacant eyes. Tiffany reached for the tumbler, and their fingers touched for a brief moment. It looked as if they would struggle over the glass, but Tiffany managed to pry it from her mother's grip. As if she couldn't maintain her posture without the glass of whiskey, Audrey's head suddenly fell forward and her chest heaved with a deep sigh. Another deep breath followed, then her body fell sideways, the legs dangling over the sofa. She started to snore, and a thin thread of spittle ran down her chin from the half-open mouth. Carefully Tiffany lifted her mother's legs onto the couch. The bathrobe split open, and involuntarily Tiffany looked at the white, soft flesh of her thighs. She quickly spread a blanket over the inert body.

In her bedroom Tiffany collected a few articles of clothing. In the attic she found her father's cardboard box. In the living room she took his picture off the wall. There wasn't much else she cared to take with her. On her way out she slowly walked past her mother. Would Audrey wonder who had wrapped her in the blanket when she woke up from her stupor? Would she realize that her daughter had tried one more time to take care of her? Before the hopelessness of the moment could overcome Tiffany, she rushed out of the house.

The trip was an agony. Anxiety about the passports, exhaustion from lack of sleep, fear of flying and bewilderment at the crowds in the airports made the journey miserable for her. She couldn't eat anything on the airplane. The whole time, she felt like throwing up and constantly rushed to the bathroom, but it was just her nerves. Every time she walked back to her seat with shaking legs, she was convinced that she would not be able to endure this journey any longer. And before she sat down between Michael and Emma, the nausea was back. She knew she looked as pale as a ghost.

Michael tried to comfort her. He put his arm around her shoulder and whispered into her ear that everything would be all right. Sometimes she could relax for a brief moment, but it never lasted long. The next attack seemed always worse than the previous one. How she envied Emma, who had fallen asleep shortly after boarding. Tiffany gazed at the sleeping girl, curled up in her seat, breathing softly. She had taken this trip before and didn't have a worry in the world. But she, Tiffany, wasn't sure that she could ever go through this ordeal again.

It was on the flight from Paris to Nice that she finally mastered her nausea and her fear. By that time, she was too exhausted to be afraid. In Paris, men in uniform had glanced at their passports. One of them had looked at her and said something in French. Michael had laughed and answered him in this strange, beautiful language. Later he told her that the official had welcomed them to France, telling Michael that they were a handsome family, especially the young woman. Frenchmen like beautiful women, he had explained, and they thought nothing about telling them so. She found it all very strange. In Junction City, nobody would think about complimenting a stranger, and they surely wouldn't single her out. Maybe the man was making fun of her, but Michael assured her that this was not so. It must be the clothes, she decided. They had bought them at the airport in Denver at an outrageous price because Michael didn't think she needed Aunt Susan's hand-me-downs any longer. In the bathroom, she had put on the dark-blue pants and the pink sweater made from some fuzzy material. When she had reappeared, Michael kissed her and told her that she looked like a new person.

She had started to doze off on that last flight when Michael touched her shoulder. He pointed out of the window and she gasped. Before she had only seen clouds and blue sky, now they were flying over mountains, endless ranges of majestic mountains whose snowcapped peaks sparkled in the sun. The Alps. She had never seen anything like it. For the first time on the trip, she allowed herself to feel joy.

When they drove through the French countryside, the soft vibration of the car lulled her to sleep, while Emma's excited voice drifted in and out of her consciousness. She sounded happy, which reassured Tiffany. Maybe everything would be all right. When she woke up much later, she felt sluggish but calm. She glanced at Michael's angular profile. The deep lines around his mouth had disappeared, as had the rigid tension of his body. There was a softness about him now, and he looked young and relaxed.

He turned to her and smiled. "We'll be there pretty soon."

She pushed herself up on the seat and looked out of the window. Behind her, Emma chattered about the house and the swimming pool.

"It's fall, honey, the pool is drained. We have to wait till next year to swim," her father interrupted her.

"Will we be here that long?" Emma asked surprised.

"Yes, I think so." Michael stared straight ahead.

"But then I have to go to school here."

"Yes, you do. You'll learn French and be a very smart girl."

Emma was silent. When Tiffany turned around, she saw an unhappy scowl on the little girl's face. She stretched out her hand and touched her cheek. "Don't worry, Emma. Look at me. I've never been away from Junction City. I need somebody to help me here. You're a brave girl. Won't you help me?"

"Daddy will help you." Emma was distracted. Her own worries weighed more heavily on her than her concern for Tiffany.

"I don't know, Emma. He'll be very busy, and he knows French. He probably can't imagine how it is for us, not knowing the language. I don't even know how to buy our food here. We'll both have to learn together."

Her voice quavered, and she stopped abruptly. She had only meant to comfort Emma but instead had put into words the enormous obstacles that awaited her. How could she learn another language? She hadn't even mastered English well enough. She knew her way around Junction City; she knew the people; she knew their customs. Who were the people who lived here? How would she go about her life in a strange place? She had told herself that she would keep house for Michael and take care of Emma, the way she had done in Junction City. But now they were here, and it seemed quite impossible that she would learn the ways of a foreign country.

Michael opened his mouth to say something, but before he could do so, Emma answered. "I know a little French. I can teach you, Tiffany. If I go to school here, maybe you can go too." She didn't sound exactly cheerful, rather like a mother who had to come up with a sensible solution to a difficult situation. Tiffany smiled, and for now, her anxiety receded.

And then they arrived at the house. Michael unlocked the heavy wrought-iron gate with a key so large, it would have been fit for a castle. Behind it was the most amazing house she had ever seen. She couldn't decide if the stone walls were pink, white or the lightest brown. A red tile roof glowed in the late afternoon sun. Faded, blue shutters hid long, narrow windows. A high stone wall, overgrown with thick, thorny branches, surrounded the house and the garden with its small swimming pool. Dry leaves rustled softly across its blue bottom. Red and pink rose petals covered the terrace, but next to the house a few roses were still blooming in the warmth of the stone walls. Emma held her hand as they walked to the house. The front door was made of thick, weathered wood, and Michael opened it with another key, as large as the first one. There was a stale, musty smell inside. It reminded Tiffany of summer, dry earth, herbs and flowers. When Michael opened the windows and threw back the shutters, the soft light of the warm fall day touched the white-washed walls, the red tile floor and the simple, wooden furniture. Silently Tiffany looked around her. They went upstairs, and she gazed out of the window at the land that extended in waves of hills and valleys until it disappeared in a haze of green forest and blue sky. On top of faraway hills, she could see clusters of pink houses around churches crowned with wrought-iron bell towers. The houses looked like breezy dots that an artist's brush had daubed on a canvas. She leaned out of the window and touched the stone wall below her. It was rough and jagged, warm from the day's sunshine.

When she turned around, she saw Michael leaning against the wall, observing her. "It's beautiful," she whispered. "I didn't know places like this existed."

Chapter 33

Al gave Ed the details about the roofing job and told him to get the material. It took him two days to haul the shingles to the motel. Then he went to Marvin's place late one evening to tell him that they would have to start early the next morning. It was the first time that he had gone there since Marty's death. He dreaded it, and, sure enough, as he approached the ramshackle house with the old garage where Marty used to spend his time, he felt a lump in his throat. Marvin was sullen and unfriendly when he opened the door. Once again, Ed wondered why the guy wanted to work with him. He'd be at the motel the next morning, Marvin grumbled.

Marvin was fast and capable on the job. After two hours on the roof, they worked together as if they had been a team forever. They didn't talk much. It wasn't necessary because they both knew what had to be done. This was a new experience for Ed because with Marty there had been endless, long-winded explanations, and Marty never moved a finger without Ed giving him direct orders. In a way, Ed missed the fussing and yelling. But he had to admit that there was a benefit in working with a guy who knew his stuff. They were done ahead of schedule, and Al Wiederspan gave them a small bonus.

Several days later, Marvin showed up at Ed's house and asked him if he wanted to do another job with him, out in the country. And that's the way it went through the fall and early winter until it got too cold to work outside. When they had a warm spell in late February, old

Jeremiah hired them to repair the roof of his barn. The roof was wet and slippery, and in some places it was completely rotted through. You didn't know it until you stepped on it. Ed and Marvin were cautious, but it happened more than once that the wood gave way and they caught a glimpse of the dark space below them. They knew the work was dangerous, especially when the weather turned cold again and the wet wood was covered with a sheet of ice. But neither one of them wanted to call it quits. So they continued to work, and Jeremiah was rubbing his hands, well satisfied.

It had to happen. Ed knew it. He just didn't know which of the two of them would be the one. Marvin was working high up on the roof, and he was a few feet below him, when he heard a loud crash followed by a scream. He never thought that Marvin, who only grunted and spoke in short, chopped sentences, could utter such a loud sound. When he looked up, he saw his partner frantically grasping at the slippery wood. Half of his body had disappeared into a hole that was big enough to swallow him up. Ed dropped his tools and threw himself flat on the roof, grabbing one of Marvin's legs that was desperately clinging to the crumbling roof. Both men were quiet, breathing white clouds into the cold air. Cautiously Marvin tried to hoist himself over the edge of the opening, sliding his arm forward and trying to lift his leg that was dangling in the empty space below. It appeared as if he would be able to scoot over the edge, and Ed thought of releasing his grip on Marvin's leg because he was not in a very stable position himself. But suddenly the wood gave way, and he felt the leg pull away from him. He tightened his grasp and yelled at Marvin to hold on to an exposed beam, but it was clear that the rotten wood could not support their weight much longer. At the top of his voice Ed screamed, "Jeremiah! Help!"

The old man came fast and saw right away what needed to be done. It still seemed like an eternity before he had climbed up the ladder and thrown Ed a rope to tie around Marvin's leg. Throughout the whole ordeal Marvin remained quiet. Only once he yelled at Ed to hurry up. Carefully they lowered him through the gaping hole onto the floor of the barn.

They didn't talk about it afterward. Maybe Marvin grunted something like thank you, but Ed wasn't sure. It didn't matter. Ed was dumbfounded that he had managed to get Marvin safely off the roof. There was a time when Marty had been alive that he would have rejoiced if his brother had fallen and broken his neck. Up there on Jeremiah's roof it hadn't even occurred to him to let him fall to his death. And when he thought about it afterward, the idea didn't appeal to him. It was the money, he decided. He was making more money with Marvin than he had ever earned before. He had so much money now that he had started giving some to the old woman. For food, he had told her. She was still a lousy cook, but at least he had better cuts of meat.

Sometime, not long after Tif had left, he started going over to the motel. He'd have a cup of coffee in the office and chat a bit with Liz. He didn't know why he went because Liz had never been all that friendly with him, and she wasn't very talkative now; neither was he. But he got the feeling that she didn't mind him. They sat there, smoked, sipped coffee, and watched TV together. She once asked him if he had heard from Tif, and he told her that he hadn't. Sometimes they wondered where in South America she was. Liz thought that Tif and Barron made a good couple. Maybe she was right. He didn't have an opinion on that. At first, he only went to the motel once a week. By Christmas time, he dropped by more often, sometimes two or three times a week. It took him a while to figure out Liz's schedule, but once he knew it, he planned his visits accordingly. And then, in a vague sort of way, he felt a need to go there every day, sometimes in the morning, sometimes at night. The day wasn't right if he didn't stop by the motel. Occasionally, he asked himself if Liz felt the same. She smiled when he walked through the door, and there was this comfortable familiarity between them that people have who are at ease with each other.

It was just after Christmas when she started looking at him in this curious way. She'd light a cigarette, inhale deeply and then gaze at him through the smoke. It was like that for several days. At first, he thought it had to do with the fact that he felt low because he hadn't worked in a couple of weeks. He still had plenty of money, but nothing to do, nowhere to go. Maybe she noticed it and felt sorry for him.

It was Monday night and very dark outside. She always closed early on Mondays. The thought of going out into the gloomy, cold night and looking for another place to hang out depressed him. He watched Liz walk around the counter and turn the sign in the window over to "Closed." Her hips brushed against him as she passed by. She was a big woman, and the office was small. He was more surprised than excited, but he was ready when she switched off the lights and took his hand into her warm, fleshy palm. They looked at each other in the blue, garish neon light that shone through the window. He'd always had a liking for big, soft women.

Liz smiled, and then she pulled him into the back room that was used for storage. There were crates with cigarettes and pop, boxes with soap and plastic cups. And there was also an old sofa. Sometimes Al took a nap on it. The room had no windows, and Liz didn't switch on the light. It was pitch-black. They bumped into each other and stumbled over the crates until they reached the sofa, and then they stood there for a moment and listened to each other's breathing. When Liz lifted his hand and gently thrust it into her ample bosom, it was all he needed. Her softness closed in on him like a pool of warm water.

Afterwards they sat on the sofa, smoking a cigarette. He sat close to Liz and savored her touch, the faint smell of sweat and excitement. Ed felt as if he had champagne in his veins. He wanted to laugh, but at the same time he wanted to preserve their silence. When she told him that she had to go now because Ernie would be getting home and she had to warm up his dinner, he still felt good. He didn't dread the dark night outside any longer. And when he saw Grace in the tavern later that night, he didn't care. He couldn't understand why he had ever been so crazy about her. Sitting at the bar and slowly drinking his beer, he let his mind wander over what had happened in that small, dark room. He could still feel Liz's soft skin against his.

And so it stayed from then on. Sometimes they made love, sometimes they talked and smoked. Life wasn't bad. It was around that time, when strangers appeared at the motel. One of them a big, burly man in an expensive suit, the other a younger man, who did all the talking. The older one just stood there looking around, checking out the place. They rented two rooms. City people, Ed guessed, and he had a hunch that they had something to do with Barron. He wasn't keen on strangers, so he didn't stick around. When he walked by their car, the door opened and a woman stepped out. She was beautiful, and for a moment she took his breath away. How did he describe her later to Liz? Glamorous in her fur coat, like an exotic bird that had lost its way. She tried to smile at him, but it wasn't real. It was a mask, and behind that fake smile lurked something else. He hurried to get away.

The next day, Liz told him that they had asked for directions to the Nielsen house. They drove out there, and when they came back they were in a real foul mood. Since when had the house been empty, the woman wanted to know. Did Liz know Michael Barron? Did he have a little girl with him? Liz shrugged her shoulders and told them that she barely knew Barron. She didn't like these people, she told Ed, and neither did Ed. Later that day he saw them at Dub's. This time the older guy did all the talking, while the woman poked around in her food and threw him angry glances. The younger man didn't say much. He drank a lot. Occasionally, he bent over and whispered something into the woman's ear. But she didn't pay much attention to him. They stayed for three days; then they vanished. Liz thought the woman was the little girl's mother and they were looking for her. The older man had told her that he was a lawyer. He could save Barron a lot of trouble if he found him, he said. Ed swore under his breath as he listened to Liz, and she laughed out loud, which made her bosom quiver. They talked about these strange people for a few days and then forgot about them.

The next summer he got a postcard. He had never in his life received a postcard. It was from Tif and showed a picture of Amsterdam. He wasn't quite sure where that was. It didn't sound like a place in South America. Someplace in Europe, Liz told him, when he showed her the card. She wanted to pin it on the wall behind the desk, but he thought they should be more discreet. What if these strangers came back? The text on the card was a surprise too. At first he thought that Barron had written it for Tif because it was in cursive. She always used to print except for her signature, a childish scrawl that looked like a third grader's. The writing on the card was fluid and firm, yet tentative and careful. There was something delicate about it. He recognized Tif's old signature.

Dear Ed, it said on the card, *we are having a stopover in Amsterdam on our flight back to the U.S. I am doing well. You can't imagine how* amazing *it is here. We won't stay long, but I'll try to come and see you. Love, Tiffany.*

He never did see her. She never came.

He wished he could have told her that he didn't have anything against Barron, that he was happy for her. But it wasn't important.

He thought she knew.

ABOUT THE AUTHOR

Christel Detsch is a native of Germany. She lived in Nebraska for 20 years and now resides in Colorado. She has studied German and History and has an M.A. from the University of Colorado, Boulder.

www.ingramcontent.com/pod-product-compliance
Lightning Source LLC
Chambersburg PA
CBHW021957170626
46808CB00001B/191